SHIMMER

'What an amazing sequel . . . Kick-butt action-scenes, perfect characterizations and a mesmerizing storyline that gets better and better.' OBSESSION WITH BOOKS

'If you like feisty characters, heart-pumping action and sexy romance then this book is for you . . . *Haze* is a must-read.' INSIDE MY WORLDS: R. L. SHARPE

'What makes it a standout read in this genre is the clever writing, with witty dialogue and a believable cast of characters . . . Packs a punch.' READPLUS BLOG

'Some books you crave. You keep returning to the cover art and re-reading the blurb, you stalk the authors' Twitter, Tumblr, Goodreads profiles in the hopes of gleaning morsels of information . . . you count down to release day. Paula Weston's *Haze* was just such a craving . . . Weston is something special indeed, and The Rephaim is one of the most original and intriguing new young adult series available.' ALPHA READER

'Paula Weston hasn't let the ball drop in the sequel to the hugely successful *Shadows*. Everything I loved from the first book—the cleverness, the mythology, and of course the romance, are still there.'
FIRST IMPRESSIONS BLOG

'Paula Weston brings the amazing to the table once again, with the brilliant and exhilarating *Haze* . . . I love this series. It's one of the best angel-themed series available now, and it's Australian to boot!'
SPECULATING ON SPECFIC BLOG

SHADOWS

'One of the best YA novels I have ever read.'
DARK READERS

'One of the best angel books I've read, if not the best,
with brilliant characters and its own take on the genre
which I had previously sworn myself off.'
THE OVERFLOWING LIBRARY

'*Shadows*' fast-paced narrative, risqué romance and snappy
dialogue kept me absolutely hooked and I stayed up late into
the night to finish this book . . . The smart-mouthed character
of Rafa kicked the Edwards, Peters and Jacobs of the YA
world to the [curb]. If only he were real . . .' SUN BOOKSHOP

'Forget everything you think you know about angels and
demons . . . *Shadows* is, by far, THE book to read . . . [it
is] beyond explosive with a kickass heroine, an amazing
storyline with incredible mythology, and a romance
sure to heat up even the coldest of hearts.'
WINTER HAVEN BOOKS

'Fans in need of another angel series after finishing Lauren
Kate's *Fallen* will devour *Shadows* . . . there's a heroine—
Gaby—to get behind, a boy—Rafa—to fall in love with,
as well as the many sides fighting to win you over.'
BOOK PROBE BLOG

'I have to say that this is in my top of 2012 reads
and I'm so glad I picked it up. I can't wait for the next
in his series. If you're looking for the next incredible
paranormal, fallen angel type story . . . look no
further because this is it.' FIC FARE

'Oh my God (almost literally)! If this doesn't drag young adult readers away from their computer screens, nothing will. It will entrance many oldies too. Aussie author Paula Weston's debut is a fast-paced, sensational ride, which screams "read me" and "turn me into a movie" . . . it's a wild start to what should be an even wilder series.'
ADELAIDE *ADVERTISER*

'A breath of fresh air in an over-saturated market . . . I urge any paranormal fiction fans to pick up a copy immediately.' WONDROUS READS

'O-M-freakin-G . . . This book was AWESOME! So, so, good. Quite possibly my fave Aussie release this year.'
BOOKSWOONING

'If you told me last week that I'd be fan-girling over a YA urban fantasy series I would've stared at you blankly then hurled a copy of *Friday Brown* at your face.
Quietly eats hat I loved this book. Loved.'
TRIN IN THE WIND

'Tough, smart and refreshing . . . not to mention it's the best angel-themed book I have read.' ALPHA READER

'This book should be right at the top of your wishlists.'
INKCRUSH

'It's got angels, it's got demons, it's got hot guys, it's got sword fighting and it's got a strong female lead. What else could you ask for?' SHARPEWORDS

BOOK III

SHIMMER

PAULA WESTON

Copyright © 2016 by Paula Weston
Published by arrangement with The Text Publishing Company, Australia
Published in North America by Tundra Books, 2016

Tundra Books, a division of Random House of Canada Limited,
a Penguin Random House Company

Library and Archives Canada Cataloguing in Publication

Weston, Paula, author
        Shimmer / by Paula Weston.

(The Rephaim ; 3)
Issued in print and electronic formats.
ISBN 978-1-77049-848-8 (pbk.).—ISBN 978-1-77049-850-1 (epub)

        I. Title. II. Series: Weston, Paula Rephaim ; 3.

PZ7.W5266Shi 2016   j823'.92   C2014-903895-X
                                             C2014-903896-8

Published simultaneously in the United States of America by
Tundra Books of Northern New York, a division of Random House of
Canada Limited, a Penguin Random House Company

Library of Congress Control Number: 2014941898

Cover designed by Us Now
Cover image: © Mark Owen /Arcangel Images
The text was set in Warnock Pro
Printed and bound in the United States of America

www.penguinrandomhouse.ca

1 2 3 4 5 6   21 20 19 18 17 16

FOR MUM AND DAD

THE REPHAIM — WHO'S WHO

Gaby/Gabe   Recently discovered she's not completely human—and that she knows how to kill creatures from hell with a sword.

Jude   Gaby's twin brother. Also not who he thought he was. Not necessarily unhappy to discover he's more than a backpacker.

Rafa   Jude's best friend. Had a complicated history with Gabe. Now has a complicated relationship with Gaby.

Jason   Gaby and Jude's cousin. Keeper of secrets. Not keen on the rest of the Rephaim.

Loyal to the Sanctuary

Daniel   One of the Council of Five. Gabe's ex. Nathaniel's right-hand man. Snappy dresser.

Taya   Designated head-kicker. Punches first, asks questions later.

Malachi   Taya's battle partner. Prone to trash talking.

Daisy   A close friend of Gabe's. Impulsive, loyal. Not a fan of Mya.

Micah   Another old friend of Gabe's. Laid-back. Deceptively effective in battle.

Calista   One of the Council of Five (ex-soldier). Limited sense of humor.

Uriel   Another member of the Council of Five. Also an ex-soldier. Still jumps into the fray as opportunities arise.

Magda   The academic on the Council of Five. Not a fighter.

Outcasts

Mya   Volatile, unpredictable. Anti-authoritarian. Has a tendency to overuse kohl eyeliner.

Ez   Calm and level-headed. Emotionally intelligent *and* deadly with sharp weapons. One half of the Rephaim's only functional couple.

Zak   A man mountain of few words. Trusts Jude and Rafa implicitly. The other half of above-mentioned couple.

Jones   Easy-going, lethal. Doesn't hold grudges. Has more patience with Mya than most people.

Seth   Always up for a fight. Tall and strong—even for the Rephaim.

PROLOGUE

There's a lot I don't know about my life. But here's what I do know.

Eleven days ago I was living in Pandanus Beach with my best friend, Maggie, holding down a job at the library, grieving for my twin brother Jude. I thought I was a backpacker; I thought I'd watched Jude die in a crumpled mess of metal and petrol and dust. I thought I was learning to get on with my life, despite gruesome dreams of hellbeasts and mutilations.

Then Rafa came to town. Violence followed—and some mind-bending news. I'm not nineteen: I'm a hundred and thirty-nine. And I'm not a high school drop-out estranged from my parents: I'm part of the Rephaim—a society of half-angel, half-human beings. My father was one of the Fallen, two hundred and one archangels originally sent to hell thousands of years ago because they couldn't resist human women. A hundred and forty years ago, led by Semyaza, they broke out and did the same thing all over again. And then they disappeared without a trace. The only one of the Fallen who abstained was Nathaniel. He's the one who gathered together the Fallen's bastard babies and made us into a society. Raised us into an army. Called us the Rephaim.

Not that I remember any of that.

Nathaniel claims our destiny is to find our Fallen fathers and turn them in: hand them over to the Angelic Garrison. But we're not the only ones looking for them. Hell's Gatekeeper demons are also tracking them, and are itching to destroy the Rephaim along the way.

So where do I come into all this?

About a decade ago, there was a major split among the Rephaim over what should happen if we actually did find our fathers. Jude and twenty-three others, including Rafa, rebelled. I should have walked out with them, but I stayed. They became Outcasts.

Then a year ago, Jude and I made up. It turns out it was because Jason—our cousin, who'd been hiding from Nathaniel all these years—reached out to us. He told us about a young girl in his family who had visions. She'd seen something important involving me and Jude, so we went to see her. And then we disappeared. Both factions of the Rephaim assumed we'd betrayed them and had found the Fallen—and it got us killed.

But we were both alive, with no memory of being Rephaim or what we'd done. Both thinking the other was dead.

Rafa helped me find Jude. My brother took the truth better than I did—and he's fitting into his Rephaite skin so much quicker than me.

Along the way we've discovered a new threat. There's a farmhouse in Iowa that contains an iron-lined room. It can do something that should be impossible: imprison the Rephaim. It was built by a family who know about the Fallen and the Rephaim, and who hate us. A family who claim to receive divine guidance about how to protect the world from us.

Somehow the Gatekeepers found out about that room. And they were quick to put it to use. But not before they murdered a sixteen-year-old girl and her mother and left them to rot in a cornfield.

I still don't remember that old life. Or what Jude and I did a year ago. Neither does he.

But I vividly remember everything that's happened these past eleven days, since Rafa tracked me down. And it's those memories I cling to now.

HAPPY THOUGHTS

'What did I tell you about scratching that?'

I look up, my fingers still digging into the scar above my collarbone. I didn't hear Rafa come out of the bungalow.

'It's itchy.'

'It's itchy because it's healing.' He sits next to me on the top step of the deck. 'Let me see.'

I stretch the neckline of my T-shirt so he can see the puncture marks: a sharkbite-shaped souvenir of my hellion cage match on Monday night. I keep my eyes on the sea beyond the town as he studies it. The sun slips behind a cloud, casting the water in gray shadow. I listen to the low pounding of the surf down the hill, the chatter of lorikeets in the trees up the street. Breathe in morning air sharp with salt and eucalypt.

'It doesn't look too bad. Moisturizer would help, though,' Rafa says.

'Moisturizer. And you give Jason a hard time because he can tie a scarf.'

'No,' Rafa brushes his thumb over the scar tissue, 'because he's a tool.' His touch and that hint of sandalwood are as distracting as ever. I let my T-shirt settle back in place.

'And speaking of tools,' he says, 'we've got places to be.'

'I can think of better ways to start the day than with the Butlers in the front bar of the Imperial.'

'I don't plan on making it a long visit.'

'That's my point.'

'You can handle a couple of meatheads in steel-capped boots.' He stretches an arm across his chest away from me, biceps flexing.

'Rafa . . .'

'Do you want to keep getting hurt?' He drops his arm. 'Because I don't find watching you in pain to be much of a spectator sport.'

Two lorikeets sweep past us, squabbling. They land on the grevillea next door and start to wrangle over a pink flower.

'You have to know you can fight when you need to,' Rafa says. 'Not just defend: attack. And if it takes a scuffle in a pub to get you ready for the shit that's coming, then that's okay with me.'

I finally look at him, his green eyes watching me, waiting. 'Is there any other way with you lot except violence?'

He shrugs, a lazy gesture. 'It's what we're built for.'

I stretch out my fingers. No sign of the grazes and bruises from the cabin brawl three nights ago, but I still feel them. 'But not every Rephaite is a fighter, are they?'

'You see me as a scholar?' He cracks a knuckle and laughs without humor. 'Funnily enough, when Nathaniel was handing out careers that option never came up.'

The sun moves out from behind the cloud, turns the sea silver.

'Don't you ever get tired of it?' I can't imagine what it must have been like, the life I've forgotten. Always fighting or training to fight.

'Brawling? Nah, keeps me fit.'

'I'm serious.'

His shoulders tense. He looks out to the water, eyes tight against the glare.

'I don't know if you've noticed, Gaby, but violence is the only thing I'm good at.'

Violence is the only thing I'm good at . . .

The Pan Beach morning fades and with it the noisy lorikeets and the pounding surf. And a bone-deep chill cuts through the warmth of the sun . . .

THE COLD LIGHT OF DAY

Cold. God, I'm so cold.

I'm wrapped in two blankets, knees tucked under my chin, waiting. Waiting for my sliding thoughts to find traction. Waiting for the crushing panic to pass. Waiting for Rafa to appear in the middle of this ancient chapterhouse, bloodied, injured, pissed off. Alive.

But Rafa's not coming.

My breath shortens; my head swims with jasmine, incense, and musty wool. I blink, try to focus. My eyes skate over white marble columns, towering arches, heavy glass panes; angels tearing demons apart in a thickly textured oil painting.

The winged figures blur. All I see is the demon blade thrusting out of Rafa's stomach, wet with his blood, his eyes searching for mine in the darkness. Black spots stain my vision. I bite the inside of my cheek, taste copper.

'Gaby, stop.' Jude's fingers press into my shoulderblade. 'You're doing it again.'

I take a long, shaky breath. The spots recede. Jude is still with me. Rafa is at the mercy of demons in Iowa and I'm in a monastery in Italy with the Rephaim, but I have my brother back.

It's something. A big something.

I wipe my face. The tips of my fingers are numb from the cold.

Rafa was taken no more than twenty minutes ago. The longest twenty minutes of my life. My eyes travel to the domed ceiling high above us. The point where the arches meet is shrouded in shadow and cobwebs.

I do not want to be here; I don't want to have to deal with Nathaniel and his Council of Five. Anger, flaring under my ribs, burns off the fear, just for a moment.

Screw Nathaniel.

Screw the fallen angel and his Rephaim for snaring me in this shitty blood-soaked mess of angels and demons. Screw them for dragging me into their world and then ripping mine apart. Everything they touch leads to violence, and somehow that's cost me the memories I should have of a whole other life, the one with the Rephaim: it's cost me a year without Jude and gifted me a year of gnawing grief and emptiness. And now it's going to cost me Rafa.

My fingernails dig into the worn timber pew.

'Gaby.'

Jude is still watching me. I force myself to focus on him. His brown eyes—so much like mine—are searching, worried. He smells like campfire and the sea.

'Are you sure this is where you want to be?'

'There is nowhere else,' I say and I hate the truth in those words.

'That's assuming Nathaniel's not lying through his teeth. But if you change your mind—if you want out of here—we're gone.' He holds my gaze. 'It won't take too much to convince these guys to leave.' He nods at Ez and Zak, standing with their heads together a few meters away. Mya paces the chapterhouse behind them, cheeks still flushed from arguing with Nathaniel. Her shirt and jeans are covered in gore and grass, her hair loose, wild.

Ez sees us looking and comes over. 'Are you ready?' Her lips are pale, the scars on her cheek and neck stark against her caramel skin.

I sit up. 'Yeah.' It's the first time I've lied to Ez. She pretends not to notice.

'You can't let the Five see weakness,' she says. 'Remember: the last time you were here you killed a hell-beast.'

I push away the memory of the blood-stained sawdust and chain-link wire. Try to focus.

'The Gabe you were in the cage, that's who they need to see here today.' Ez checks I understand what she's saying. I do. I need to be the fighter they've known for more than a century. It doesn't matter that I don't remember ever being that person: it's the only version of me they'll respect. I've already let Nathaniel see me lose it in the last ten minutes. This conversation has to go differently.

Zak gives me a quick once-over. 'You can do this.' Solid as always—but even he looks smaller in this cavernous place. His blue eyes are paler than usual, his ebony skin dull, as if just being here somehow diminishes him.

Mya comes to a standstill in the middle of the chapterhouse. 'It's a waste of time.' She's talking to Jude but she's angry with everyone. Me for choosing to stay here and ask for help; Ez and Zak for agreeing to it. 'Nathaniel will find an excuse not to attack the farmhouse.'

'Maybe,' Jude says. 'But we need to try.'

Mounting a rescue for Rafa and Taya shouldn't even be a discussion. And it shouldn't be me arguing for it. It should be Daniel. Of those of us who were ambushed on the mountain twenty minutes ago, he's the only one on the Council of Five.

I close my eyes and I'm back there. The chorus of cicadas, the tang of eucalypt and damp soil, diesel and campfire smoke. Warm night air. Rafa and Daniel arguing because we'd told the Butler brothers and their crew about demons and hellions. Taya and Rafa arguing about my trip with the Outcasts to Los Angeles.

I saw the blade slice through Rafa, then I saw flaming eyes in the dark. And then chaos. Blood. Terror.

'This place stinks.' Mya is pacing again. The monks have mostly cleaned up the mess of our arrival but the air is still pungent with charred flesh and vomit. 'We need to open a window.'

Zak shakes his head. His long black curls are still plastered against his scalp and barely move. 'It's freezing out there.' He holds out his katana, checks it in the faint light straining through windows high above us. It's sticky with demon blood. He picks up an unused bandage and wipes the blade clean. I look around, find my sword propped beside Jude's at the end of the pew. Somebody must have grabbed it because I don't remember having it when we left the mountain.

Mya finally comes over.

'When is Jones getting here?' Zak asks.

'Soon.' She hands him her katana. He wipes it down, hands it back. 'He's waiting for the rest of the crew. Strength in numbers.'

I sit against the pew. Nathaniel will be back with the Council of Five any time now. It's about to get crowded in here.

Jude is watching the door. 'Everyone who walks through there is going to know us, aren't they?'

'Yeah,' I say. 'But they won't all come through the door. The Outcasts will shift in.'

He blows out his breath. The Rephaite ability to be anywhere in the blink of an eye is still new for him. 'We really used to be able do that? On our own?'

I nod, and have a sharp memory of dark trees in Melbourne. Cool air against my skin. Insects chirping. Rafa trying to teach me to shift. The terrifying sensation of being sucked into a vortex—and then slamming into the concrete path about a meter from where I started.

'Then we can do it again,' he says. 'I'd feel a lot better being here if we could come and go as easily as everyone else.'

Mya sits on his other side, ignores me. 'So what's the plan?'

'We listen to what Nathaniel has to say. If there's a chance he'll help, it's worth sticking around for a bit longer. If not, we'll get the rest of your crew—'

'Our crew,' Mya corrects.

Jude pauses. '*Our* crew together, and work out our own plan. Deal?'

'Deal.' Mya, Ez, and Zak say it together. As if it's the most natural thing in the world for him to be taking charge.

There's a heavy scraping over the stone floor. The big timber doors opening. I sit up straighter, try to steady my pulse.

Time's up.

BLAME: A GAME FOR ALL THE FAMILY

Daniel walks in first. His dark hair is sticking up in all directions and there's still a streak of dried blood on his neck. The sight of him looking so disheveled crushes any hope this is anything other than a full-blown crisis.

Next is a redhead with cropped hair and seventies sideburns, followed by two women I don't recognize and a monk with wispy white hair. And then Nathaniel. Too late, I realize my sword is out of reach. I'd feel better if I was armed, but going for it now would look like a provocation.

They cross the room and we stand up. All of them stare at Jude except Daniel, who's staring at me. They stop a few meters away, Nathaniel in the middle, taller even than Zak. His irises flicker with those unnatural blue flames.

'I'm guessing this is the Council of Five,' I say to Jude.

I'm thrown by the presence of the elderly monk, though. 'That one's Uriel—Uri.' I point to the redhead. 'I don't know the others.'

'This is Magdalena,' Daniel says, gesturing, 'and Calista.'

I look from one to the other, try to remember what Rafa said about the Five . . . *Nathaniel likes to have all three Rephaite disciplines covered: military, religious, academic . . .* He was sitting at the bench in my kitchen, reading the paper and winding up Jason about his beautifully tied scarves. I shut the memory down quickly, before the panic starts to rise.

Everything about Calista says soldier: broad shoulders, cropped hair, scarred arms. Her coal-dark eyes graze over us, wary; some of the hardness softening as those eyes meet mine. She wants me to remember her.

Magdalena—Magda, Rafa called her—stands back. She grips her elbows, her hands pale, her nails short and manicured. A strand of dark hair hangs loose around her face. She's fiddling with a string of prayer beads; they clack against each other in a strange rhythm.

'Where's the other one?' I ask.

'Zebediah is in the scriptorium. Brother Stephen will brief him.' Daniel's voice is thin. 'What have you decided?'

I glance at Mya. She won't meet my eyes. 'We're staying. For now.'

'And the others?'

'Here soon.'

Jude is still scrutinizing the four council members. Measuring them. Like the rest of the Rephaim, they look about twenty, not a hundred and thirty-nine. They don't look like the governing body of a society of half-angel bastards.

'Jude.' It's Uri who speaks. 'Did you come here for a fight?'

My brother shrugs. He seems relaxed; I know he's not. The muscles in his neck are taut, his eyes wary. 'That depends on what happens next.'

Mya spins her sword, threatening. Nathaniel and the Five are unarmed and I realize this could go off the rails before the others even get here. My heart gives a hard rap on my ribs. I have to keep this on track.

'When are we attacking the farmhouse?'

All eyes shift to me. A gust of wind rattles a pane somewhere above us. Magda's beads clack once, then again, and fall silent.

'Gabriella.' My name echoes back from the buttressed ceiling. 'I have called everyone here to keep them safe. These walls—'

'I know, I know, they're warded against demons. What about Rafa and Taya?'

'In a moment. We cannot overlook the significance of what has befallen you and your brother.'

'Are you shitting me?' I glare at Daniel. 'Tell me again you didn't orchestrate that attack simply to get us all here.'

His jaw tightens. 'What sort of monsters do you think we are?'

'The sort that thought it was a good idea to put me in a cage with a hellion.'

'*One* hellion—and you killed it. I didn't set a horde of Gatekeepers on you while you had your back turned.'

'This is what you wanted though, isn't it? Jude and me, here?'

'Not like this. Never like this.'

'Please,' Nathaniel says. 'Zachariah, Esther, Mya. We need a moment with Judah and Gabriella before the others arrive.'

'I said no.' I let my blankets drop to the cold floor. Ez, Zak, and Mya move closer. It's more in defiance than solidarity, but I'll take what I can get.

Nathaniel's eyes don't leave mine. 'Why will you not talk to us alone?'

'Because I don't trust you.' I let my eyes narrow. 'And since we can't shift . . .'

He has the gall to look offended. Beside him, Calista squares her shoulders. As if she's heard enough to know I'm not the Gabe she remembers.

Nathaniel shifts his attention to Jude. 'You say you do not remember your past. Will you allow me to search your mind?'

Jude flicks me a glance.

'He can read our thoughts, but we have to let him,'

I say. 'Unless we're drugged or beaten unconscious.'

He snorts. 'No fucking way.'

'Show some respect.' Calista's face is pinched, flushed.

'That's one thing he certainly hasn't learned,' Daniel says. Uri steps up beside him, flexes his fingers. The cool air fizzes with anger.

Which is when Jones and the rest of the Outcasts materialize in the middle of the chapterhouse.

Armed.

DISOBEDIENT BASTARDS

My stomach lurches the way it always does when Rephaim shift. Nathaniel and the Five turn and face a forest of swords, glinting in the dull morning light. Zak, Ez, and Mya shift and reappear almost instantly in front of the other eighteen Outcasts.

Brother Stephen and Magda scuttle out of the way but Jude and I don't move. We're stranded by the wall, between the two groups. Too far from our swords.

'Lay down your weapons.' Calista's voice rings off the walls. 'Lay them down or we'll take this as an act of aggression.'

'Did you think we were going to come here unarmed?' Mya says, all barbs and hooks. Lit up somehow, as if this is what she's been waiting for. I feel a surge of pure exasperation that nearly floors me. How are we going to get Rafa back if these people can't be in the same room without it turning into a brawl?

Jones moves into position next to Mya. Straight black hair sticks out from under a knitted beanie and frames his angular face. He's wearing black jeans and a black woolen sweater. The Outcasts rejected many things when they walked away from the Sanctuary, but not the Rephaim penchant for black on black. He glances at me—the last time I saw him I was outside the club in LA with a knife sticking out of my leg—and then his eyes snap to Jude. First time since finding out my brother's alive. His face crumples a little.

'You are guests,' Calista says. 'Show some respect.'

'Or what?' Mya says.

'Or we're going to see if you've gotten any better at swinging that sword.'

I look to Nathaniel. Why isn't he stepping in? But then I understand: he's too busy counting. He's looking the Outcasts over, checking they're all there. My stomach drops again. The Outcasts as one reposition their weight and lift their weapons.

A small army stands behind Nathaniel and the Five. At least thirty Rephaim. Some I recognize from my first trip up the mountain last week. Most I don't. They're lined up with military precision, armed with swords and poleaxes. That night on the mountain—the night we got Maggie back after Taya took her to get to me—Rafa, Ez, and Zak fought against a handful of Sanctuary Rephaim. At least until the Gatekeeper demons arrived. Then they put aside their grudges and fought shoulder to shoulder. Now, without an immediate threat from a third party, the tension between the two groups has snapped back.

Malachi is front and center. Eyes only for me. Glaring. Does he blame me for what's happening to Taya? Or does he blame himself? If he'd been there, his battle partner wouldn't be imprisoned with Rafa, horribly injured and fighting off demons while we . . .

No.

I'm not game to move, anyway, the slightest gesture could set off either group. Eyes on both sides flick to Jude and me. We're unarmed. Jude raises his eyebrows and I have no idea what to do. What was I thinking, bringing the Outcasts here?

I search for red hair, find Daisy in the crowd of Rephaim. She's eyeballing the Outcasts, but a tear tracks down her freckled cheek. She's seen Jude. They might have been enemies for the past decade but there's no doubt how much it means to her that he's alive. Micah is there too, tall and blond, absently spinning the hilt of his katana. He catches my eye, nods a quick greeting, and then fixes his attention back on Mya. I'm glad he and Daisy are in the room: they're the only Sanctuary Rephaim who haven't treated me like a sworn enemy over the past week.

'Everyone needs to calm down,' Daniel says. He accepts

the sword Malachi offers. Calista and Uri are armed now too.

'You want us to stay calm?' Mya points her katana at Calista. 'You just called in two squads.'

Calista knocks the blade away. 'Watch your tone.'

Three blades whip up to replace Mya's—Jones, Ez, and Zak, their swords all trained on Calista's throat.

'Lower your weapons.'

Nathaniel. Finally.

'Them first.' Mya gestures to the Rephaim behind Nathaniel.

'Lower your weapons,' he repeats.

Nobody moves. Nathaniel shouldn't be surprised the Outcasts don't obey: they've been in open rebellion against him for a decade.

'Don't think we won't take you on,' Calista says. 'This is long overdue.'

God, there's no way this is ending without carnage. Blood pounds at my temples. 'What is wrong with you people?'

The coiled rage in the room shifts, winds around me. I feel blurred, smudged, as if I don't quite fit in my skin. I jump up on the pew, stare them down. 'While you're busy with your pissing contest, Zarael has Rafa and Taya in that farmhouse.' My voice is too loud, I can't help it. I'm buzzing with fear and anger and panic. 'You should be falling over yourselves to save them. Or is this crap so important you'll let Gatekeepers do what they like to them?'

'You're not in a position to make demands anymore, Gabe,' Calista says.

'Those demons killed a sixteen-year-old girl and her mother. I shouldn't have to demand anything.'

Calista shakes her head. 'Can't you see the mess you're in? I never accepted that you betrayed us, but now you turn up here with *them* pushing for an Outcast-style attack—'

Jude springs up next to me. 'Betrayed you, yeah? What do you actually know about what we did last year? Know for a fact? Any of you?' His eyes rake over the Rephaim on both sides of the room. He waits. Nobody speaks. 'Then back the fuck off. I don't remember being tight with you guys'—Jude gestures to the Sanctuary side of the room—'or you'—to the Outcasts.

Calista shifts her weight and something about the movement catches my eye. Her track pants are oddly loose around her left calf, like there's something different about that leg.

'And I sure as hell don't remember deserting my sister a decade ago.' His voice wavers but he doesn't look away from the sea of faces. The chapterhouse simmers with recrimination but both sides wait for him to continue, lower their swords a fraction. I feel pride—and a prick of regret that they don't respond to me like that. 'Whatever we did last year brought us back together again, so don't expect an apology from either of us any time soon.'

For a steadying moment, I fit back in my skin.

'And we're not talking about it anymore until we get Rafa back,' Jude adds.

'And Taya.' Malachi—still glaring.

'And Taya.'

The only sounds in the chapterhouse are boots on stone, clinking steel.

'You are in no position to make demands either.' The skin around Daniel's eyes is taut: a hint of the old rivalry between him and Jude that I've heard so much about.

'I don't give a shit what position I'm in. That's where we stand.'

They eyeball each other.

The cold gets the better of me. I shudder and instantly regret it. Daniel breaks eye contact with Jude. He waits a beat and passes his sword to Malachi. Then he comes over and picks up a blanket from the floor, offers it to me. I hesitate. Is this a test? What message will I send if I take the comfort he's offering? I shiver again. Dammit.

'You're freezing,' Daniel says, matter-of-fact. 'You'll be no use to anyone if you fall ill.'

I vaguely register that Rephaim can get sick. It makes sense: *I've* been sick. I take the blanket, wordlessly throw it around my shoulders and wait to feel its warmth. Daniel returns to Nathaniel's side.

'Nathaniel,' Jude says. His bare arms are covered in

goosebumps, but he shows no sign of feeling the cold. 'What's your call?'

The fallen angel is statue-still, his chiseled face impassive. 'The Council and I shall meet. Then we shall send for you.' He gestures to both groups. 'All of you.'

I tighten my blanket. 'How long's that going to take?'

'As long as necessary. It will give you the chance to shower and eat. Brother Stephen will show you to the guestrooms.'

'We don't have time—'

'Gabriella.'

I bite back my next words.

'This is not a skirmish with a handful of Gatekeepers. What you are asking for is a full battle against Zarael and his entire horde. We do not attack, Gabriella. If you had not been robbed of your past you would know and understand this, as you always have. We have authority to defend ourselves when necessary, but have no commission to seek out demons for conflict. I do not risk Rephaite lives lightly.'

'What about defending Rafa and Taya? What about not wasting the opportunity of knowing where Zarael and his horde are for the first time in over a century?'

He makes a show of looking around the chapterhouse. 'Have you called the lost Rephaite?'

I falter. 'Jason?'

'Yes. Have you phoned him?'

'Not yet.'

'Please do so now. He is at risk every second he is not here.'

Which means Maggie is too. Oh god, Maggie. No matter what I do, I can't keep her safe. And I have to tell her about Simon and the Butlers. I touch my phone in my pocket. I hate that I have to drag my best friend back into this shitty mess. But what choice do I have?

I'm not letting any more people I care about get hurt.

GATHERING CLOUDS

On Nathaniel's signal the Sanctuary Rephaim file out of the chapterhouse, resentful. I sit on the pew and cradle my phone. It's cold and lifeless, or maybe the phone's fine and it's me. Daisy and Micah both catch my eye before they leave; both take one last look at Jude.

'You may follow Brother Stephen,' Nathaniel says to the Outcasts, and gestures to the monk waiting by the door. His head is bowed, his gnarled hands folded over his brown robe. Magda has already left.

'We'll wait for Gabe,' Ez says.

Nathaniel tilts his chin a fraction as if he's considering a tricky question. 'As you wish.' He makes no move to leave. Daniel, Uri, and Calista stay in position as well; the Outcasts hold their line. Nathaniel's attention flicks to them, frequently. Another gust of wind outside. The draft brushes past my ear, shifts a stray hair clinging to my neck.

Mya lets out her breath, incapable of hiding her frustration. 'We know the way to our rooms. There's no need to babysit us.'

'You think we kept your rooms?' Calista says. 'Honestly, Mya, your delusion knows no bounds.'

Malachi lifts the tip of his sword in Mya's direction. His eyes are hard, his skin washed out under the jet-black goatee.

'This is your fault.'

Mya smiles, dangerous. 'How do you figure that?'

'You caused the split: you kept Gabe and Jude apart. Whatever they did a year ago wouldn't have happened if they'd both still been here. This attack today wouldn't have happened.'

Whatever they did a year ago.

'I'm not the one who led Zarael straight to them and got a bunch of rednecks butchered,' Mya snaps.

'No, *you're* the one who keeps putting people I care about in danger—'

'Enough.' Ez steps between them, her plait swinging across her back. 'We're not doing this now.'

Jude picks up the other blanket and turns his back to the others. 'Better make that call before this turns ugly again.'

I check my watch. It's been forty-seven minutes since

the attack. I try not to think of all the things Zarael could do to Rafa in forty-seven minutes. My breath shortens again. Jude grips my elbow.

'You don't know what's going on at the farmhouse, and imagining the worst doesn't change that. All it does is paralyze you, which helps nobody.'

He's right, I know he is. But the fear is deep in my bones now. A part of me. And then the realization hits: I know how I can find out exactly what's happening in that room. I take a deep breath and tap in Maggie's number. I need to hear her voice before I talk to Jason. Her phone rings six times. It's about to go to voice mail—

'Gaby.' Her voice is bright, warm. I can hear soft music in the background, tinkling glasses. I close my eyes and wish I didn't have to take this moment from her.

'Mags . . .'

'What is it?' Her fear is instant. 'What happened with the Butlers?'

I focus on the worn pew so I don't have to see everyone watching me deliver the news. I stall. 'Is Jason with you?'

'Of course.'

'Are you still in Melbourne?'

'Yes—babe, where are you?'

'The Sanctuary.'

I hear her intake of breath. 'Why? Is everything okay? Is Jude—'

'Jude's fine.' I dig my fingernail into a gouge in the

timber, remember that three of the Five are still in the room. 'Zarael attacked. He got Taya and . . . and Rafa.' I bite the inside of my lip. Jude takes the phone from me.

'Hey, hey. It's okay, Maggie, they're alive.' He pauses, taps his thumb on his thigh. A glance at Daniel. 'Yeah, he and Taya followed us up there. He reckons the demons took them as leverage. Or bait.' He listens for a moment. 'Simon's okay. He's here with us. So are the brothers and their mates. They're a bit knocked around . . . Yeah, Maggie, we will. We'll look after them.'

I don't know if he means Rafa and Taya or Simon and the Butlers. Guilt stabs at me. Rafa warned the Butlers their guns were no match for demons, and now they know. Beyond any doubt.

I force myself to concentrate on the feel of the cool air filling my nose and lungs. I exhale. Breathe deeply again. When I feel closer to calm, I ask for the phone back.

'Oh god, Gaby . . .' Maggie's voice cracks. 'Are you okay?'

'I'd be better if everyone here stopped arguing long enough to come up with a plan.' I meet Daniel's eyes. He doesn't blink.

'Are you safe? I mean, last time you were there . . .' She doesn't finish the sentence. She doesn't need to.

'Jude's here. So are Ez and Zak.'

'It's the Sanctuary, Gaby. They hurt you.'

'I know.' I turn away from the Rephaim and Outcasts, tuck my knees to my chin. I wish Maggie and I were at the old table in our kitchen, hands wrapped around chipped coffee mugs, talking about books she loves and places I've seen and wishing it was Friday already.

'Then why—'

'We need them. There's not enough of us to go after the Gatekeepers on our own.'

'Why do you have to go?'

'Because it's Rafa,' I whisper. 'And this is my life now.'

A sigh. 'Babe—oh, hang on. Jason wants to talk to you.' There are muffled words before she hands the phone over.

'Gaby, I'm sorry.'

I swallow. 'Me too.'

'What do you need?'

'You and Maggie here, safe.'

A long pause. 'Gaby, I'm not coming to the Sanctuary.'

I close my eyes. I get it. I get that he's avoided the Sanctuary his entire life. But I need him to see beyond all that, as hard as it will be. This is more important. *Rafa* is more important.

'Nathaniel's done something here that keeps demons out.'

A beat. 'How?'

'I don't know, wards that work like the iron room. Ask him when you get here.' Jason doesn't respond so I push on. 'Look, you don't have to side with anyone and nobody can force you stay here.'

'I'll think about it.'

'Jason—'

'We're safe where we are for the moment.'

'How can you be sure? The Gatekeepers found the house in Iowa, and we didn't lead them there. And you can't go back to Pan Beach, not now.'

'I know.' I hear a frustrated sigh. 'Let me think about it.'

'One more thing.' I swallow, drop my voice. 'I need to see Dani.'

No response.

'Jason?'

Still nothing.

I stand up and clutch my blanket tighter, head to the far end of the chapterhouse. 'Jason.' I move further into the shadows, check that nobody has followed me.

'Have you told them about her?' His voice is stiff, distant.

'Of course not, but—'

'She's not getting involved in this nightmare.'

My heart squeezes. Of course he's resisting this, but he needs to remember what's at stake. Who's at stake. 'At least give her the choice. Give me the number.'

'You know she won't answer.'

'Then I'll leave a message. Jason—'

'You can't ask me do to this. I've kept my family—*our* family—safe from Nathaniel for all these years. If he finds out what she can do . . . We can't un-ring that bell.'

'And we can't reattach Rafa's head if Zarael hacks it

off.' I feel the strain in my voice. Too loud. I check over my shoulder. Yep: everyone's watching. I breathe in, try to calm myself. 'We need to know what's going on in that room.' I lower my voice again. 'And we need her here. We can protect her. Please.'

'Gaby . . .'

'I'm not asking her to go in there and get them out.'

'No, you're asking her to give up a family secret that could get her killed—or worse.' He pauses. 'Why does she have to be there?'

'Because even if she agrees, her mother's just as likely to disappear with her again and leave us in the dark. Will you call her?'

More silence. And then: 'Give me a minute.'

I strain to hear the hushed conversation on the other end.

Why don't you let Dani decide?

It's not a decision for a twelve-year-old.

She strikes me as an intelligent girl, Jason. Just ask.

There's a crackling noise as the phone is handed over. 'He'll call her.'

'Are you sure?'

Maggie hesitates, and I can picture her silently confirming it with Jason. 'Yes.'

I sag back against the cold stone wall, close my eyes.

'Is it really safe there?' She sounds edgy.

I look over at Nathaniel and Daniel, both watching

me; at Jude standing rigid, waiting, a huddle of Outcasts behind him.

'I honestly have no idea. But it's the safest place for all of us right now.'

FIRE AND ICE

Nathaniel moves towards me as soon as I hang up. Can't he give me a second to breathe?

'He's thinking about it,' I say.

'What is there to think about?'

Do I tell him how much Jason hates him for what he did to our mothers? It's not going to help get Rafa back. Nathaniel's icy gaze flickers. Does he know I know?

'Shouldn't you and the Five be off somewhere making a decision about Iowa?'

He watches me a moment longer. It's like being caught in headlights on the highway. In the middle of winter. 'Brother Stephen will show you all to your rooms now.'

'We won't be here long enough to need a bed,' I say.

Nathaniel's expression doesn't change. 'When you are ready a meal will be waiting in the commissary.'

He leaves and Uri and Calista follow him out. Daniel lingers. He waits until the door rasps shut and then crosses the room. Gives me a subtle once-over, even though he knows I wasn't physically hurt during the attack. 'Are you all right?'

'No, Daniel, I'm really not.'

Behind him, Brother Stephen waits for the Outcasts to acknowledge him, but they're too busy with Jude. Ez, Zak, and Mya have known for a few hours that he's alive. For the rest of them it's only been a matter of minutes.

Daniel follows my gaze and watches Jones drag Jude into a man hug. Next in line is the tall Scandinavian, Seth. It's just like with Ez, Zak, and Mya: nobody cares what Jude did a year ago. They're too elated to have him back.

Daniel turns back to me. 'You really did a mercenary job with them.' It's not a question.

'Don't.' I breathe in camphor from the blanket. 'Just . . . don't.' I can live without hearing his opinion yet again on how I should be thinking and behaving. How I should be more like the Gabe he remembers. Whatever he sees in my face stops the rest of his lecture. He reconsiders his approach.

'You need to stop pushing Nathaniel.'

'Why? Is he that fickle that he'd leave Rafa and Taya to Zarael just to teach me a lesson?'

'Nathaniel is an angel, Gabriella, he's not prone to petty human emotions.'

'Then what does it matter how much I push him?'

'The rift between the Rephaim was caused because that group'—he tips his head in the direction of the Outcasts, their voices getting louder around Jude—'lost respect for Nathaniel as our mentor and protector.'

'I thought it was because Nathaniel refused to explain what the archangels want from us, beyond finding the Fallen.'

'If Nathaniel doesn't share information, it's for our own protection.'

'Is that why he never told you this place is warded against demons? To protect you?'

Daniel's nostrils flare the tiniest bit. 'I trust Nathaniel's judgment.'

'Well, I'm glad one of us does because Rafa and Taya's lives are in his hands.'

'Nathaniel is not a dictator. The Five will have just as much of a say—'

'Then go and make sure the right decision is made.'

Now that he's close, I can see the lines around his mouth; the dark shadows under his eyes. The stress he's been working so hard to hide since we got here. God, he's a mess: this is bad. The grip on my heart tightens.

'We have to get them back, Daniel. Please.'

Something changes when I say his name. He's not seeing me; he's seeing the old Gabe, the Gabe he knew and trusted. For a few seconds, it's just Daniel and his memories.

'I'll do what I can.'

'Thank you.'

He looks around, remembers I'm not Gabe and that we're not alone. He straightens his shoulders and his shirt. 'This may take a while.' He says it loud enough to carry to the others. 'Stay out of trouble.'

I don't know if he's talking to me, Jude, or all of us and I don't get a chance to ask because he shifts as soon as he says it.

Not: walks calmly from the room to demonstrate how in control he is.

Shifts.

YOU CAN CHECK OUT ANY
TIME YOU LIKE . . .

Brother Stephen leads us out of the chapterhouse into a chilly gray morning. Low clouds blanket the mountains, pressing down on the ancient sandstone building ahead of us. High walls hem us in. I breathe in the sharp scent of pine needles and cold air nips at my nose and ears.

We cross a courtyard, swords in hand. The Outcasts follow, framed by carved columns and the domed roof of the chapterhouse. We pass a marble statue of a warrior angel twice as tall as Nathaniel, streaked and cracked from decades of wind, snow, and sunshine. The angel's wings are outstretched, sword raised in triumph, his expression grim. Trees whisper beyond the wall. Boots crunch on gravel.

Jude stays close, keeps glancing my way. 'You okay?'

'Better now I'm moving.' The anger's gone. It drained away in the quiet of the chapterhouse. Now I'm numb again, which is still better than the panic hovering somewhere behind me.

We walk under an archway and into an expansive piazza, flanked on all sides by three-storey buildings and cloistered walkways. A fountain dominates the manicured grass; water spills over the lip of a large stone bowl and splashes softly into a pond below. The piazza is familiar—it's the one I saw out the window when I was last here, although from this angle it looks more like one in the photos from the iron room.

The iron room . . .

I crush that thought, focus instead on following Brother Stephen's shuffled steps along the cloister. Try to ignore the churning in my stomach. I need to move faster; I need to run until my vision blurs and my legs are on fire. I might not be able to outrun this feeling, but pain would at least be a distraction.

This place is so . . . medieval. Lanterns hang from brass chains above us. Cracked wooden benches sit against the walls under windows dull with age and grime. We pass a clay pot filled with lavender and I pick off a leaf and crush it between my fingers. The smell is almost calming. Almost.

We reach the end of the cloister and Brother Stephen holds open a carved door, waves our group inside. The Outcasts mill about at the base of a wide staircase, fidgeting. The air is warmer in here. The stairs creak as we climb to the first storey. At the top, my stomach twists. This could be the same hallway I was dragged down last week. It's a lot like it—beige walls, beige carpet. There's even a lift at the other end.

'Gaby?' Jude's hand is on my elbow again. I didn't realize I'd stopped walking. I'm bone cold, despite the central heating.

'It's . . . I'm fine,' I say. 'Just thinking about the last time I was here.'

'This will be nothing like that. This time you've got backup.' He gestures to the Outcasts around us.

I've got some currency with the Outcasts thanks to the job in LA, but I'm not going to kid myself: they're here for Rafa and Jude. They're not here for me. And there's no love for me from the Sanctuary Rephaim either—except for maybe Daisy.

Brother Stephen gives Jude and me the first two rooms. I wait while Jude does a quick lap of his. The monk directs the others down the hall but hesitates when I touch the sleeve of his robe.

'Where's Daisy's room?' I ask quietly. I'd feel better knowing she's not too far away.

He considers the question. His eyes are pale blue and faded with age but still sharp, intelligent. 'Her quarters are on the next floor. But you will find she spends most of her spare time in the gymnasium.'

Brother Stephen follows after the Outcasts and I go into the room next to Jude's. It's exactly like the one Daniel brought me to last week: polished furniture and white muslin curtains over old-fashioned timber-framed windows. Sterile.

I toss my sword onto the bed. I drop the blanket and go to the window, look down at the piazza. I can't believe I'm back here. This time Rafa's not coming to save me; this time, I have to save him. I grip the window ledge. I can do this. I have to do this. If ever I needed to channel badass Gabe, now's the time. But she's as far away from me as Rafa.

'We used to live here?' Jude asks, joining me.

'Do you feel anything . . . familiar?'

He stares out at the mountains hemming in the ancient buildings. 'No. Why?'

'It's just—I thought maybe it might be like everything else. You know, that something about this might feel . . . *right*.'

He looks at me, a slight crease in his forehead. 'Nothing about this place feels right.'

I think about him staring down Nathaniel and then being group-hugged by the Outcasts.

'What?' he says.

'Nothing.' I sink onto the bed. I pluck at my shirt, smell wood smoke, grass, dirt. Tears threaten. Again.

Jude sits beside me.

'What happened when you were in that room in Iowa?'

I close my eyes and see the plaster torn back to reveal giant wings etched into a solid iron wall. My stomach knots, remembering Rafa hurling himself against the unrelenting metal, unable to shift beyond those walls until the Outcasts broke us out.

'I was trying to protect Maggie. I wanted her to be safe when Rafa and I came searching for you. Jason thought those women could help.'

I tell Jude what we found in that room: photos of the Rephaim. Photos *stolen* from the Rephaim. Floor plans and drawings of the Sanctuary. And a journal with sepia-tone photos of men burning a body in a cornfield.

'Rafa thinks someone here at the Sanctuary has been feeding information to them for years—that's how they know so much about the Rephaim.'

'He have any idea who would do that?'

'No, he didn't know.'

Jude thinks for a moment. 'Those Iowa women know how that room works.'

I nod.

'And Nathaniel has one of them here?'

'Yeah, Virginia—Sophie's grandmother.' I think about Sophie lying dead in the cornfield beside her mother, torn apart by demons. I feel sick. 'Debra—Virginia's other daughter—she's safe. Mya took her to a cop the Outcasts know in LA.'

Jude drums his fingers on his knees. 'We need to find out how the family created those wards and if there's any way we can get around them.'

'I know.'

'What do you know?'

Mya is in the doorway, Ez and Zak behind her. She's looking at Jude, not me.

'That we need to talk to Virginia,' I say. 'Or even better, Debra, given she designed that room.'

Mya comes inside, drops a duffel bag at Jude's feet. 'I got Jones to grab some clothes for you.'

'What about Gaby?'

'Her stuff's already here.'

I give her a level look. 'And how am I going to get it?'

She shrugs. 'I guess you're about to find out if you have any friends left here.'

Nice. Apparently we're only on the same side when she needs backup in an argument with Nathaniel. Ez and Zak stay by the door. Ez catches my eye, gives me an apologetic smile.

'We need to talk to Debra,' I say again to Mya.

'We will.'

'When?'

'When we need to.'

'We need to now.'

'I thought you wanted us here. Make your mind up, Gabe.'

I kick the duffel bag at her. 'What the fuck is your problem?'

Mya leans over me, her neck reddening. 'What do you want to do, Gabe—go to LA and interrogate Debra or stay here and beg Nathaniel for help?'

I'm on my feet in an instant, in her face. 'I want Rafa and Taya back, that's what I want.'

'You don't think I do too?' We're centimeters apart. Close enough that I can smell the peppermint on her breath. Anger surges through me, crackling, familiar. Comforting.

'Then let's go in on our own,' Mya says. 'Right now.'

'No.' Ez comes further inside. 'Not until we know how that room works. Maybe we need more numbers, maybe we don't. But we'll lose the option of a bigger force the second Nathaniel finds out we've gone.'

I tear my eyes from Mya to see what Jude's thinking. He runs a hand through his hair—the same thick dark hair that always looks untidy on me. Everything about him is so familiar and yet . . . different. Different from the brother of my fake memories: the brother who loved to drink and surf and laugh. I still see that Jude in him, but *this* Jude is more focused. More take-charge.

'Then let's talk to Virginia,' he says and I nod, emphatic. 'She's in the Sanctuary somewhere. It's the obvious move.'

Mya makes an impatient sound and turns away.

'I agree it's a better option,' Ez says. 'But not yet.'

'Why not?' I ask.

'Because if we get caught, it's over for us here. We can't risk it.' She looks away for a moment, frustrated. When her eyes meet mine again, I see how uneasy she is. 'I hate this as much as you do but everything is different now. Zarael can *imprison* us.'

Zak shifts his weight in the doorway. 'Ez is right. It'd be better if we didn't have to face that farmhouse on our own. We need to give the Five at least half a chance. Who knows: maybe they've grown a set.'

Jude presses his lips together and nods, but his eyes flick to me. I give a tiny shake of my head. We can't just sit around waiting. I rub at the dirt smudged on my forearm. Maybe he and I can find out where Virginia is being held. Someone must know . . .

Of course. *Daisy.*

I think about the fine line she treads between obedience and defiance. She hasn't crossed it yet for me, but if *Jude* was asking for help, the response might be different. Brother Stephen said she hangs out in the gym. My skin chills at the thought of the dank training room with its wire cage and blood-stained sawdust. But if it's where Daisy's most likely to go, it's where we need to be. Jude and I have to talk to her away from the Outcasts. Away from Mya.

I walk to the window again, jerk the curtains apart, walk back to Jude. 'I really need to hit something. Right now.' I give him a meaningful look.

He frowns, trying to read my mood. 'What did you have in mind?'

'Nobody said the gym was off limits. We could work the bags down there for a while. You and me.'

'Okay . . . sure.'

I let my breath out.

'That's not an entirely stupid idea.'

Crap.

Mya raises her eyebrows at me. 'What? You think you're the only one who needs to blow off steam?' She walks between Jude and me on her way to the door, eyeballing me as she passes. 'I'll get the others. We could *all* do with a session downstairs.'

NOTHING SAYS 'I CARE' LIKE A PUNCH IN THE FACE

We need to get to the gym before Mya and the others. There's no chance Daisy will help us—no way she'll break Nathaniel's trust—if Mya knows about it.

I turn to Ez. 'Can we go now—meet them down there?'

Her brow creases, but she nods. 'Sure.'

'Can we shift?'

Ez hesitates for just a second and then reaches for Jude and me. We arrive next to one of two boxing rings. I twist around before I've settled properly back into my skin. Search the shadows for movement, strain to hear sounds of activity. I sweep the room twice, wonder if the shift is messing with my senses. I try to steady my breathing but the result is the same.

The gym is empty.

Banks of fluorescent lights hang from the ceiling; weights and barbells are stacked against the walls; exercise mats cover the concrete floor. But no Daisy. All the strength drains out of me. Where the hell is she?

I rub my bare arms. There's a hint of warmth in the basement, but it's struggling to take the chill out of the air. The place smells of leather, sawdust, and sweat.

Ez touches my elbow. 'Are you really okay being down here?' The question is cautious, careful. It's then the full reality of where I am hits me. My scalp prickles. I turn back to the middle of the room. Jude is already heading for the cage and I can't help it: I'm drawn too. There's no trace of blood in the sawdust—mine or the hellion's—but the bile rises in my throat. What did they do with its body? With its head? My heart stumbles. What if Zarael puts a hellion in that room with Rafa and Taya? Or two hellions? Ten? The sawdust comes at me and I grip the chain wire to steady myself.

'Bloody hell, Gaby,' Jude says. 'They locked you in there with one of those hell-beasts?' His fingers find mine on the wire. 'Those arseholes . . .'

I drag myself back to the moment. *This* moment. 'We need to talk to Daisy,' I whisper. 'She'll know where Virginia is.'

'That's why you wanted to come down here?' He glances back at Ez and Zak, frowns.

'It has to be just us. Nobody else ends up in the shit if

we get caught. Jude.' I wait until he's looking at me again. 'We'll tell them if we get to Virginia. But first we need to talk to Daisy. Alone.'

There are more voices behind us: the rest of the Outcasts have arrived. I squeeze Jude's fingers, hold his gaze until I see he's with me. And then I put my back to the chain wire and face the Outcasts. Mya, Jones, Seth. Others I recognize from the LA job. I get longer eye contact from Jude's old crew now, a few tentative nods. An improvement on the open hostility we started with two days ago in Dubai. If they resent being here, they keep it to themselves. Right now, Jude is all they care about. Within seconds he's surrounded. More hugging and hand-shaking.

I push away from the cage and head for Ez. She's helping Zak rig up a punching bag. The panic is still there, pulling at me, but if I keep moving I can almost ignore it. I need to give Daisy time to show.

'Gabe.' Jones breaks from the group.

'Oh. Hey.'

'How's the leg?' He gestures to my thigh. My hand goes to the stab wound, fully healed thanks to half a dozen shifts. The love fest for Jude continues behind us, Mya in the middle of it.

'It still itches a bit.' For a few seconds I'm back pinned against the fence, feel the sickening sensation of pushing the knife through sinew and muscle into Bel's chest, and that brief moment of triumph before the demon staggered away, pulled it out and threw it at me.

Jones shoves his hands in his pockets. Looks away, back again. 'Was Rafa . . . Did he . . . ?' He can't finish.

'He didn't see it coming. Neither of them did.' I can't stop the tremor in my voice and it's like I've punched Jones. He closes his eyes, fights the image.

'I didn't think I could hate Zarael any more than I already do.'

'Has anything like this happened before?'

'Gatekeepers killed Cass back in 1912, took his head. But that was in battle—'

'You've lost Rephaim?' For a second I can't feel my legs.

'We can die, Gabe, just like they can. But they've never been able to hold us prisoner. And we've never been at their mercy, not like this.'

'Can we beat them?'

'I don't know.' He slides off his beanie and tucks it in his back pocket. Long dark hair sits flat against his head. 'But we've got half a chance now you and Jude are back.'

I hope he's right. I hope Jude and I can be who the Rephaim need us to be. Who Rafa needs us to be.

'How about we burn some energy.' Ez says it loud enough to get everyone's attention. 'Gabe, Jude, over here.' She and Zak have the bag up and ready.

The Outcasts linger near Jude for a few seconds more and then fan out on the mats. Jude falls into step with me as we cross the room. He glances at Jones and Seth, squaring up against each other. 'I hate having all these people know more about us than we do.' He stretches an arm across his chest as we walk. 'We still need to sort that mess out. The laptop you found might help.'

'It's in Pan Beach.'

'I know.'

We reach Ez and Zak before I can find out where the conversation was headed. Zak pushes the bag away from him and the chain squeaks. When it swings back, he traps it against his broad chest. 'Gabe, you first.'

I glance at the tarnished bronze door on the far side of the gym. Still closed. I take the fingerless gloves Ez offers.

Jude strips off his sweater and continues to limber up. I stretch out my shoulders, wait for Zak to get in position behind the bag and hold it steady. His head pokes around the side. 'Start with jabs.'

The rest of the room has gone still; everyone's stopped to spectate. Jude's watching too. I wasn't lying: I do need to hit something. I'm fizzing with nervous energy but my first punch is light, self-conscious. The second not much better.

'That the best you've got?' Zak says.

I grit my teeth and throw a hook as hard as I can. It jars my shoulder and Zak takes a step back to absorb it. 'Better. Give me combinations.'

It's like sparring: after two more punches the moves

come naturally, instinctively. The intensity builds as I mix it up: jabs, hooks, power punches, leading first with my left and then my right. Feet always moving.

'Keep your guard up.'

I bring my other fist up protectively to cover my face. Everything in the room fades except Zak and the bag. I slam my fist into the leather. Again. And again. My breath shortens. My knuckles sting.

'Roundhouse.'

I lash out without thinking. My shin makes a satisfying *thwack* halfway up the leather bag.

'Other leg,' Zak says, and braces as I connect again.

I pummel the bag with punches, kicks, elbow strikes. Sweat runs down my neck. A dull ache spreads across my shoulders. I need to go harder. I need to punish the bag, drive out that image of Rafa and that sword. I need—

'That'll do,' Zak says.

Already? I smack the bag with a final combination of punches and step back, panting, let my hands drop. My pulse thuds in my temples. It's not enough. Nowhere near enough.

'You're not that rusty,' Jones says, exchanging places with Zak. He positions himself behind the bag, gestures for Jude to step up. 'Just watch the face.'

Jude rolls his neck from side to side, glances at me as I stand with my hands on my knees, catching my breath. Hesitates for a heartbeat. And then he goes to work. Just like with his sword skills, his technique is controlled and accurate, his strikes forceful enough to occasionally knock the wind from Jones. He's kept fit—obviously—but it's more than that. He's hitting the leather as if he's been doing it every day for years. I've known about this other life for over a week: Jude's known for a few hours. Why does all this come to him so much more quickly than it did for me? It took an attack from a hell-beast for my body to remember how to fight. And even then it was patchy. I'm getting better, but only in fits and starts.

Mya sits on the mats a few meters away, legs crossed, watching Jude as if he's the only person in the room. Jude is oblivious to the attention: he's too focused on pounding the bag.

Why isn't he more freaked out? About being here, about meeting Nathaniel, about all the talk of taking on a horde of Gatekeeper demons and their hellions? The last thought stops me cold. What if I lose him again? The shadowy wall beyond my brother looms dark, threatening. Blood rushes in my ears. What if I lose him *and* Rafa?

A loud scrape snaps my attention back to the gym. The old bronze door slides open and a shot of adrenaline spikes through me.

Daisy and Micah.

About freaking time.

They don't seem surprised to find their gym crowded with Outcasts. Seth and the others immediately close ranks to form a barrier between Daisy and Micah and Jude and me. I shift my weight, feel the muscles in my shoulders bunch up again.

'Let them through,' Zak says.

Seth mutters something to the guy next to him and steps aside. The others follow, creating a gap barely wide enough for Micah and Daisy to pass single file. Micah is taller than everyone except Zak and Seth, and I track their progress by his spiky blond hair. The last time I spoke to him he was guarding Maggie with Malachi and Taya. He'd seemed happy to see me—or at least happy to see Gabe—even though I'd turned up looking for a fight. He and Daisy can hold their own, but they're seriously outnumbered here. I need to keep things calm. I try to catch Daisy's eye but she's preoccupied watching her back.

Micah clears the pack first. 'You know, Gabe, it would be nice to see you sometime when the shit hasn't hit the fan.'

'Who's this guy?' Jude asks.

'That's Micah.'

Micah studies Jude. Hesitant. 'Memory loss or not, it's good to see you, man.'

'Did you hurt Gaby when she was here?'

'Dude, *I'd* have to lose my memory to even try it.'

Daisy checks me over. Her straight red hair is pinned back and her face is paler than usual: the smattering of freckles even more pronounced under the fluorescents. Her eyes flit back to Jude, almost involuntarily.

'How the hell did the Gatekeepers find you guys?' she asks.

'Remember the hell-beast that fed on Taya last Tuesday night?' I say.

Daisy blinks. 'It tracked her? But that was five days ago.'

'Apparently it still had her scent.'

She glances at the hellion bite on my neck. 'How bad was it?'

And just like that, my throat is all cotton wool.

'Rafa took one through the stomach,' Zak says. 'Taya, here.' He demonstrates a chopping motion above his collarbone, angled towards his shoulder.

'Why didn't they shift?'

'It happened too fast.'

'How many were there?' Micah asks.

'Too many. Including Zarael.' Zak and Micah exchange a look heavy with understanding. Their fear stokes my own.

'Shit,' Daisy whispers.

Mya pushes her way in front of Jude. 'Like you care whether Rafa lives or dies.'

Everything about Daisy hardens. 'Don't tell me how I feel about Rafa.'

'Yeah, God forbid someone should judge *you*.'

'Glad to see you appreciate the hospitality of the Sanctuary.'

'It wasn't my call.'

'And yet you're still here.'

'Not for long. Count on it.'

Micah puts his arm out as if to hold Daisy back. 'We didn't come here for a fight.'

Ez steps up next to Mya. 'You want to tell Daisy that?'

'That's Daisy?' Jude gives her an appreciative once-over that brings a flush to her neck. 'You're the one with the twin-bladed sais?'

She dips her head. 'That's me.'

It takes a second for me to realize he means the skinny daggers she uses. Of all the things I've told Jude in the past few hours, I can't believe that detail stuck.

'I'd like to see those in action,' he says.

'I'd say that's a given at this point.' Her eyes roam over him. 'You look good.'

Mya clucks her tongue. 'That's why you came down here—to check Jude out?'

'Believe it or not, Mya, people here care about Jude too.'

'Yeah.' Mya smiles, taunting. 'I bet *they* do.'

Micah steps between them, exasperated. 'Why don't you two sort this out on the mats?'

Daisy's green eyes shine. 'Excellent idea.'

'No, it's not,' Ez says before I can think of a way to stop it. 'That's hardly a fair fight.'

'I can handle myself.' Mya shakes out her wrists.

'Yes, you can, but not against Daisy. You and everyone here knows it. Don't make this about more than it needs to be.'

Jones raises his hand. 'I'll take on Daisy. Unless she's got those blades tucked somewhere I can't see them.'

Daisy measures him. 'In there?' She points to the boxing ring.

Something flickers in Jones's face—satisfaction? 'Absolutely.'

Jude looks from Daisy to me. 'Is this okay?'

I blow out my breath. It's not okay—it's wasting time we don't have—but that's not what he's asking. 'This is about as healthy as it gets between this lot. It doesn't matter what the question is, the answer is usually a throw down.' I follow them to the ring.

Jones and Daisy climb through the ropes and stretch out their arms and shoulders. Jones is already in track pants and fitted tank top; Daisy strips down to a T-shirt, tossing her hoodie at Micah. The Outcasts gather around the ropes with an odd sense of anticipation.

Daisy and Jones circle each other, cautious. I grip the middle rope—too tight, impatient—and vaguely wonder how long it's been since they faced off.

Daisy attacks first, quick and fast. Jones ducks her punch and then drops into splits to avoid a roundhouse kick. He doesn't just have the body of a dancer; he moves like one too. Still on the floor, he swings his legs around in a scissor kick but Daisy jumps up to miss them. He rolls out of the way to avoid being stomped. She leaps at him again but he's gone before she lands. Not shifted—just moving insanely fast. Their movements are fluid, like an aggressive ballet.

They've done this before.

Daisy takes off away from Jones, plants a foot on the second rope, spins, and launches at him. He dives out of the way. She curls up and lands in a commando roll. I look around at the ring. Everyone is caught in the moment—except Mya. She looks on, stony-faced.

Daisy and Jones continue their dance. It takes as much skill and concentration to attack each other at this speed without making contact as it does to connect. I've never seen the Rephaim like this. I have to admit, it's mesmerizing. Beautiful, even.

And then, when they're both in the air and it looks like one of them has finally misjudged their flight, a third person materializes between them and king-hits Jones to the canvas.

Malachi.

I'm through the ropes before I think about it. 'What the fuck are you doing?'

Jones is already on his feet, wiping blood from his mouth. Movement to my left catches my eye. It's Zak. He's ready to tear Malachi apart.

'Hang on,' I say, eyes back on Malachi. 'I've got this. Daisy, don't go anywhere.'

'Wasn't planning on it.' She's somewhere behind me.

Malachi grunts. 'Get out of the ring, Gabe.' His eyes are overcast with anger and grief.

'They're just blowing off steam.'

'Zarael has Taya. You think this is the time for games?'

'It's better than staring at those beige walls upstairs going crazy, waiting for someone here to make a decision about that farmhouse.'

His lips press together so hard they turn white. 'Get out of the ring or it'll be you and me.'

The Outcasts fall still. Jones and Daisy slip between the ropes and join them. I should walk away, get what I need from Daisy. But the Outcasts are all waiting to see how far I'll take this. I can feel it now: the fear, the unknowing. Theirs and mine: it's all there under my rib cage, churning. A burst of adrenaline hits my heart and strength surges through me like an aftershock. I drop and sweep Malachi's legs out from under him, just like Rafa did to me on the training mats in Dubai.

Malachi hits the canvas hard. He springs back up almost instantly, shoves hair out of his face. 'Cheap shot, Gabe.'

'I still owe you a couple.' I turn side-on, unable to keep still.

'Gaby . . .' It's Jude, but I can't think about him right now.

Malachi stalks closer. This is the first time I've fought him without a sword—or a toilet brush. I need to keep moving—

Malachi's boot flies up at me before I finish that thought. I jump back and block the kick just as his fist connects with my kidney. I forgot how quick he is. Dull pain radiates across my hip but I slam my knee into his chest before he straightens. He hops back.

I crack a knuckle like Rafa would. Feel stronger hearing that sound.

Malachi comes at me again, feints right, left, and then throws a lightning-fast punch. I don't get my hands up quick enough. It connects with my cheek and the world momentarily explodes into tiny white shards of pain. I keep my feet and dodge Malachi's next punch, striking out blindly with my heel and connecting with the side of his knee. He drops down and I slam my elbow into his nose.

My cheek is throbbing. I'm bleeding, but now so is Malachi; his goatee is shiny with it. He gets to his feet. He's nowhere near done yet. We wipe away blood, eyeball each other, and go at it again. Malachi gets in another solid punch—my ribs this time—before I finally catch on to his timing and rhythm. And then we fall into our own, more brutal, ballet of kicks and punches, blocks and strikes.

There's no sound in the room except our breathing and shuffling, fists smacking on flesh. And Zak reminding me to keep moving, keep my hands up.

I crunch a knee into Malachi's thigh; he elbows my lower back. I punch the side of his head; he kicks my ankle. I feel nothing except pain. Think of nothing except attacking and defending.

I don't know how long we keep going; long enough for the blood on our faces to dry. Long enough for the sting to go out of our anger. We keep swinging at each other like heavyweights in the twelfth round of a championship bout, getting slower and slower. Not taking our eyes from each other.

Finally, Zak climbs into the ring. 'How about we call this one a draw?'

Malachi and I stop throwing punches but keep circling, dragging our feet. My limbs are heavy; my heart feels like it's pumping molasses.

'Enough already,' Zak says. 'There's enough pain headed our way.'

One of us has to call it quits, and I can see from the set of Malachi's jaw that it's not going to be him. And I still need to talk to Daisy about Virginia. My feet stop.

'Draw?' I manage between breaths.

He takes two more steps. Waits a second to make sure I'm not playing him. 'Draw.'

We drop to our knees together. I slump to the canvas, stare up at the fluorescent lights. Bloody hell, everything *hurts*. I feel a thud beside me. Malachi is on his back too. His nose is swollen and bloodied, his left eye purple and closed shut. Blood cakes his mouth and goatee and his hair is slick with sweat.

He turns his head towards me, lets out a ragged breath. 'Thank you.'

I close my eyes, absorb the waves of pain pulsing through my body; the bone-deep ache in my cheek. It was brutal and exhausting but for a brief moment we were distracted.

'You're welcome.'

HISTORY COUNTS

'Fuck, Gaby, what were you thinking?'

Jude slides a hand under my shoulders and sits me up. I lean into him a little. He still smells of the ocean, even underground.

'I wasn't,' I say. 'That was the whole point.'

Daisy touches my shoulder on her way past and offers to help Malachi off the canvas. He waves her away.

'Daisy,' I rasp. 'Can we talk?'

'Let me sort out this idiot first.'

Jude wipes dried blood from my face. 'God, you're a mess.'

I bat his hand. 'Stop it.' I half-laugh, but it hurts too much. At some point Malachi split my lip.

'How are you going to fight in Iowa now?'

Oh. He doesn't know the Rephaim can heal each other.

Something else I need to explain.

'I'll take care of it,' Ez says. She's been waiting beyond the ropes, giving Jude and me a moment. Now she climbs into the ring and helps him lift me to my feet.

'Where are you going?'

'Not far. You'll see.' Ez puts an arm around my waist, takes my weight from him.

And like that, I'm being stretched thin and crushed back together—and then I'm across the room by the door. I raise my hand to Jude. By the time he responds we're back in the ring. He flinches, gives us a filthy look. 'Thanks for the warning.'

My insides settle and I test my muscle soreness. Better. Jude is staring at my lip. I check and find it's not fat anymore and the split is almost completely healed.

He stares at Ez. 'You did that?'

'I shared enough energy to speed up Gabe's natural healing process. Nothing more. One of the benefits of shifting together.'

'That's . . . handy.'

Malachi hauls himself up by the ropes, sways on his feet. His eyes fix on me. There's no anger left, just pain and worry.

'Don't push Nathaniel too far.' The words come out thick. 'Don't give him an excuse not to go after them.'

I nod, unsure if I mean it.

'Right,' Daisy says to him. 'Are you going to let me help

you or are you going to keep being a dick?'

He glowers at her through his swollen eye. 'When you're ready.'

'I'll catch you in the commissary,' she says to me. Then she ducks under Malachi's arm and they disappear before I can think of something to make her stay. *Shit*.

The Outcasts drift off into pairs to spar. Mya waits while Jude, Ez, and I climb out between the ropes. For once Mya's more interested in me than Jude.

'What?' I say to her.

She shakes her head. 'You. Every time I think you're sliding back into being Gabe you go do something like that.' She flicks her fingers in the direction of the ring. I try to read her expression. One minute she's sniping at me, blaming me for all that's wrong with the Rephaim; the next she's putting bullets in Bel, saving my life in LA. Her mood swings are exhausting.

'You still want a workout?' Ez asks Mya, massaging the tension from her arms. She needs a release too.

'What about Jude?'

Jones slaps his palms together. 'I'll take him on.'

'I don't have the moves to match your footwork, buddy,' Jude says.

'That's all right, we'll go old school. You know, actually hit each other.'

Jude checks I'm okay and they find space on the mats. I look around for Micah, find him sitting cross-legged on a weights bench watching the Outcasts, holding Daisy's hoodie. I ease myself down next to him, still a little tender.

'You want to go a few more rounds? I'll take you on.'

I push his shoulder.

'Soft,' he says. His eyes skim over the Outcasts. The sparring is urgent, frenetic. They're all wound as tight as I am. Maybe tighter: they've never been powerless before.

'They've kept up their training, I'll give them that,' Micah says.

'It's not like they've been lazing around on a beach for the past decade.'

He glances at me. 'I'm sorry, did you just defend the Outcasts?'

'No . . .'

'You did a job with them yesterday, though, didn't you?'

I rub my eyelid, nod.

'So. What was it like?'

I look past him, remember the raid on the nightclub. The stench of stale beer and cigarettes. The pulsing lights and throbbing music. Immundi demons with sharp suits and sharp teeth. Screaming kids. Bel pinning me to the fence, spraying blood on my face. Promising to hurt me.

'Mostly terrifying.' I don't have to check Micah's reaction to know that's not the response he was expecting.

'Who called the shots?'

'Mya came up with the plan but Rafa and Zak took over once we got there.'

'Huh. Maybe she's not as reckless as she'd like us to believe.'

'I wouldn't go that far.'

'Is it all about the money or is she still obsessed with killing every demon walking the earth?'

I find Mya in the crowd of sparring Outcasts. Loose blonde hair falling across her eyes as she protects herself from a barrage of Ez's kicks. She definitely wanted to kill Immundi in LA—but then so did I once I understood what was going on in that basement.

'They save humans. They kill demons. They get paid. What's so bad about that?'

Micah opens his mouth, falters. 'Nothing. But tell anyone I said that and there'll be no more of these little chats.'

I'm cooling down now, feeling the chill in the room. Thoughts of Rafa crowd in again. I push them back, concentrate on Micah. Wonder if I can trust him.

Screw it, it's worth the risk.

'Do you know where Virginia is?'

He gives me a level look. 'Why?'

'I need to talk to her.'

'Give the Five a chance to interrogate her.'

'She's been here for a day, they've had their go.'

'Antagonizing Nathaniel is not the way to help Rafa.'

I sit around to face him. 'So, what, you always do what you're supposed to?' He doesn't answer so I push on. 'If that's true, then why didn't you tell anyone about Jason? You saw him shift up at the Retreat and yet nobody here knew about him until a few hours ago.'

'I figured you knew what you were doing.'

'Why would you think that?'

He shrugs. 'Because I've known you my entire life and I trust you.'

'So trust me now. Help me with Virginia.'

'I can't.'

'Why not?'

'Because this is bigger than you and me.'

I wonder if that's the truth. I reach under my hair, touch the thick scar on the back of my neck. 'It's because I'm not Gabe, right?'

Micah's eyes darken. 'That's not true and you know it. It took me about five seconds at that cabin to see you're the same person you've always been. You've got the same quick temper, same impulses. Same fighting style. Same lack of tact.'

I pick at the loose stitching on the weight bench. I feel the Sanctuary pressing in around me. The weight of my history here. The reason we're all in this mess right now.

I have to ask.

'Do you think I betrayed everyone last year?'

He studies me. 'Because you ran off with Jude? I don't know what you did, but only an idiot would think you'd do something to hurt any of us. And Jude might not have wanted to be here but he'd never hurt us either.'

'What about all these run-ins I keep hearing about between the Sanctuary crew and the Outcasts over the past decade? You know, with swords and poleaxes? I'm guessing he was trying to hurt someone then.' And did Micah just call Daniel an idiot?

'That doesn't count. Nobody's ever trying to *kill* anyone. Whatever you and Jude did, no matter how bad it turned out, I've never doubted your intentions.'

I pull on the thread and it snaps free. I roll it into a tiny ball and flick it from my thumb. Around us the gym is a blur of energy and movement, bodies connecting. Forearms, elbows, fists, boots. 'I can't work out if you're naïve or if I should be flattered you trust me so implicitly.'

'Be flattered: I trust you more than anyone else alive.'

'Why?'

'Because you've been bailing me out of trouble for decades. That's what you do.'

I meet his eyes, curious. 'Define "trouble".'

A pause. 'In the early days it was sneaking off to bars. You always covered for me, and not just when I was out with Jude and Rafa.'

My pulse catches at Rafa's name. For a second, the room tilts and I dig my fingertips into the bench to keep myself upright. The cold gets back into my bones.

'I had some addiction issues in the '90s.' Micah glances away, self-conscious. I look more closely at his face, his clear eyes, smooth skin. 'You won't find any traces of it now. Shifting's good for more than bumps and bruises.' I catch the sadness behind his smile. I'm surprised I haven't recognized it before—or maybe he's only just now letting me see it. 'I had a rough time over a girl. Rafa, Jude, and Daisy knew what was going on, but you were the one who stepped in. You faked a mission to get me out of here and then kept Daniel off my back while I got clean. Made me get help. Shifted with me every few hours to make recovery easier. Daniel knew something was going on, but you never told him . . . even after you hooked up with him.'

I stare down at the mat under my feet, worn and cracked from years of wear. For the first time I feel a flutter of pride in Gabe. And relief: I was a good friend. We sit in silence for a minute or so, watch Jude block punches from Jones, counter with a solid kick to his thigh.

'You and Jude . . .' Micah shakes his head. 'I never thought I'd see either of you alive again, let alone together as a team. When you two weren't talking, it was like the world turned inside out.'

I probe the bruise on my ribs. It's still sore. I don't want to think about Jude and me being angry at each other, but I have to ask. 'Do you know why I didn't leave with him when they all walked out?'

Micah shakes his head. 'I honestly thought you were going. And I got it, completely. Things had gone too far with Nathaniel and he needed to give Jude answers. It came down to leaving—accepting there was more to know—or staying and pretending it didn't matter.'

'Why didn't you go with them?'

Another sad half-smile. 'Because you stayed.'

I close my eyes. It always comes back to this: Why? Why did I stay behind when Jude and the others became Outcasts? What did Jude and I find out that brought us back together? And what did we do that led to us having our pasts taken from us? Does any of it have anything to do with what's happening to Rafa and Taya right now?

Micah glances at his watch and stands. He brings his fingers to his lips and lets out a piercing whistle. Everyone stops.

'Lunch is in twenty. You might want to think about showering beforehand.' He waits until he's satisfied the Outcasts are wrapping up and then turns back to me. 'Those roughnecks you brought with you will get fed in the infirmary. They've been giving the brothers a hard time.'

The Butlers. And Simon.

'Has anyone told them where they are or what's really going on?'

'Brother Ferro thought it would be better coming from you.'

Yeah, because they trust me so much. But whose responsibility are they if not mine? I was the one who wanted to warn them about an imminent demon attack.

'Now *those* guys I can take you to,' Micah says.

I drag my fingers through my hair, retie my ponytail. I imagine explaining to Mick Butler that he's in a monastery in Italy with a fallen angel and more half-angel bastards than he can count. And then I think about Daisy, and realize my next chance of seeing her will be at lunch.

'Let's eat first.'

BREAKING BREAD

I'm in the shower when I lose it. The blast of warm water dissolves the lie that I'm okay. I drop to my knees under the weight of the truth, feel it twist my face, my insides. My shoulders heave with the effort of not sobbing: I don't want Jude to hear me in the next room.

All I can see is the demon sword coming out of Rafa. Rafa's eyes searching for me in the shadows, full of pain. Full of fear. He's been trapped in that room for an hour and forty-six minutes. An hour and forty-six minutes for Zarael to hurt him—

Stop. Just . . . stop.

Rafa is alive. We're getting him back.

I lose time watching dirt and blood swirl down the drain. The water finally runs clear. I find the strength to stand, force myself to wash my hair and scrub my skin, scrape the black grime out from under my nails.

This gleaming white bathroom is exactly like the one I almost drowned in last Monday. Am I ever going to have an experience at the Sanctuary that doesn't involve me sobbing, fighting, or aching?

I dry my hair and wipe steam from the mirror with a damp towel, get a good look at myself. Great. My face is blotchy and my eyes look like I've been drinking rum for twelve hours. I look exhausted.

Someone has left clothes on the bed: jeans, T-shirt, and a fleece-lined hoodie. I get dressed and pull back my hair, repeat my new mantra: Rafa is alive. We're getting him back. I wish it felt like the truth.

A knock on the door. It's Jude. He hasn't shaved, but his hair is damp. It hangs almost to his shoulders, uncombed. I'm met with a waft of mint toothpaste. He takes in the state of my face. 'You should stick your head outside for a few seconds.'

I go to the window and push it open. Cold air stings my cheeks and slaps all the breath from me. The clouds have lifted enough that I can see the steep, rugged face of the Alps, dark clumps of pine trees, valleys of snow. Patches of pale blue sky far above.

'That'll do or you'll end up with frostbite.' Jude leans out and pulls the pane shut. I shiver in the warmth of the room. Brown eyes watch me through thick lashes. My brother, alive—not decapitated on the side of a deserted road. Not lost to me forever. Ready to face Gatekeepers and hell-beasts.

'Shit, princess.' Jude pulls me to him. I bury my face in his neck, breathe him in: pine forest and sea salt. We stay like that for a moment until I can form words again.

'I'm sorry,' I manage when I finally pull back. The neck of his shirt is wet. 'I can't get a grip on any of this. And I'm terrified something's going to happen to you—'

'You don't think I'm scared of losing you again? It doesn't matter how much we learn about that farmhouse or how many Rephaim are with us when we storm it, we'll still be fighting demons.'

I nod, wipe my cheek on my shoulder. 'Demons who want us. That's all taking Rafa and Taya is about: getting to us so they can find out if we had contact with the Fallen last year.'

Jude walks to the window and stares down at the piazza, not really seeing it. When he turns back, he's focused. 'Let me see that scar again.'

I lift my hair and turn around. He touches the thick skin on the nape of my neck, the wound that destroyed the mark of a crescent moon he and the rest of the Rephaim have in the same spot.

'Bel said he put a blade through my neck last year and you begged for my life.'

Jude says nothing for a good ten seconds. 'If he did, he either pulled back before it severed your head or someone stopped him.' His gaze drifts as he tries to force the pieces together. 'Do you think I did a deal with that demon to save you?'

My skin chills to hear him say it out loud. There's a knock on the door before I have to answer.

Ez is waiting in the hallway. She glances at my face and gives my shoulder a quick rub. 'Let's eat.' Jude and Zak fall into step behind us. It's eerie up here, silent except for the quiet hum of ducted heating and muffled steps on endless carpet.

'Where is everybody?' I ask.

'Already downstairs. I'm not the only one who's missed the cooking.' Ez gives me a small smile. I had a taste of Sanctuary food when I was here last week—mushroom risotto—but I'd been half-drowned by Malachi and drugged by Daniel, so I wasn't exactly primed to savor it.

Ez leads us downstairs and along a wide hallway lined with enormous works of classical art—the largest I've seen hanging outside a major gallery. Certainly more impressive than anything the Pan Beach Gallery has ever exhibited. And again, they're all battles between angels and demons. More carnage.

It's as if the Rephaim need constant reminders of what's in store if the so-called prophezied war between angels and demons eventuates. Of what will happen if they (we) fail to find the Fallen and hand them over to the Angelic Garrison. My scalp tightens. God, I hope Jude and I didn't have contact with the Fallen last year.

'No word from the Five?' Jude asks Ez as we pass a life-size image of an angel impaled on a spike, his helmet askew, wings broken and torn.

'Not yet.'

We reach a set of carved timber doors. Jude steps in front of them, blocks the way. He tells Ez and Zak about our plan to get Daisy alone and ask for her help—without anyone else knowing.

'You need to tread carefully there, Jude,' Ez says. 'Daisy's loyalty is to Nathaniel, no matter how misty-eyed she was to see you.'

But she doesn't tell us not to try.

We pass through another building, another hallway. Mya is waiting at the end of it in front of double doors, hands in the pockets of her leather jacket. As we get closer, I hear clinking cutlery and low voices in the room beyond. The commissary.

'So you do still have friends,' she says, nodding at my clean clothes. She checks Jude over, meets his gaze fleetingly and then opens the door.

I'm expecting a boarding-school–style dining room. By now, I should know better than to make assumptions about the Rephaim. Jude and I prop in the doorway. His jaw drops a little.

The room is modern, airy and *huge*. On one side, floor-to-ceiling windows give a clear view of the pine forest; on the other, an open kitchen bustles with activity. Men in chefs whites line up behind steaming pots, ladles in hand. White laminate tables are grouped together in long rows, set with silver cutlery, wine glasses, miniature lamps, and fresh purple flowers. The chairs are made from funky curved timber and the floor is covered in dark slate. A wall of wine dominates the back of the room, dwarfing a polished timber bar. The air is heavy with roasted tomatoes, basil, and garlic. My mouth waters. Apparently not even high levels of anxiety kill my appetite.

It takes me a moment to realize the chatter has stopped. Completely. My eyes skim over faces of Rephaim I don't know but vaguely recognize from the chapterhouse, and then Daisy—thank god—and Micah, Malachi . . . more strangers . . . and finally a cluster of Outcasts in the far corner. They've pushed three tables together. Jones waves us over.

We cross the room, pretend everyone's not staring at us. I flex my fingers, try to coax out this constant tension, but I'm still acutely conscious of each footstep.

'Who pays for all this?' Jude asks.

'Nathaniel and a fleet of financial advisers.' Mya says the last four words as if they taste bad. 'He has more money than he can spend, and this is what he does with it: provides a luxury mountain resort for these bastards.'

I think about the cramped quarters the Outcasts use in Dubai: stuffy, hot and stinking of charred food and sweat.

It's a long way from this. A long way from the place they once called home.

Jones and Seth move down the table to make room. I sit between Ez and Jude, position myself opposite Zak—his shoulders are so broad I'm effectively screened from most of the room. Mya sits at the head of the table. Of course.

'All good?' Zak asks.

Jones nods. 'So far.'

'That could be about to change.'

Malachi is headed our way, hands in his pockets, shoulders slightly hunched. Apart from the faint shadow of a bruise around one eye, there's barely a sign of our brawl. He looks up and down the three tables. 'Why aren't you eating?'

Jones half-turns towards the hostile crowd of Sanctuary Rephaim. 'We're trying to work out if it's an "act of aggression" if we all get up at once to eat. Not that I mind a good melee, but I don't think it would go down well with the kitchen. I am peckish, though.'

'Just grab a plate and go to the counter,' Malachi says, weary, and walks away.

Jones rubs his hands together. 'You heard the man.'

Chairs scrape on the slate floor. I catch Daisy's eye, briefly, before we approach the service counter in a pack. There, a young guy with curly black hair sticking out from under a chef's hat points to each dish and explains them to us. In Italian. I glance at Jude. He doesn't understand a word of it either, which I find a strange relief. The chef is talking to me now, asking me something. There's recognition in his eyes: he knows me. I shake my head, embarrassed.

'That's goat ragu with pappardelle pasta,' Ez says beside me. 'This one is *gnocchi tartufo*—the gnocchi's made from parmesan, truffle, and potato—and that's the best onion soup you'll eat this side of the French border.'

I accept a bowl of ragu, earning an approving smile from the chef. Jude chooses the same and we head back to the table. He's also juggling a tall glass filled with skinny breadsticks and a jug of red wine. We get settled and he pours us both a glass. I raise my eyebrows.

'It's Italy,' he says, as if it's a no-brainer to drink in the middle of the day. For a heartbeat I'm back in Monterosso with him, sipping limoncello in a café by the sea at ten in the morning. Another memory from a trip we never took. Another lie.

'We need to stay sharp,' I say.

'Says the girl who just got the shit kicked out of her.' He looks past Zak. 'Bloody hell, he's persistent.'

Malachi is coming back, this time with Daisy and Micah. All three cradle half-eaten meals. Jude knocks my knee under the table. *Be patient.*

'You want to make room?' Malachi asks.

Zak measures him, seems satisfies with what he finds. 'Fine. But don't think we won't throw down in here if you pull any of your usual shit.'

'Noted.' Malachi sits in the spare seat beside Zak. Daisy puts her plate on the table and drags a chair over, squeezing next to Jones. Micah finds a spot further along. The two Outcast girls he sits between don't seem too put out at having to make room for him.

'Hey,' I say to Daisy. 'Did you bring me these?' I pluck at my hoodie.

'Yeah, your stuff is in boxes in the storeroom.'

Something quivers in my chest.

'Do you have anything of mine?' Jude asks her.

'No.' Daisy concentrates on her bowl, pushing the thick soup around. 'You took most of your stuff when you left.'

Of course he did. When Jude left the Sanctuary, he had no intention of coming back.

'What sort of stuff?' he asks.

'Books, clothes, weapons.' All the things in the cottage on Patmos. 'You guys didn't leave much behind when you left. Except Rafa's motorbike.'

'Rafa had a motorbike?' I look to Ez. 'Seriously?'

'Yes,' Ez says. 'The guy who thinks cars are a waste of time decided he couldn't live without an overpowered motorbike.'

'Why?'

'To annoy Daniel. And then he learned to ride it and loved the speed. Never rode with a helmet, of course.'

I nod. 'If he lost control, he could shift before he hit the ground, right?'

Ez smiles at her gnocchi, shakes her head.

'What?'

'You're the reason he wrecked the first bike.'

'That's right,' Zak says. 'You wanted him to red-line it through the Alps. He flipped it on a corner north of the border and lost it over a cliff. You two thought it was a hell of a joke.'

'I dared him to do that?'

'Gabe,' Ez says, almost chiding. 'You were on the back with him.'

I try to picture it: me on a bike with Rafa. Fearless. Laughing. Before he and Jude left the Sanctuary. Before whatever happened between Rafa and me. Whatever it was, it stopped Rafa finishing what we started in his bedroom in Pan Beach; has held him back every time we start to cross that line. And now I'll never feel his lips or his hands on me again unless we get him out of that room.

'He bought another one,' Daisy says, and I'm dragged back to the moment. She catches Jude's eye. 'You used to ride it too, just not like a lunatic.'

A crooked smile. He can't help himself. 'Is it still here?'

'It's in the garage as far as I know. Nobody's been on it since you guys left.'

'We should check it out,' he says to me.

See Rafa's motorbike? One that I used to ride with him? Just thinking about it makes me feel hollow. 'We need to check on Simon and the guys at some point too.'

Nobody seems excited by that prospect. The room hums with chatter now, the occasional chink of glasses and cutlery. A gust of wind disturbs the pine trees outside, the tops bending and swaying.

Jude finishes his meal first, scrapes his plate and licks the knife clean. 'Could Rafa and Taya shift *inside* that iron room?' he asks.

Malachi's fork pauses at his lips. He looks at me, questioning.

'When we were there, Rafa shifted as far as the wall. He'd disappear until he hit it.' I try not to think about how many times he slammed back into the floor. How his rage filled that tiny room.

'That's good,' Malachi says, eyes distant. 'It means he and Taya can heal each other. Theoretically.'

A tiny spark of hope. 'Could they keep shifting—not stay still long enough to be pinned down?'

'Not indefinitely.'

Ez pours herself half a glass of wine. 'Those women must have factored that in when they built the room. What would be the point of trapping us if we could escape the second the seal on the door was broken? They'd need to incapacitate us.'

'Maybe it wasn't set up properly. It's not like the kid was expecting you,' Zak says.

The kid. Sophie. Dead after something far worse than

us turned up at the farmhouse. The goat ragu sits heavy in my stomach.

'So Rafa and Taya might not be conscious?' Jude looks from Ez to Malachi.

Malachi lowers his fork, pushes his plate away. 'That's about the best we can hope for at this point.'

TIME TO SMELL THE ROSES

Jude nudges my foot.

'Daisy, you got a second?' he asks.

Her head comes up. She blinks at Jude and nods. He stands and I follow. I don't look at Micah—he must know what we're doing. Mya starts to rise too but Jude shakes his head. The skin around her eyes tightens but she doesn't leave the table.

Daisy waits until we're out in the hallway. 'What's up?'

'We need to talk to Virginia,' Jude says.

'Good luck with that.'

'I'm serious. She knows how that room works. We need information.'

'What do you think Nathaniel and the Five have been trying to get out of her since she got here? You think either of you will be more persuasive than him?'

'I can guarantee I'm more charming,' Jude says.

She studies him for a long moment, his eyes, his hair, but when her gaze drops to his mouth she shakes her head as if annoyed with herself. 'You've been back here five minutes and you want to pull a stunt like that?'

'Daisy,' Jude says quietly. 'Do you know where she is?'

'Wow. It's a been a while since you used that look on me.'

'What look?'

'The one that says, "Daisy, don't let me down." That stopped working the day you followed Mya out the door.' She doesn't look away and neither does Jude. I shift my weight, force myself to stay out of it.

'This is about getting to Rafa and Taya, not who I used to be or how I used to look at you,' Jude says.

A faint flush creeps above the neckline of her sweater.

'Hey.' I touch her arm. She jerks away and then looks embarrassed. I guess the old Gabe wasn't much of a toucher. 'You don't have to be involved,' I say. 'Just tell us where to find her.'

'You can't shift. What are you going to do if someone finds you?' Her eyes narrow. 'Or is someone else coming along?' She doesn't mention Mya but that's obviously who she means.

'No, just us. And if you want to keep it that way we should move now.' I give the commissary doors a meaning-ful look. The hum of conversation continues on the other side. I pick at the hem of my T-shirt, impatient.

Daisy runs her tongue across her teeth, stares past me for a second, and then turns and walks down the hallway. Jude and I exchange a quick look and follow. She doesn't speak as she leads us through more buildings and then outside. Water splashes in a fountain under the muted sky; the breeze carries hints of lavender and rosemary. We're back in the main piazza. I step out beyond the cloister and look up, try to get my bearings. We're surrounded by three-storey buildings on all sides—our rooms are somewhere above us to the left. I think.

'As far as I know, Virginia's in guest quarters in Nathaniel's compound.' She scans the cloisters as she speaks, her voice quiet. Jaw tense.

'And that's in which direction?' Jude asks.

She nods at the building on the other side of the lawn. 'Past the infirmary, near the chapterhouse.'

'Is she alone?'

'Doubtful. But at least Nathaniel's with the Five in the library'—she stabs her thumb in the opposite direction—'so you shouldn't run into him.'

My pulse picks up. 'Can you shift us in there?' I ask.

Daisy shakes her head. 'Bad idea. Someone would feel it.' It would be quicker to cross the grass but Daisy stays under the cover of the cloisters, walking the length of two sides of the piazza. When we reach the other corner, she stops in front of tall doors. They're bronze and tinged green with age, and both have ornate carvings. On one, a giant lion stands on its hind legs, teeth bared and mane flowing. A flock of sheep cowers on the other. Either the lion is protecting the sheep from an unseen enemy or it's about to eat them, it's hard to tell.

'Nathaniel's garden is on the other side, in the middle of the compound. The guest quarters are all on ground level so you can use the bushes for cover while you find her room. It should be on the western wall. Then you need to get inside without being seen.'

I give a short laugh. 'Just like that.'

'Hey, this is your plan, not mine.' Daisy walks over to a bench by the wall, sits down, and crosses her ankles. 'Don't be seen.'

Jude raises his eyebrows at me. 'Ready?'

My pulse is more insistent now. I see Rafa in agony, collapsing to his knees in the forest. I nod. Jude lifts the ring under the sheep and turns it. A bolt slides on the other side, too loud in the hushed piazza. My mouth is dry. Bad idea or not, I wish we could shift.

The door swings open slowly, ancient bronze scraping on ancient stones. I step into the short, dank passage and Jude closes the latch behind us. It takes a moment for my eyes to adjust: the garden is at the other end. We press ourselves against the damp wall, creep to the opening. Jude is breathing quicker now too.

I take a nervous look outside and duck back into the

shadows. The garden is about the same size as my front yard in Pan Beach. Wrought-iron tables and chairs are clustered together in the middle, surrounded by a sea of white, pink, and purple roses. Patches of wild mint and basil; tomatoes climbing a trellis; thick blueberry bushes along all four walls. There's nobody in sight.

'Which is the western wall?' I whisper.

Jude points to his left. I have no idea how he can tell when the sun is hidden behind an endless bank of rain clouds. He drops into a crouch and I do the same. We wait a heartbeat and then make a run for a clump of blueberry bushes screening the first window, press ourselves against the wall. I take a second to steel myself and then peer inside. It's a guest room. Empty. I shake my head at Jude and we move on to the next one in a half-crouch. Empty. So are the next two. I feel ill. And exposed. We're a long way from the bronze doors.

I check the fifth room and my pulse jackhammers.

It's her.

Virginia is sitting in a high-backed chair facing the window, head bowed, lips moving. Slender fingers clutch the armrest. Her tailored suit is immaculate, her gray bob neat. Face unmarked. However Nathaniel's been trying to coerce her, it hasn't involved violence. Yet. The room is full of antiques: a four-poster bed, a dresser with a washbowl and water pitcher, a tall bookcase packed with books bound in matching dark leather.

She's right *there*.

Jude and I reach for the window at the same time. It's shut, but maybe it's not locked. We try to find a place to grip. The pane rattles.

Virginia lifts her head. We freeze.

She gasps—soundless through the thick glass—and twists in her chair to see if she's still alone in the room. Her head whips back around, chest rising and falling. Now I realize her pale blue eyes are underscored with shadows and the lines around her mouth seem deeper than a day ago.

Adrenalin builds. We're so close. I point to the window. 'Open it.' I mouth.

She stares at me and it's like the farmhouse all over again: fear and loathing and grief.

'Go to hell.' She says it slowly so I can lip-read.

Jude drops to the ground. I don't break eye contact with Virginia. I hear a snap, and he's back a second later, stripping leaves from a torn branch. He jams a jagged end between the window and the frame, tries to pry it open. Virginia jumps up, checks over her shoulder again.

The branch breaks. 'Fuck,' Jude mutters, goes for another one.

Virginia is behind her chair now, eyes wide. But her spine is straight and her shoulders square: still defiant. Does she know Rafa and Taya are trapped in the iron room with demons? Does she care?

Jude's back with a new branch, stronger. This time, the window starts to give. Come on, come on. Jude puts all his weight into it.

Footsteps crunch on the gravel path. Shit. I pull Jude down behind the bushes and we press our backs to the wall. The grout between the stones is rough under my fingers. Maybe it's just someone passing. Or maybe it's Uri or Calista or any one of the Rephaim itching to take a swing at us.

Whoever it is is closer now, their steps slow, uncertain. Jude and I lock eyes. I know what he wants to do, and it doesn't involve getting caught hiding behind blueberry bushes and going down quietly. I nod.

We spring to our feet together, launch ourselves around the shrub—

—and come face to face with Brother Stephen.

We jolt to a stop. The monk staggers back. He drops the bunch of mint he's carrying and clutches the neck of his robe with a gnarled hand.

'Hello, Brother,' Jude says, breathing hard. 'You scared the hell out of us.' He scans the garden, settles his weight.

'You should not be in here.' Brother Stephen's faded eyes flit to the window behind us.

My heart gives another hard thump. 'We just want to talk. We're not going to hurt her.'

'That is not the point, Gabriella. Nathaniel has forbidden anyone to speak to this woman.'

'She knows how to help Rafa and Taya.'

'I understand your anxiety. I fear for them too, but now is not the time for disobedience.'

My fingers have tightened to fists. If we can't get to Virginia, then all that's left for us to do is to wait for Nathaniel to make a decision. Pressure builds behind my eyes.

'Please, Gabriella. This woman has not said a word to Nathaniel or the Council. She will not talk to you and it is not worth the strife you will stir up by forcing the issue.' His shoulders are hunched, his gaze stern. 'Go, now, and I will not speak of this.'

I check the window. Virginia is still behind the chair, watching. So, so close.

'Brother—'

'*Please.*' The monk steadies himself against a trellis thick with tomatoes. It shakes at his touch.

Jude brushes my wrist and I meet his eyes. All the air goes out of me.

We're running out of time and we both know we're not beating up an old monk to buy more.

THE AUSTRALIAN PATIENT

We creep back out the way we came in and I expect to get caught with every step. I check over my shoulder only once, find Brother Stephen watching us, troubled. I have no idea if we can trust him—but I doubt he'll be so forgiving if we're caught in here again.

We slip back out into the cloisters. Daisy is right where we left her.

'Well?'

I shake my head and tell her what happened. She scans the piazza but it's still empty. The rain clouds are lower, the breeze sharper. 'Are you sure it was Brother Stephen?' she asks. 'He's usually in the chapel this time of day.'

Jude gives her a flat look. 'My short-term memory is fine. It was the same monk who took us to our rooms.'

'You're lucky. You two need to quit while you're ahead.'

Panic flickers. 'And do what?' I ask. 'Sit around and wait?'

Daisy stands up, wipes her palms on her jeans—just how nervous was she out here?—and gestures to the building closest to us. 'You could check on your mates from Pandanus Beach.'

Jude knocks dirt from the soles of his boots onto the cobblestones. 'May as well while we're here.'

I rub the corner of my eye, try to focus. I can't find an excuse to put off seeing Mick and his boys. Simon. A strand of hair catches on my lip and I drag it free, gesture for Daisy to lead the way. We're almost to the double doors when Ez walks around the corner at the far end of the cloister. Daisy keeps going inside, but Jude and I wait in the doorway. Ez raises her eyebrows in a silent question. I shake my head and catch a hint of disappointment in the set of her mouth.

Daisy is waiting in the hallway, restless.

'I thought I'd say hi to the brothers,' Ez says. Daisy looks from her to me and back again and then walks off without a word.

The cloying smell of antiseptic hits me a few steps from the infirmary door. It all comes back in a rush: stark white walls, gut-churning fear, torn flesh—a reminder of hellion teeth and claws. I stop, take a breath. Disinfectant coats my tongue. Daisy glances at me, her hand on the door. 'All right?'

I swallow. Nod.

'If you come any closer with that fucking needle I will ram it so far up your arse it'll make you cough.' Mick's voice carries from inside. His snarl is so familiar it's almost comforting.

Daisy rolls her eyes and opens the door. I brace for another assault of memories but all I see is Mick in the middle of the room wearing a crisp white hospital gown. One arm is strapped to his chest. With his good hand, he's waving a scalpel at one of the monks who helped him from the chapterhouse. The monk has his palms out, like he's trying to settle a spooked horse.

I stop halfway across the room, try to ignore the gurney by the wall. I was laid out on it not that many days ago. Ez is watching Mick, but her attention keeps drifting to the monk.

Mick turns on us, his half-beard still matted with grass and mud. The room is heady with something that smells like wet lawn clippings and marjoram.

'Where the fuck are we?'

'Italy,' I say.

Mick's eyes flick from me to the monk and back again. 'Bullshit.'

'Yeah, you're right. We're obviously still in Pan Beach. Where's everyone else?'

Mick thrusts his chin towards swinging doors behind him. The infirmary is how I remember it—sterile, cold, white—but I don't remember the doors. Of course, I was in excruciating agony at the time.

'They okay?'

Mick lowers the scalpel. 'Joffa's leg's a mess, Woosha's missing a thumb, and Rusty's got twenty stitches in his chest. What do you think?'

'What about Simon?'

'Still shittin' himself.'

'But is he all right?'

'He's better than the boys who didn't make it.'

I bite my lip. 'Who?'

'Maxie. Hawk. Gus. Tank.' He fires their names like bullets.

Tank, with the Southern Cross tattoo on his throat. Rafa snapped his wrist at the Imperial two days ago. I don't know the other three and now they're all dead.

'Sorry.' The word is so inadequate. Mick's boys are rough and fond of violence but they didn't deserve to die.

'Tough pricks. Went down fighting.' Mick turns his face away, but not before I see the pain there. He rubs a palm over his shaved head, meets my gaze again. 'You going to tell me what's going on?'

'Lose the blade first,' I say.

'Only if that medieval wanker gets the needle away from me.'

The monk holding the syringe looks at Daisy, pink spots on his cheeks. 'It's a mild painkiller.'

'I don't give a shit. You're not sticking that thing in me.'

'Let him suffer,' Daisy says. 'And you'—she stabs a finger at Mick—'show some gratitude.'

Jude walks over to the stainless steel bench. It's covered in bandages, swabs, and surgical instruments. 'Where's the doctor?'

'Brother Ferro is medically trained,' Ez says. 'Brother, is it still only you or did Benigno finish his studies?'

Brother Ferro—a middle-aged man with intelligent eyes—nods. 'Brother Benigno received his qualifications five years ago.' He speaks with a strong Italian accent. He takes a moment to check Ez over, lingering on the scars on her cheek and neck. 'I was saddened to hear of your injuries, Esther. How are you?'

'I'm fine, Brother, thank you.' She doesn't turn away or make any attempt to cover the hellion marks.

'I have missed you, Gabriella. Judah.' Brother Ferro nods. 'You need a haircut.'

Jude's fingers stray to his hair. He realizes what he's doing and lets his hand drop.

'Oi.' Mick flips and catches the scalpel with his free hand. 'Someone needs to tell me what the fuck is going on.'

I point to the swinging doors. 'In there, with everyone else.'

Mick shoots a sour look at Brother Ferro and limps off. His gown flaps open to give us a startling view of his bare backside. I glimpse an aging black and gray Grim Reaper across his shoulders, and try very hard not to notice the weird tufts of hair further south.

'Good god, I just ate,' Daisy says and screws her eyes shut.

Mick bangs open the doors and shuffles into a larger room with eight hospital beds, four against each wall. Woosha and Joffa are on the left with two more of Mick's guys—one with a blond mullet, the other with tribal tattoos. Rusty and Simon are on the right. The smell of grass and marjoram is stronger in here.

Mick wasn't exaggerating: Joffa is a mess. His burnt leg—the same one I stabbed—is heavily bandaged. His nose is taped where I hit it, and he's hooked up to a drip. He glares at me through bleary eyes, his bald head shiny with sweat. On the next bed, Woosha's shoulder is strapped, his left fist completely lost in bandages. His lip is torn where a silver ring used to be.

'Brace yourself for more bullshit boys,' Mick says, lowering himself on to his brother's bed. Rusty is wearing white boxers, and a wide strip of dressing covers the stitches across his chest. Simon lies shirtless, his back to us. A bandage bisects the sleek tiger prowling the length of his spine. He rolls over gingerly and sits up, pressing a wad of fabric against his ribs.

'Are you okay?' I ask, not moving any closer. Right now he must be wishing he'd said no when Jude asked him to take us up the mountain.

Simon's eyes graze over me, settle on Mick. He doesn't answer.

'Simon reckons you're all half-angels or some shit like that,' Mick says.

Nobody corrects him.

'I *knew* it. No human fights like that prick Rafa.'

My breath catches. I hear Rafa's softly spoken words to me outside the hospital in Melbourne: *Harden the fuck up.* It's almost my undoing. I take a breath.

'Those half-angels are called the Rephaim—'

'You one of them?'

I hesitate. 'Yeah.'

Mick measures me, nods. 'That's the only way you could've got the better of my boys.'

I let the comment slide.

'They—we—can travel in the blink of an eye.' I gesture to the walls around us. 'Right now, we're somewhere the demons can't come. In northern Italy.'

Mick chews on his thumbnail. Spits out what he harvests onto the floor. 'Are we prisoners?'

'Technically, no. But you're stuck here for a while with the rest of us.'

'How long?'

'I don't know.'

Rusty rubs his chin through his scruffy dark beard. 'Who runs the show here?'

'Nathaniel. He's a fallen angel.'

'Fuck off,' Mick says, but Rusty nods slowly, as if that makes some kind of sense to him. As usual, he's quicker on the uptake than his brother.

Fluorescent lights hum overhead. Simon lifts the bundle he's been holding against his ribs and wrinkles his nose. A poultice. That explains the smell.

'Is Taya . . . ?' Simon's eyes don't meet mine. He saw Taya take a blade: invincible, snarky Taya. Arse-kicking Rephaite. He's had a soft spot for her since she broke up the all-in brawl at the bar and beat the crap out of the drunk who glassed him.

'Taya and Rafa are alive.' I keep my voice steady. 'And we're going after them as soon as we have the numbers.'

Rusty swings his legs over the side of the bed to sit beside Mick. 'Why hasn't your fallen angel gone after them?'

'Excellent question.'

Daisy fires me a look, annoyed. 'It's not that simple, Gabe. We're under instructions to defend ourselves only, not attack.'

'Instructions from who?' Rusty asks.

'The Angelic Garrison.'

'Why? They scared of demons?'

'They're archangels, you moron. Demons are scared of *them*. It's a big decision to attack the Gatekeepers. Nathaniel won't risk our lives lightly.'

'Come on Daisy,' Ez says. 'You know it's more a case

of him not wanting to risk his chance to redeem himself. To do that, he needs to find the Fallen—and for that he needs us.'

'And here we go.'

They face each other. Almost resigned.

'You honestly believe Nathaniel's in contact with the Garrison?' Ez asks.

'That's not the point. The point is whether or not you lot can be back here without pushing your own agenda.'

'Daisy, the only agenda we have is to rescue Rafa and Taya, and Nathaniel's either on board with that or he's not.'

Simon's bed squeaks. 'The demons want you,' he says to me. 'You said it yourself.'

Jude closes the distance to Simon in three steps, gets right in his face. 'You want to hand my sister to demons?'

Simon leans as far back as he can to get away from him. 'No, of course not. I'm just saying—'

'Even if she had what they wanted—which she doesn't—that's never going to happen. You keep talking like that and I'll ask Ez to drop you straight back to that camp. See how you go on your own.'

The color leaches from Simon's face. 'Bloody hell, give me a break. I just watched demons hack Mick's crew to pieces. *Demons*.' His voice cracks.

'You weren't the only one there,' Jude says.

'Yeah, but it's different for you—you're one of *them*.'

'Which means nothing if I don't remember how to *be* one of them,' Jude snaps. 'If I did, maybe I could've been more help in that fight.'

'Hey.' I pull him away from Simon. 'Don't even start with that crap. We're swimming in the deep end doing the best we can. What happened on that mountain wasn't our fault.' Although even as I say it, I'm not sure I believe it.

'It's my fault if I'm the one who changed our memories. Made us less than what we should be.'

'What did you say?' Daisy stares at Jude. 'You did this?'

'We don't know that,' I say. 'It's a theory—based on pretty flimsy evidence.'

Daisy is about to press the issue when her phone vibrates. She stabs at it, impatient. Reads her screen.

'Okay, we've got company.' She turns to Ez. 'Get your crew to the chapterhouse, and then nobody moves from there without orders.'

My skin chills. 'What is it?'

Daisy jams her phone in her back pocket. 'Demons at the gate—literally.'

KNOCK, KNOCK

The wind up here chills me bone-deep. Or maybe it's the view. I'm on the roof of the Sanctuary looking down on Zarael, who's at the edge of the trees. My heart's going like a road drill. Has he brought a body? A head?

I bite the inside of my lip. Remember to watch where I put my feet.

Keep your shit together.

The leader of the Gatekeepers stands forward of two other demons, long black hair blowing away from his face. He's all angles and scars. The last time I saw him he was centimeters from me, breathing sulfur into my face—a heartbeat before Ez shifted with Jude and me to the chapterhouse. I'm three stories above him now. It's nowhere near far enough.

The other Gatekeepers are disturbingly uniform, with

their black trench coats and long white hair. Even from up here I know that's Bel closest to Zarael; there's something about the way he stands, the tilt of his chin. Which means the demon on Bel's other side is most likely Leon. Why are they here? Did they bring Rafa? The forest fades.

Jude takes my elbow, steadies me. Everything sharpens again.

'Thanks.' It comes out in a plume of vapor.

We're on top of the westernmost wing of the Sanctuary, lined up with the Outcasts. The smell of pine needles, cedar, and wood smoke cuts the air. Steady wind gusts stir trees older and taller than the monastery. We're rugged up, gloved fingers clutching cold swords. The roof pitch is steeper than it looks from the ground and my calves are already aching from the effort of staying upright on the grimy terracotta tiles.

The demons have seen us. I know because they've turned their faces skyward and I can see flickering orange eyes.

'We're about to find out if Nathaniel's wards cover the roof,' Zak says to nobody in particular.

I change the grip on my sword. 'Why are they here?'

Ez shakes her head and her plait swishes on her black ski jacket. 'I have no idea.'

I glance back at the demons and then try to get my bearings. The roof we're on extends more than a hundred meters in either direction, forming one side of the elongated Sanctuary compound. Behind us is the piazza I can see from my room. Further north is another collection of wings and courtyards where I think the infirmary might be. To my left, a huge tree sprouts out between buildings, taller than the Sanctuary. This place is the size of a university. The chapterhouse is at the opposite end, closer to the mountains. Where we should be. We skipped the briefing: we had our own in Jude's room. And as soon as Daniel sets foot outside he'll see us up here.

Jude touches my elbow again. I follow his gaze to the line of trees. A hellion lumbers up behind the demons: seven-foot tall with a huge misshapen head. In chain mail. Two more appear behind it, one of them missing half an arm.

'Holy shit . . .' Jude whispers. It's the first time he's seen a hell-beast outside of his nightmares. 'You killed one of those?'

I shudder, remember the beast crushing me, teeth buried in my neck, sucking at me. The searing pain when it ripped open my side. The smell of blood and sawdust, that rush of strength—my first taste of what it means to be Rephaim—and the shock of being able to throw the monster off me. That moment when I brought my blade down on its bared throat . . .

'I don't recommend the experience.'

Mya picks her way across the tiles, steps around a brick chimney billowing white smoke.

'We need to know if there are more down there,' she says.

'No, what you need to do is learn to follow an order.'

Daniel.

I turn to find him on the roof with us. A dozen Sanctuary Rephaim flank him, including Daisy, Malachi, and Micah. I'm so wound up I hardly felt them shift.

'You were told to come to the chapterhouse.' Daniel's eyes pass over Mya and Jude, linger on me.

'Nobody here re-enlisted in your army.' Mya's face is pink from cold, her blonde hair tied back and tucked inside a faux-fur collar. 'If there's a threat we act, not wait for an *order*.'

'That's why your people get hurt.' He doesn't look at Ez. He doesn't have to.

'How else are we supposed to see what's happening out here? There are no windows on this side.'

'If you'd come to the chapterhouse as instructed, Mya, you would've learned there are other ways to see what's happening outside our walls.' Daniel's hands are tucked inside his suede jacket. 'Our surveillance systems have advanced here in the past decade.'

'Maybe someone could've mentioned—'

A loud crack pulls our attention back to the trees.

Zarael and Bel are meters from us at eye level, balancing in a cedar tree. Bel's branch has snapped, sending a shower of leaves to the forest floor. He jumps to the next one as the broken limb breaks free. Leon and a hellion skitter out of the way before it crashes to the forest floor.

'It's a miracle.' Zarael's voice is smoky like Bel's, but deeper. More threatening. 'Both twins here, alive.'

He's close enough that I can make out the crisscross of deep red marks across his face. The other Gatekeepers are pale, almost beautiful in a terrible way, but not Zarael. Rafa told me he was torn apart when the Fallen escaped hell, and then put back together. I didn't realize the story was literal.

'It seems the rumor of their demise was exaggerated,' Daniel says. There's something missing in his voice—condescension? His usual self-assurance? It's enough for me to wonder if this is the first time the Gatekeepers have dared come this close to the Sanctuary.

Zarael is smiling. One side of his trench coat is tucked behind the heavy sword on his hip. It's hard to tell if he's looking at Jude or me. Jude takes a long, slow breath. It's my turn to steady him. Are there enough of us to stop Zarael if the rest of his horde are hidden in the forest and they can shift to the roof? Nobody else on our side speaks. Maybe the Rephaim have never been this close to Zarael without trying to kill him. Or maybe he's as terrifying to them as he is to me.

What would Rafa do?

I force myself to face Bel. 'It suits you.' My mouth is cotton-dry, but I say it loud enough for him to hear.

The demon's eyebrows twitch together and I tap my fingertip in the middle of my forehead. He lifts his free hand. As soon as he touches the scars there his lip curls. A reminder of two of the bullets Mya fired into him in LA.

'Wait until you see what I've done to Rafael.'

My entire body flashes hot, then cold. 'Hurt him and I'll cut your head off.'

'Too late,' he says, and shows me unnaturally white teeth. 'It is amazing how much blood you bastards can lose. Immortality in a human vessel certainly has its drawbacks.'

'What do you want, Zarael?' Daniel asks.

I force myself to focus on the question rather than the horrible possibilities implicit in Bel's taunt.

Zarael strokes his jaw with a long black fingernail. 'I want these two to tell me what they did—and why it is that Bel and Leon were so convinced they killed them.'

'You're wasting your time. The twins don't remember who they are, let alone what happened a year ago.'

'I am confident my method of interrogation will be more thorough than yours. Give them to me now, and I will return the other two while they still have their heads.'

Zak and Malachi step forward together, swords drawn.

'No,' Daniel says. 'Hold position.'

Zarael casts his flickering gaze over the roof. Hungry, predatory. 'Your days are numbered, all of you. We will find the Fallen. They will return to hell—*all* of them—and without Nathaniel to protect you, we will pick you off like fieldmice.'

'Except Gabriella,' Bel says, pointing a bony finger in my direction. 'I will have my fun with you before I let the hellions strip your bones.'

He wants my fear. I struggle not to give it to him. 'You're going to find that difficult without a head.'

'We shall see who keeps their head the longest.' Zarael changes his grip on the branch above him. 'Now, children, as much as I am enjoying this rare chance to exchange insults, there are others here we need to see.'

And then he and Bel are gone, the leaves of the great cedar shaking in their wake.

SMILE . . .

'The library,' Daniel says. 'Now.'

The Rephaim behind him disappear.

Mya holds her ground. 'How is that going to—'

'We have cameras. Stop arguing.'

She has no comeback for that.

The shift is short and it's gentle—as it always is with Ez—but still leaves my skin chilled. The first thing I smell is musty paper. The second, fresh espresso. We're in a long, narrow room. The walls either side of us are lined with shelves, stretching up so far I can't make out the highest ones. There are more books in here than I've seen in my lifetime, and I work in a public library. In the middle of the room is a long row of desks and chairs and a bank of computer screens.

Daniel and three other Rephaim are clustered around

the largest. The library is a strange hybrid of medieval and modern: the tables are antiques, the chairs ergonomic; the parquetry floor worn with age, the screens flat and shiny. This is probably where the Rephaim tracked Rafa online and found my short story: the one that set all of this in motion.

'Technology's improved since we left,' Ez says to Mya. Mya doesn't respond.

Daisy registers our arrival but her attention is fixed on whatever's on the screen. We hang back. Jude is still craning his neck, checking out the library, while the other Outcasts shuffle behind us, impatient. The screens at our end of the table are all cold, blank.

I unzip my jacket. 'Who's Zarael going to see?'

'Tourists,' Ez says. She's trying to peer over shoulders to see what's in front of Daniel. 'Hundreds come by bus twice a week.'

I stare at her. 'Why would Nathaniel encourage that?'

'The Sanctuary is a thousand years old. Pilgrims were coming here long before Nathaniel moved in.'

'But it's crawling with Rephaim.'

'The tours never come past the front chapel. The rest of the world thinks this a closed order. Everyone trains indoors the days the buses come.'

And obviously the buses are here now.

Magda breaks away from the cluster around Daniel and comes over to us, cautious. Intelligent brown eyes shift from me to Ez to Mya and back to Ez. She's still clutching her beads.

'Let me turn this on for you so you can see what they're looking at.'

Ez steps out of her way. Mya doesn't move, forcing Magda to walk around her. She turns on the nearest screen and brings up images from four cameras, each showing a different angle of the front entrance.

'It's a live feed.' Magda moves aside so we can crowd around the screen.

'Oh god, it's peak hour out there,' Ez says.

There must be a hundred tourists milling about the gravel parking lot, most with silver hair and rounded shoulders. Some are climbing out of buses and forming groups around their guides, others line up for the chapel. A monk poses for photos while two others usher the visitors towards the main steps.

No sign of the Gatekeepers.

'What do we do?' I ask.

'We wait.' Daniel doesn't look away from his screen. At least he's acknowledged we're here.

'For what?' Mya demands. 'Zarael to send out a hellion?'

'He won't attack humans. He knows better than to draw that sort of attention.'

'Of course they'll attack. That's what they do.'

Daniel finally turns his head. 'No, Mya, they threaten humans to bait you. You take the bait, the demons attack, and then they kill the witnesses. The Gatekeepers have never openly attacked humans unless you and your *crew* have been in the vicinity.'

'That's not true,' Jude says. 'What about the ship? Zarael let hellions feed on aid workers—'

'Do you remember that incident?' Daniel straightens from the desk.

'I've dreamed about a hellion on a ship. I didn't know what it meant until today.'

'So your dreams differ from Gabriella's?'

'Who cares?' Mya shifts her weight, taps her fingers on the edge of the worn desk. 'You should be more worried about what's happening out there.' She's wound tight. Too tight. She wasn't even like this before we went to LA.

Daniel's gaze slips to me for a second before returning to Mya. 'I'm not inciting a battle in the front parking lot. We will not engage with the Gatekeepers unless there is absolutely no avoiding it.'

Jude scratches his jaw with the hilt of his katana. 'Wouldn't it be easier to get the tourists inside the walls *before* something happens?'

'That's what the monks are doing.'

'Maybe they should pose for a few less photos and hurry the process along.'

'Yes, panic would be perfect out there right now.' Daniel turns back to the screen and a second later the guy at the keyboard says: 'We're on.'

'There.' Jude points to the lower right-hand image. A woman in a red coat has turned away from the group, her attention caught by something off screen. Behind me, Magda's prayer beads clack.

Zarael, Bel, and Leon step into the frame. The three demons stop in the shadow of the trees and look up at the camera. It takes a second for me to register what's different about them: they're wearing sunglasses and their swords are hidden under their coats. Nobody is screaming or running, so the hell-beasts haven't shown themselves.

Zarael speaks to the woman. The breeze ruffles her short gray hair. She's about the same age as Mrs. Williamson in Pan Beach, though not as fit. The woman turns her head to catch his words. There's no audio from the security cameras but we all stay quiet anyway.

The woman seems startled, but then nods and looks over her shoulder at someone we can't see. I scan the other camera angles, notice a youngish monk—mid-twenties maybe. He sees the three demons and his head jerks towards the camera. He stares at us for a long, agonizing moment, eyes wide, pleading. Then he turns and ushers the rest of the group up the chapel steps and into the safety of the Sanctuary walls.

The woman in the coat has something in her hand now: a phone. She sees the group heading inside, doesn't follow. Zarael strolls closer. Bel and Leon wait at the tree line. Bel taps the hilt of his sword through his trench coat.

My heart climbs my throat.

'You're going to cower in here and let this happen?' Mya's voice cracks on the last word.

'Nothing has happened yet,' Daniel says. 'And Nathaniel is watching.'

'If you think I'm going to stand here—'

'You will *not* leave this room, any of you.' He says it with force.

I feel more than see Ez stiffen beside me. God, I hope Daniel knows what he's doing. Zarael is beside the woman now, towering over her. He puts his arm around her shoulders, and she holds out her phone to take a selfie with him. She's all nerves, fingers twitching. Her smile falters: she's seen his scars. The demon's grin widens, as if posing for photos with tourists is his favorite thing in the world.

A movement catches my eye. Another monk, much older, is walking towards them. Wispy white hair floating in the breeze.

'Brother Stephen,' Jude whispers, eyes fixed on the screen. 'He gets around.'

'What is he *doing*?' Mya's voice is stretched thin.

Brother Stephen's palms are up, as if apologizing for interrupting. The woman tries to step away. Zarael pulls her closer, laughing, as if they're both in on a joke. The monk holds out his hand for her phone. She hesitates and then hands it to him. He steps back to fit her and Zarael in the shot.

'Go closer,' Daniel says. The Rephaite at the computer in front of him clicks three times and the camera zooms in. Magda's beads are clacking double-time now, in sync with my heart.

The demon strokes the woman's hair so hard her head moves back with his hand. Brother Stephen says something to her. She nods, eager, and pulls away from Zarael. This time he lets her go.

'Don't . . .' Mya whispers.

But Brother Stephen has already stepped in to take her place. My skin chills.

The elderly monk and the former head gatekeeper of hell stand side by side, posing for her. Zarael doesn't put his arm around Brother Stephen: he clamps fingers around his neck. The woman takes a quick snap and then hurries towards the chapel, her red coat stark against the gravel car park. She doesn't look back.

Zarael turns so he and Brother Stephen face away from the chapel. He wrenches the monk's arm behind his back and Brother Stephen's face contorts.

'Daniel . . .' I barely get his name out my mouth is so dry.

And then the demon lifts his face to the security camera, smiles, and snaps the old man's arm.

HOOK, LINE, SINKER

My stomach drops and Mya appears onscreen a split second later.

'Nobody else leaves!' Daniel orders.

Ez looks to Jude and me, urgent, and we reach for her at the same time. I'm in the vortex for a heartbeat— and then I'm on solid ground again, buffeted by cold wind. The air is thick with the smell of pine trees and bus fumes.

Zarael is dragging the monk towards the forest, the tip of his sword pressed under his chin. Brother Stephen moans in our direction. Terrified. Blood trickles down his throat.

'I love that you are so predictable,' Zarael says. The Outcasts are all here now. He grins at us, eyes still hidden behind his sunglasses, and disappears. Brother Stephen slumps to the gravel. I check the trees. Bel and Leon are gone.

Mya races for the monk but Daisy and Micah materialize before she gets there. Micah kneels and gently lifts Brother Stephen onto his lap, cradling his arm and putting pressure on his bleeding neck. I stand guard with Jude and the Outcasts, watch the forest for movement. Blood thuds at my temples.

'I can help,' Mya says, panting.

'You've done enough,' Daisy snaps. 'We've got this.' Micah and Brother Stephen disappear.

'Shifting will heal him?' Jude asks me.

'No. It doesn't work on humans. He'll need stitches and that arm set.'

Jude runs a hand through his hair. 'I thought that prick was going to take the monk with him.'

'Me too.'

'Why didn't they stay and fight?'

'Because that's not what he came here to do,' Daisy says. She faces down the Outcasts, not caring she's outnumbered. 'He came to bait you lot, pure and simple.'

'Shut up Daisy.' Mya ties her hair up with a violent twist of her wrist.

'Think about it: Zarael knows your crew is here. He knows your first instinct is offense, and ours is to wait. He knew he could stir up strife just by being here.' Daisy spins the sword in her hand. 'Daniel wants everyone back in the library. Now. And don't you dare shift anywhere else, you chickenshit.' She points her katana at Mya.

'Hey.' Ez blocks Daisy from getting any closer. 'That's enough.'

Daisy eyeballs Ez for a second and then disappears.

'She can go screw herself,' Mya says. 'I'm going to check on Brother Stephen.'

Ez sighs. 'Do you really think that's smart?'

'I don't care, I'm going.' And she's gone. Dry pine needles stir on the ground where she was standing.

Zak looks to Jude and me. 'We going back in there?'

'Nothing's changed,' Jude says. 'We still need them. Gaby?'

My thoughts slide back to Rafa. How long has it been now? I check my watch. Three hours and four minutes. *Three hours and four minutes.* It's always there, the sickening feeling that twists everything inside me when I think about him. What's happening right now? Is he conscious? Is he fighting? Is he even alive?

The knot tightens.

'Yeah,' I say. 'We go back in.'

Everyone else has left the library except Daniel and Daisy. Ez, Zak, and Jones stay close to Jude and me. The rest of the Outcasts fan out behind us. Daniel's chest rises and falls. His eyes find mine. Furious.

'If you intend to stay here, you need to follow orders.' He measures his words. 'If any of you pull a stunt like that—'

'You call saving an old monk from a demon a stunt?' Jude challenges.

'You lost the right to worry about anyone here when you walked away a decade ago. You and your *crew*—' Daniel stops, takes a slow breath. Takes a moment to gather himself. God forbid he should lose control.

Jude turns to Daisy. 'You say Zarael came to stir us up, so why didn't he do more damage while the tourists were still in the parking lot? Why not bring out the hellions?'

'Gatekeepers don't make a habit of showing themselves and their pets to humans,' Daisy says.

'Why not? What are they afraid of?'

She pauses, as if it still surprises her he doesn't know the answer. 'The Angelic Garrison.'

'Okay, so why haven't the archangels taken them out already? Why let demons exist in the world at all?'

Daisy turns to Daniel.

'Because there are greater battles building.' Daniel's voice is steadier now. 'There are boundaries between heaven and hell: lines that exist until the end of the age.'

'What's that supposed to mean?'

'It means some knowledge is not for us.'

'That sounds like the kind of bullshit doctrine you trot out when you don't know the answer.'

A small, bitter laugh escapes Daniel. 'The more things change, the more they stay the same.'

I massage my temples. I need to stop this before it

deteriorates into yet another slanging match.

'Daniel.'

It's an effort, but he shifts his attention from Jude.

'Did you know you have a mole here at the Sanctuary?'

Daniel blinks. 'Don't be ridiculous.'

'That room in Iowa? There was a drawing board covered in floor plans for this place with notes about who lives where, and the walls were covered with photos of Rephaim—'

'Photos of whom?'

'You, me, Jude, Rafa, Mya, Nathaniel . . . Photos taken when everyone was still together. Rafa did an inventory and everyone was accounted for. The women who built that iron room know a hell of a lot about the Sanctuary, for people who've never been here.'

'You didn't mention that yesterday.'

'I didn't get a chance.'

'Your friend Jason is the only one who's been in contact with those women.'

I shake my head. 'Whoever it is has had access to computers, phones, and photo albums over decades; has known where Rephaim would be so the surveillance shots we saw could be taken. They know where Nathaniel sleeps, Daniel.'

'Nobody here would betray Nathaniel.'

'Great. Then don't give it another thought. Keep on pretending nothing's wrong. Or you could go talk to the one person who knows exactly who your mole is: your house guest.'

Daniel inhales slowly, lets it out even slower. Searches my eyes. And then he walks away without another word.

DID YOU HEAR THE ONE
ABOUT THE LLAMAS?

The door at the far end of the library clicks shut behind him and Daisy's eyes skim over the Outcasts.

'What's your next genius move?'

Jones sits on the edge of a table, straightens his beanie. 'Well, first we'll wring our hands over upsetting Daniel'— he pauses for a response; she gives him nothing—'and then if the rec room's not off limits, we might amuse ourselves while we wait for the Five to finally make a decision.'

There are noises of agreement, a few nods. Zak pulls Jude aside and they have a quick chat, too quiet for me to hear. Then Zak disappears.

Daisy raises her eyebrows at Jude. 'Where's he gone?'

'To check in on the Pan Beach lads.' He doesn't look at me, which makes me uneasy.

Ez touches my arm. 'You coming with us to play pool?'

'Actually,' Daisy says, 'if you want to see your old stuff, now's probably the time.'

Oh. The thought squeezes all the air from my lungs. Do I want to see evidence of my old life? I swallow, glance at Jude. 'You coming too?'

'Are you kidding? Of course I am.'

We pass through a tiled foyer and then we're in another piazza, smaller than the one with the fountain, more manicured: clipped lawn, trimmed lavender bushes, polished timber benches along the walls. The chill out here is deeper now, more insistent. The breeze has dropped and a light drizzle falls, so fine it doesn't make a sound. Jude walks close enough that our shoulders occasionally bump. I want to ask where Zak's gone, but not in front of Daisy in case I don't like the answer.

'Daniel doesn't seem to be a fan of mine,' Jude says as we move along the cloister.

Daisy gives a short laugh. 'That's an understatement. You've been his number one rival for the last hundred and thirty-nine years.'

'Rival for what?'

'For the hearts and minds of the Rephaim. And you were winning, until you ran away from home when you didn't get what you wanted.'

I actually *see* Jude's guilt slide back into place. Daisy must see it too because she softens a fraction. 'You never would've challenged Nathaniel to call down an archangel if it wasn't for Mya. She stirred up a lot of shit.'

He gives a humorless smile. 'I imagine I was more than capable of stirring up shit without help.'

We walk on in silence until we reach a set of weathered double doors. Inside is a brightly lit garage the size of a small aircraft hangar. Half a dozen cars are lined up on the polished concrete against the wall, most at least a decade old. The place smells of motor oil and rust.

'Who drives these?' Jude asks.

'Mostly the brothers.'

I notice a smaller shape under a cover in the far corner.

'Is that Rafa's bike?' I ask.

Daisy gives me a sideways glance. 'You're not planning on riding it, are you?'

'Not in a million years.'

Jude gets to it first and rips off the cover, lets out a low whistle. It's lean and shiny and lethal. Jude runs his fingers over the handlebars and I find myself reaching out too. The silver tank has ridges on the side like shark gills. I couldn't care less about the bike except for the fact it belonged to Rafa. I know so little about him. Why didn't I check out his room at Patmos, see more of his things? For a heartbeat I have no breath. Oh god, let him survive this.

'Holy shit,' Jude says. 'Do you know what this is?'

'A death wish?' Daisy offers.

'It's a Kawasaki Ninja ZX-11, the fastest road bike on

the planet—at least it was a few years back.' He sits on his heels to inspect the motor. 'Does a quarter mile in under eleven seconds.'

'Since when did you become a bike expert?'

Jude looks at me over the leather seat. 'I've always—' He stops, frowns. 'Huh.' He stands up and steps away. Daisy covers the bike again.

'You love bikes,' she says to Jude. 'You and Rafa are obsessed with anything involving speed.'

He touches the handlebars through the fabric. 'Do you think I could—'

'Not on my watch.' She crosses the garage and disappears through another door. I hesitate, torn between wanting to know what that other version of me left behind and worried what it might say about who I was.

Daisy waits in a narrow storeroom. She pulls half a dozen boxes down from shelves and sets them out on the floor. One is already open, scarves, beanies, and sweaters hanging over the side as if someone has been rifling through looking for clothes. Which they have—twice now in the past week. Daisy was obviously here last; Daniel would never leave clothes this untidy.

I sit down on the cold concrete and open the other boxes one at a time, spread things around me on the floor. It's like breaking into someone else's time capsule. Three boxes are full of books. The first is packed with biographies—Aung San Suu Kyi, Nelson Mandela, Che Guevara,

Gandhi. The second, manuals on weapons and martial arts; hand-to-hand combat through the ages; traditional katana sharpening. The third, paperback novels in languages I can't read, plus a guide in English to the top twenty-five places to drink espresso in Europe. In another box, there's a paperweight made from what appears to be real amber; a small Grecian urn, possibly authentic; worry beads; a wheat pack; maps and photos of Monterosso. Yet another jammed with shoes—combat and hiking boots, runners, sensible walking shoes.

Nothing remotely feminine. I need Maggie to see this; it explains a lot about my fashion sense.

Jude is picking through another box. 'What the hell?' He holds up a tatty hand-stitched dog, stuffing poking out between its ears.

Daisy smiles, her frustration gone for the moment. 'We all had one when we were kids. You kept yours.' She reaches out, gives the long-eared mutt a scratch behind the ear. 'Your weapons are in the armory.'

I take the dog from Jude, ignore his teasing smirk.

'What sort of weapons?' I ask.

'Three katanas, a dozen or so knives, a crossbow, quarterstaff, mace—'

'A mace?'

'You went through a medieval phase. It led to the demise of at least three training dummies.'

'Did I have a computer?'

Daisy nods. 'Laptop. You must have taken it with you when you did whatever you did. It wasn't with this stuff when I packed it up. But this was.'

She digs around in a box I haven't yet looked in and pulls out a photo album. Its padded cover is faded, the spiral binding tarnished and peeling. I take it carefully, as if it might bite, open it slowly.

The first image is a blown-up shot of Jude and me, sitting side by side in a café, suntanned and grinning. His arm is slung around me and he's holding a glass of wine in his free hand. There's a donkey poking its head over my shoulder and I can just make out the brim of a straw hat belonging to someone off camera. I'm wearing a red, blue, and green knitted beanie, tassels hanging down to my shoulderblades. The photo is stuck down under a plastic protector.

'Look at that,' I say to Jude softly. 'We did make it to Peru.'

He nudges me. 'And *you* wore the chullo.'

We smile at each other. There's something deeply comforting about this image—not everything we remember is a total lie.

'Turn the page.'

I do and my heart stutters.

It's Rafa. And me. We're both wearing black tank tops and track pants, doubled over with our hands on our knees like we're catching our breath. His head is lifted so he can see me, and he's grinning, triumphant. I know the expression: he's just beaten me in a foot race or some test of strength or skill.

It takes me back to Pan Beach, our race on the sand. Rafa pulling ahead, pushing himself to beat me. Me catching my breath and then losing it again, wrapped around him, peeling his shirt up his back. The pang that hits my chest is so much sharper than desire.

I turn the page, then another. There are so many shots of Jude—in front of pyramids and ancient ruins and massive trees—but most are in cafés or bars, grinning at the camera over a table loaded with food. And almost all of them have Rafa sticking his head in the frame or pulling a face behind Jude's back.

Here it is, evidence of what I keep hearing: that Rafa, Jude and I were inseparable. A team. What the hell happened to change that? To make that other version of me choose the Sanctuary over them?

However angry I was at Rafa when he left the Sanctuary—however much I wanted to hurt him—it wasn't enough to destroy these photos. All of them are faded and printed on old-school photo paper. By the state of the album, they predate the digital age by a decade or two.

'This is . . .' Jude doesn't finish. There are no words.

We keep going.

More photos: Ez and Zak, Daisy, Micah, Jones. Even

Malachi and Taya, a reminder they were once a part of my life too. The photos were probably taken in between tracking and fighting Gatekeepers. Here's one of Ez—without scars—arms stretched across a tree trunk so wide it doesn't fit into the frame. There's Malachi holding Micah in a headlock in front of a crumbling stone wall, both of them laughing.

And here's Daniel in workout gear: standard Rephaim black tank top and track pants. It's the first time I've seen him wearing something other than a collared shirt, and it's a little startling to see so much toned flesh. He's smiling at the camera, katana hanging loose by his side, hair slicked back with sweat.

'Is he any good with a sword?' Jude asks.

'Fairly handy.' I think of how he and Rafa tag-teamed against Bel that first night on the mountain. How easily they fell into a rhythm fighting side by side instead of against each other.

Daisy keeps digging around in the box. 'There's also this.' She holds up a leather-bound notebook.

'I kept a journal?' Please tell me I wasn't naïve enough to record deeply personal thoughts and then leave them behind for everyone in the Sanctuary to read.

She snorts a laugh. 'You weren't a journal-keeping kind of girl. It's more a collection of quotes, random facts, a couple of short stories. You liked writing longhand, don't ask me why.'

A soft leather cover wraps around the notebook, held in place with a long piece of cord. I carefully unwrap it, press open worn pages made from recycled paper. They're covered in doodles and random lists and sentences in my scratchy handwriting. A catalog of favorite novels that takes up more pages than I have time to read. A flyer for a production of *Much Ado About Nothing* in Turin. Postcards for a surrealist exhibition in Prague and a taiko drumming school in Japan. It's nice to know I was interested in something other than swords and maces.

I keep flicking through, find the first short story. It's titled 'Twelve Angry Llamas' and starts with: 'I never pack my backpack the same way twice.'

I look up at Daisy. 'Have you read these?'

She ducks her head and straight red hair falls across her face. 'Only after you were gone. I thought you were dead—'

'Did I ever go backpacking?'

'Of course not. You used to threaten to run away and see the world like a normal person. As if that was ever going to happen.'

Jude and I exchange a long look.

'Did I know about those stories?' Jude asks.

Daisy shrugs with one shoulder. 'You were the only one allowed to read them.'

Footsteps echo in the garage. I freeze and then jam the photo album into the nearest box. I feel exposed, having my old life spread out on the floor. My skin tingles a second before Nathaniel steps into the storeroom. All three of us spring to our feet.

'Desdemona.'

Daisy winces.

'I wish to speak to Gabriella and Judah.'

'Of course.' She dusts off her jeans.

I raise my eyebrows at her. 'Desdemona?'

She shrugs. 'Desdemona, Desi, Daisy . . .' She taps a stack of books with her foot. 'You okay to pack this up?'

I nod and, like that, she's gone. I slide the notebook behind me. It reminds me of something . . . The journal from the iron room. Mya has it and we still don't know what it means.

'May I?' Nathaniel gestures to the boxes and the concrete. Without waiting for a response he sits on his heels, spine straight, perfectly balanced. He's wearing jeans and a pale blue polo-neck sweater.

'Don't you have something more important to do?' I ask.

'The Five can spare me for a moment. I wanted to see you both.' He picks up a book and flicks through a few pages. I can't see the cover. 'Has seeing these possessions helped either of you with your memory?'

I pause. Did Daisy bring me in here to jog my memory? Was it an order? It might explain why Nathaniel's not reaming us out about the parking lot incident right now: jogging our memories is more important.

'No, Nathaniel, this hasn't worked any better than holding my head underwater or putting me in a death match with a hell-beast.'

He ignores the jibe. 'Have you heard from the lost Rephaite?'

'He'll be here.' At least I hope he will.

Nathaniel's attention snags on the stuffed dog hanging out the side of the box closest to him. He puts down the book and touches its head almost affectionately.

'Have you made a decision about the farmhouse?'

His eyes lift to mine. Those icy, flickering eyes. They're not as unsettling as the Gatekeepers', but they're just as hard to read. 'Virginia has not yet been forthcoming with useful information.'

'Can't you read her mind?'

'No, she is human.'

I think about her reaction to seeing Jude and me outside her window. 'You must terrify her, given how she feels about the—' I stop before I refer to him as one of the Fallen. From Daniel's reaction last week, I'm guessing it's not a term the Rephaim use around him.

'Virginia is a strong woman. Stronger than I would expect, given her current circumstances. She continues to withhold information from me.'

Jude leans back against the shelves, rests his forearm across his knee. 'Like you've withheld information from us?'

I catch Jude's eye, try to gauge where he's going with this. Nathaniel seems to be weighing up the same thing.

'In the past, you made demands of me that were unreasonable,' Nathaniel says.

'It was unreasonable to ask to speak to an archangel?'

'You do not summon the Host of Heaven, Judah. Any more than you summon God.'

'Then how *do* you contact them?'

He lets out a small sigh and I understand: this is not the first time he's had this conversation with Jude. 'That is not your concern. But if you have other questions I will attempt to answer them.'

They watch each other closely. Jude drums his fingers on the concrete. 'How many archangels are there in the Garrison?'

'Beyond counting.'

'Where does Semyaza fit in?'

'Semyaza was a captain of the Garrison.'

'And you?'

'One of the two hundred warriors who served beneath him.' There's an ache in those words, echoes of longing and regret.

'Why did you follow when he and the others fell the first time?'

I flinch at the bluntness of the question.

Nathaniel's eyes darken. 'I mistook free will for freedom.'

'Is that why you didn't go around again when you all broke out of hell?'

'Semyaza had not—' He stops, reconsiders his answer. 'I severed the bond with Semyaza and my brothers to prove to the Garrison my time imprisoned had not been in vain. That I knew my place, and I was again worthy of their trust.'

'Do you regret it?'

'No.'

'But you're still an outcast of heaven.' Jude seems to use the description deliberately.

'Because I have not yet fulfilled my responsibility to bring my brothers to justice: to deliver them to the Garrison for judgment.'

It's the first time we've heard it direct from Nathaniel.

'You talked about wards to keep out demons,' I ask. 'How do they work?'

Nathaniel hesitates. 'They are bound by a sacred bond written in my blood.'

I picture ancient sandstone smeared with angelic blood.

'When the monks agreed to give me shelter here, I pledged my bond in the language of angels on each cornerstone of this sanctuary. That bond was sealed with the brothers' blessing. The stones absorbed my blood: a sign the sacrifice was accepted. This monastery, the ground below it and the air above it, are sanctified now until the end of time. No demon can enter this place against my will until the final battle between heaven and hell.'

'Why didn't you tell the Rephaim about it?' I ask.

'I wanted them to be here by choice, of their own free will, not because it was the only place they were safe. Inviolate protection was their reward for faithfulness and loyalty.'

'Did the Five know?'

'The Council exists to guide and lead the others, not keep secrets from them. It was never my intention to create two classes of Rephaim—that is why the membership of the Council is fluid.'

'And yet the Rephaim ended up divided anyway.'

Jude watches the fallen angel with an expression I can't read. 'Does that mean blood was used to create the room in Iowa?' he asks.

'That room perplexes me. Gabriella and Rafael could enter it, and were only trapped once it was sealed. Such a thing hints of a blood ward, but one that I am not familiar with.'

'Bullshit,' I say.

His eyebrows shoot up—an extreme gesture for him. 'You question me, Gabriella?'

'You knew there was a charm protecting Virginia and her daughter from being forced to shift. You told Daniel to look for it.'

'It was an educated guess.'

'How could you guess that? You said the wards here involved blood and cornerstones. Why would you automatically think their protection came from iron?'

He places the book he's been holding in the box with the others. 'You told me the room was made from iron.'

'Nathaniel.'

His flickering eyes come back to me. 'In my library I have an ancient text that lists the gifts of iron. One of those gifts is the ability to absorb and hold wards and blessings.'

'How does that work?'

A pause. 'May I look upon the etchings from the room?'

I hand him my phone and he spends a good thirty seconds staring at the shot of the wall, the carved giant wings outstretched corner to corner. Something heavy settles in the pit of my stomach. 'You know what that is, don't you?'

'I have never seen that symbol on an iron wall.'

'But you've seen it before.'

He fixes his attention somewhere just left of me. Doesn't answer.

'Rafa and Taya are trapped by that symbol. I don't care how many secrets you've kept for the last hundred and forty years—we need to know what it means.'

He rises without looking at Jude or me, checks the garage, shuts the door. Jude and I stand, glance at each other. I've pushed him too far.

Nathaniel turns around, slowly. The calm mask has

slipped from his features. He's uncertain. Uneasy.

'I have seen this symbol before.' He studies it again, seems to go somewhere else.

'Where?'

'In heaven.'

I stare at him. Forget to breathe.

'Those symbols were marked in the air to bind us—Semyaza and we Two Hundred—before we were cast out.'

IT'S ALWAYS BLOOD

I open my mouth. Words fail me. I try again.

'What does that mean?'

Nathaniel blinks, as if remembering Jude and I are there. He hands me my phone and goes to the door. Opens it, closes it again with his back to us. A chill runs through me: he's rattled. That can't be good. His sweater is stretched tight across tense shoulders. I have a flash, a memory of giant wings unfurling in front of Bel, of demons cowering before white-blue light. My mind scrambles for traction.

'So . . .' Jude says, 'those women in Iowa recreated a symbol last seen in heaven?' He taps his thumb on the metal shelf.

I'm still staring at Nathaniel. Maybe the family really does receive revelation from God. Maybe we half-breeds truly are an abomination and these women have been given a holy mission to find a way to trap us. But then what? Kill us? Hand us over to someone more powerful to exterminate us? I stop those thoughts before they unravel me.

'Could that room hold you?' I ask Nathaniel.

He shakes his head. 'It would take the blood of an archangel. A ward like that could not work in this realm without a blood bond.'

'What about demons?'

'Not without angel blood.'

'Is it possible—'

'No. A member of the Garrison would never have authority to shed blood on earth unless the Fallen had been found. And there is no need for them to build an earthly prison for the Fallen: the Garrison can create their own whenever and wherever they require. And they do not need a prison for demons: hell already exists.'

Jude's tapping stops.

'So the trap most likely only works for Rephaim? Does that mean it would take the blood of a Rephaite to trap a Rephaite?'

Something hums. Nathaniel takes out a phone—of course he has a phone—and checks the screen. He presses his lips together. 'Thank you Gabriella, Judah,' he nods to each of us.

'Hang on—'

But Nathaniel has gone. Shifted.

'Shit.' Jude smacks his palm against the wall. 'I hate when they do that.'

I slump against the shelves. The steel digs into my back. 'Wait until it happens in the middle of an argument. It'll make your head explode.'

'Rafa?'

'He's a master at it.' I feel the familiar tug in my chest. What I wouldn't give to be arguing with him right now.

We go back to packing the remnants of my old life back into boxes. I pick up the notebook—my notebook—and flick through the pages again. My attention snags on the word *bungee*. I skim the short story. For a second my head swims and the ink bleeds together on the page. Jude stops fiddling with the box he's trying to close.

'What is it?'

I wait for the words to come back into focus. 'It's a story about jumping from a cable car in Switzerland.'

'Show me.' I hand it to him, my fingers numb. He skims a few pages. 'This one's about the Cinque Terra . . .' I hold my breath while he reads on. 'This one's about a couple of backpackers in London.' He keeps going, page after page. Finally, he looks up. 'Gaby, this is our entire trip.' He closes the notebook, hands it back to me. 'At least now we know where those memories come from.'

'Jude—'

'You heard what Daisy said: I'm the only person you

let read those stories.' His voice catches and he won't look at me.

'It still doesn't tell us who did this to us, or why.'

The opening drums of 'My Hero' interrupt that thought. I answer my phone. 'Mags?'

'Gaby, we're in the library. You have to come, now.' She's frantic. I close my eyes to concentrate.

'The library . . . *here*?'

'Please, Gaby. We're not alone.'

BLINDED BY THE LIGHT

We run.

There's no sign of Daisy so we race back the way we came, boots pounding on the cobblestones.

Shit, shit shit. What are they doing in the library? Is Dani with them? Who else is there? Panic drives my arms and knees. My lungs burn. There's the door . . . crap, that's the library, isn't it?

'Gabe!' It's Daisy, somewhere behind us. We keep running.

Jude and I hit the door together, sprint across the portico and burst into the library.

Oh fuck.

Jason has his back to us, facing down Nathaniel, Daniel, and Calista, his shoulder-length curls still wild from the shift. Calista is barely a meter from him, focused on the woman and child pressed against the bookshelves behind him. The girl is thin-boned, her skin alabaster. Blonde curls hang past her shoulders, damp like they're freshly washed. Her mother is shorter than everyone else in the room. Dark hair cropped to a pixie cut, practical, her face clear of makeup. She's wearing an oversized knitted sweater, leggings, and boots.

And Maggie.

She's pale—she always is after shifting. I've told her about Nathaniel, but she's still not prepared for him. She sees me, closes her eyes in relief. My heart gives a painful thump.

'What the hell is going on?' I demand and drag everyone's attention to me. The air in here is colder now, the mustiness heavier.

'Your friend brought uninvited guests,' Calista says. 'And the child tells us she can *see* Rephaim.'

'Gabe!'

Dani breaks free from her mother and runs to me. Maria makes a grab for her but Dani's too quick. She flings her arm around my waist, buries her head against my chest. I freeze. Maria falters. The library is blanketed in silence. The small stranger pressed against me is all elbows, and smells of pears and honey. I put my arms around her, squeeze tight. Her pink parka rustles.

The door opens and Daisy rushes in. 'What's going on—' She falters when she sees Dani wrapped around me.

'Daisy,' Daniel says. 'Guard the doors. Nobody else is to set foot in here. *Daisy.*'

She's watching me with a strange expression. Not accusing . . . confused. She registers Daniel is speaking and finally nods, heads for the door. The door clicks shut behind her.

'You know this child?' It's Daniel who asks.

I ignore him, bend my head closer to Dani. 'Are you okay?'

She peers up at me through curls even fairer than Jason's. Eyes startlingly blue. Nods. 'Mom didn't want to come but I said we had to.' Her accent is American— the faintest hint of uptown New York. She gives Jude a nervous smile.

'Gabe, answer Daniel,' Calista says.

What the hell am I supposed to say? 'Give me a minute.'

But Calista's not in the mood for waiting. She looks from Jude to me, narrows her eyes as if she's measuring the distance. She lunges. I push Dani to Jude and block Calista with my hip. She recovers, swings her fist. I duck, punch her in the stomach, and then slam my elbow into the side of her head. She staggers sideways and I kick her hard in the hip. She grabs a chair on the way down; it's on castors, so it only speeds her fall. Calista's leg twists as she lands and her track pants hitch up. I catch a flash of something—dull gray, metallic; all wrong—and then Daniel shoves me aside. By the time I get my balance,

Jude has slammed Daniel into the bookshelf, a hand tight around his throat.

'I warned you about touching my sister again,' Jude says.

Daniel swings an elbow at Jude. Jude blocks it, keeps his grip on Daniel's throat. They eyeball each other.

'Stand down!' Calista is on her feet, eyes blazing. I get between her and Jude and Daniel. Dani's back with her mother now. Maria's eyes are wide, her breathing shallow, arms clamped around her daughter. Jason is in front of them and Maggie, arms out, protective.

'You first.' Jude leans into Daniel. Daniel could shift but doesn't. Pride?

'Judah,' Nathaniel says. 'If you expect this child to stay here, she must first be tested. She may be under the influence of the demon realm.'

I glance at Dani, heart in my mouth. 'She made it through the wards, so you know she's not—'

I don't finish because I'm blinded by white-blue light. It's so fierce I have to shield my closed eyes, and even then it forces its way under my lids. I step back, involuntarily. There's an odd sound, like a crisp linen sheet being snapped out. Is he . . . ? Has he . . . ?

Next to me, Jude sucks in his breath. 'Fuck. Me.'

The light eases enough for me to peer through my fingers. Nathaniel's wings are unfurled, radiating light. They are breathtaking. Luminous. Massive. Every feather perfect. The tip of each wing touches the bookshelves either side of the library. Almost like the symbol in the iron room, except those wings weren't attached to a fallen angel. I can't take my eyes from Nathaniel, not even to check on Dani and Maria. I've seen his wings before—for a blinding moment on the mountain when he drove back the Gatekeepers—but not up close like this.

The light fades but the wings stay outstretched. Jude is so distracted he lets go of Daniel's throat. Daniel pushes past him, straightens his shirt, and walks over to Nathaniel. It's only then I see Jason has Maggie in the corner, shielding her with his body.

'It is remarkable,' Nathaniel says. 'This child is worthy to be in my presence. As is her mother.'

It takes me a second to grasp the significance of his words and when it does, it's like a kick in the chest. 'You arsehole.'

'Gabe,' Daniel snaps. 'Watch your mouth.'

'That could've killed them, couldn't it?'

Nathaniel doesn't blink. 'You brought unsanctified humans into our Sanctuary. Did you not think I would test their worthiness?'

It never occurred to me Nathaniel might show his true form to Dani and Maria. They're probably only still alive because of their fallen angel heritage. Does he now suspect that connection? And what would've happened to Maggie if Jason hadn't been so quick on his feet? He's still covering her protectively, whispering reassurances.

'Is my friend safe?' I ask. It's a struggle to keep my voice steady.

Nathaniel glances over at Maggie, almost as if he'd forgotten there was another human in the room. 'Of course.'

Jason glares at him and then helps Maggie to her feet. She's shaking and a little wobbly, but she stands on her own. 'I'm okay.'

Dani is still staring at Nathaniel. 'Your wings are beautiful,' she whispers. 'Would you flap them?'

'Baby, no.' Maria holds her daughter tight, every muscle rigid.

'Please?' Dani asks, tentative.

Nathaniel's eyebrows lift a fraction. And then he beats his wings, slowly. Once, twice. Cool air rushes over me, the smell of dry leather and old paper. The gust lifts my hair from my forehead, stirs dust and cobwebs along the bookshelves. And then Nathaniel folds his wings behind him until they disappear completely. His irises flicker, slower now.

Dani's eyes widen. 'Where do they go?'

'They are still with me. They exist on a lower plane until I manifest in glory in this one.' Vaguely, I wonder if that plane is like the one we're dragged through when we shift.

The tension in the room eases a fraction. Calista touches her head where I hit her. My eyes drop to the cuff of her track pants. The fabric is back in place but I know what I saw: a titanium prosthesis where her shin and ankle should've been.

'Lose the pity. It's been gone a long time.'

'How?' The question's out before I realize I have no right to ask.

'Zarael.' Calista makes a chopping motion in the middle of her right thigh. 'He put his sword clean through the bone. He took what he cut as a trophy.'

'But . . .' I frown. 'What about shifting?'

'It doesn't regrow limbs.'

Oh.

'Does Mya know about this girl?' Daniel asks.

'No,' I say. 'Nobody else does.'

'What about Rafa?'

'Yeah, okay. But only because he throttled it out of Jason.'

A short, unimpressed noise escapes Daniel. 'And you are critical of our methods.'

'We shall return to the child in a moment.' Nathaniel walks over to Jason.

Jason stiffens, positions Maggie so she's behind him.

'For the moment, let us talk about you, and why you have hidden from me all these years.'

THE ITALIAN INQUISITION

The pulse in Jason's throat jumps. He's not ready for this moment; not ready for Nathaniel. After a lifetime of knowing the fallen angel killed his aunt—my mother. After decades of hearing propaganda from the women in Iowa. After seeing what happened to me here last week. He's heard about the Fallen, but until today he's never been near one of them.

'I understand this is not your first visit to our Sanctuary.'

Jason is not short, but he has to crane his neck to hold Nathaniel's gaze. 'I didn't want to be here last week and I certainly don't want to be here now.'

Nathaniel waits for him to elaborate. He doesn't.

'Did you know what you were before the women from Iowa found you?'

The fallen angel sounds calm but the air around him is charged.

'I knew I was the bastard child of a fallen angel.'

'How?'

'How does a child learn anything? There were stories in my village about my mother being seduced by a "shining one", an old wives tale that I assumed was village gossip. And then one day two cousins came to the village and told me the truth: that my father was a fallen angel.'

It's a clever half-truth.

'How did these cousins know?'

'Our mothers were close; they kept no secrets from each other.'

Nathaniel shifts his weight. It's such a human thing to do. Is he uncomfortable or uncertain?

'And what did your mother tell you?'

'My mother died giving birth. I was raised by my grand-father.'

A lie.

'Where?'

'Sidi Bou Said.'

Another lie, delivered flawlessly.

Nathaniel frowns. 'There were no signs in Tunisia.'

'Signs?' I ask. The word hangs in the silence somewhere around the second storey of shelves.

'The Garrison led me to each child.'

'Archangels showed you where to find us?' I try to

hide my surprise. I find it hard to believe members of the Angelic Garrison helped him find and slaughter women and steal their babies.

'Yes.' Nathaniel says. 'By the heavens.'

'Like the virgin birth.'

'It was *nothing* like the virgin birth.' It's the first time Nathaniel's voice has been as cold as his eyes. He takes a moment to settle himself. 'Constellations aligned with the waxing and waning crescent moon to guide me to the villages and cities where the children of the Fallen entered the world. I am sure you understand the significance of the symbol.'

I have to stop myself reaching under my hair. Maybe if I still had the crescent moon on my neck instead of a thick scar I might feel more like one of the Rephaim. Even with his scars, Jude's Rephaite mark is still recognizable. Like everything else so far, he's just that little bit more Rephaite than me.

Nathaniel walks over to the shelves. He runs a finger along a row of books, selects a slim volume bound in cracked brown leather, and turns back to Jason.

'How did you know about Gabriella and Judah? Who told you they were missing?'

'Virginia.'

Another lie. But he's hardly going to tell Nathaniel he was there when Dani came back alone from wherever she went with Jude and me last year.

'When Gabe and Jude disappeared, Virginia said it was a sign the days of the Rephaim were numbered. She's been preoccupied with the twins for years. She's not the first in the family to believe they're more important than the rest of us.'

Is that true or another lie to keep Nathaniel off balance? And if it's true, why am I only hearing about it *now*? I try to catch his eye but Jason's not looking my way right now.

'Did Virginia tell you about the trap?' Nathaniel asks.

'No.'

'I shall assume you will not permit me to access your thoughts and memories?'

'You assume right.'

Nathaniel takes a long, measured breath. He's lived for thousands of years. He acts like there are no secrets in the world from him. But in the past week he's discovered two of his protégés are back from the dead with no memory of their angelic heritage; a family exists with the knowledge to build a trap for Rephaim—using symbols once used to imprison him before he was sent to hell—and another half-angel bastard has survived for nearly a hundred and forty years hidden from him. And now here's Dani. He's not as calm as he seems. He can't be.

'Do you know who your father is?'

Jason isn't prepared for the question. His resolve slips and for a second I see how much the answer means to him.

'No. Do you?'

'Child, I did not know you existed until yesterday.'

'But you know the Fallen. You know Semyaza and every one of the Two Hundred. You served with them in heaven and suffered with them in hell. There must be something you see in their children to give you a clue who belongs to whom?'

Jason's words take all the oxygen out of the chilly air. I steal a glance at Daniel and I know nobody has ever asked this. But from the unguarded expression on Daniel's face, he's thought it.

We wait.

Nathaniel turns the book over in his hands. I catch the word *Apocrypha* in gold letters along its spine. Is he holding a collection that includes the Book of Enoch—the ancient text that recounts the original fall of Semyaza and the Two Hundred? Of all the books from this library, why is he holding that one for this conversation? Does he need a reminder of why we exist?

'I know my brothers-in-arms as well as I know myself. Knowing who your father is will not change your fate. Or his.'

'We have a right to be told.'

'You are the bastard child of a fallen angel. You have no rights.'

'You don't believe that. You've spent the last hundred and thirty-nine years protecting those same bastard children, *giving* them rights—and a violent destiny.'

Nathaniel's eyes flare so bright they are almost white. 'And what other destiny would you have me give them? One that sees them obliterated from the face of the earth? You know nothing of sacrifice and loss. Nothing. You should fall on your face and weep at my feet that you exist at all.'

Jason draws breath, loading the bullets that will shred the foundations of the Sanctuary if he fires them. I grab his arm, dig my fingers into his tanned flesh. 'Let it go.'

He turns his fury on me.

'Not now,' I say before he speaks.

'Then when, Gaby?'

'When Rafa and Taya are safe.'

Jason's cheeks are flushed, his neck mottled. I've never seen him like this. So much rage. He's been waiting his whole life to confront Nathaniel, but how can I get Rafa back if the Sanctuary falls apart now?

'Please,' I say. 'You're scaring Mags.'

He glances at her, sees her breath hitch, the uncertain downturn of her mouth. Jude has moved closer now too. He catches my eye, knows how close Jason is to losing it.

'Buddy, *think*.'

Nathaniel's eyes have already returned to their normal icy blue, but his fingers are tight around the apocryphal collection. 'Do you have something you wish to say?'

Jason's hands are fists, his breathing shallow. He doesn't answer.

'Gabriella?' Nathaniel looks at me, waiting. Cold fingers wrap around my heart. He knows. Nathaniel knows Jason is different from the rest of the Rephaim; that he understands things they don't.

Finally Jason looks at me. I try to convey that it's okay, that his time will come. It takes another few seconds before he unclenches his fingers and turns away. Maggie takes his hand in both of hers.

In the quiet, I hear voices in the piazza outside, indistinct. The doors we came through are thick; whoever's out there is talking loudly. Or shouting. Daniel turns his head a fraction, like he's trying to work it out as well. There's a loud thump on the door. Then another.

Jude's eyes lock on mine. 'That sounds like a brawl.'

EVERYBODY WAS KUNG FU FIGHTING

The piazza is in chaos. It seethes with more Rephaim than I've seen in one place: punching, kicking, and wrestling each other with blinding speed. Shouting, swearing. Grunting.

'Bloody hell,' Jude says.

'At least they're not armed.'

'They don't need to be.'

We jump up on a windowsill, scan the roiling mass of bodies. I spot Ez and Zak, Daisy and Micah—not fighting each other, thankfully—Jones, Seth, Malachi. All swinging and striking with focused fury. The Outcasts are outnumbered, but in the confined space of the piazza they're holding their own.

I glance through the window behind me. Maggie, Dani,

Maria, and Jason are in the portico. I barely make eye contact with Jason before my attention is pulled back to the frenetic fighting. This isn't helping my case that we can keep Dani safe.

'Where's Mya?' Jude asks.

I expect to find her sitting out the fight, watching passively from the sidelines. But no, there she is, fending off a barrage of blows from a guy twice her size, not far from us. I haven't seen him before so he's obviously one of Daniel's guys. He lands a heavy uppercut to her jaw, snapping her head back.

'Prick,' Jude says.

'Don't—'

Too late, he's launched himself into the fray, pushing against twisting bodies to get to Mya. He takes out the big guy's knees, elbows him in the side of the head. Mya ducks a punch from another assailant, spots Jude. The look she gives him is all relief, her lip already split. Wordlessly, they put their backs to each other and keep fighting. I know he's reacting on instinct but seeing them like that, united, hollows me out a little.

If Rafa were here he'd already be throwing punches, yelling at me to get involved. But even if I jumped in, who would I help? Ez and Zak? Daisy and Micah? Either choice betrays someone. And what if I'm helping out Ez and Daisy attacks her?

When does this get any easier?

A movement catches my eye. Nathaniel is in the cloister with Daniel and Calista. He says something and Daniel gives an almost imperceptible shake of his head—a rare sign of frustration. Calista scans the brawl, fidgets. Shifts her weight to her good leg. She wants to be out there. It's hard to tell what Nathaniel's thinking. He can order his Rephaim out of the square whenever he wants. But maybe he understands that if he stops the fight now, it will only erupt somewhere else.

I can see it on the faces of the Rephaim closest to me as they duck, block, lash out: they need this. They need what I felt after my session with Malachi in the ring: pain, exhaustion, release. Maybe it will defuse the tension long enough for them to work together. Long enough to get Rafa and Taya back.

The piazza is filled with the dull smacks of fists on flesh. A mist of red. So much violence. And this is my idea of a solution now. When did I become this person? But I know the answer: somewhere between killing a hell-beast and watching Rafa be impaled by a demon blade.

Did I really think I was going to go back to my old life, working in the library and hanging out at Rick's? Who am I kidding—*this* is my old life.

Jude takes a kick to his chest, stumbles into Uri. The redhead falters for a split second and then he and Jude are swinging at each other. Jude's blocks and strikes are quicker now.

Nathaniel lets the melee continue for a few more minutes. I spend those long moments agitated, torn. I try to keep an eye on Jude. The Rephaim inflict a lot of damage on each other in that time.

'Enough,' Nathaniel says finally.

The fighting continues.

'Rephaim.' Firmer now, louder. 'Fall back.'

A split second later, the number of fighters on the lawn has dropped by two-thirds. The Outcasts look around, disoriented, surrounded by nothing but churned-up grass. Daisy, Micah, Malachi, and the rest of Daniel's soldiers have shifted to the other end of the square, fanned out along the cloister, catching their breath. A mass of discolored skin, puffy faces, torn clothes.

Jude and Zak start in their direction. Jude is favoring his left ankle. Hasn't he had enough?

I leap down from the window, ready to get between him and more bloodshed, but Nathaniel materializes on the grass and blocks our path. Everyone stops.

'No more.' The angel stands between the two groups of Rephaim. He seems taller. He checks he has the attention of his Rephaim and the Outcasts. 'The next time you fight, it will not be against each other. It will be against our enemy. This is over. Am I clear?'

I wait for Mya to argue but she's too busy gulping in air, sitting on the ground, cross-legged. Nobody from the Sanctuary has anything to say. No surprises there.

'You will heal each other. No—' he says, as the Sanctuary Rephaim start to move into pairs. 'You will heal *each other.*'

The command sinks in. He wants his Rephaim and the Outcasts to tend to each other.

'It is not a suggestion.'

There are low mutterings, a few sideways glances. I look from one side of the piazza to the other. Who's going to make the first move?

It takes three more seconds before a figure steps out from the cloisters: Malachi. His knuckles are split and he's limping, but he walks with purpose. It's obvious who he's heading for.

Mya gets to her feet, lifts her chin, defiant. Daring him. Malachi stops a few steps away and I hold my breath. I'm not the only one. This is the moment we find out if the splintered Rephaim can cooperate without an immediate threat to unite them. Mya and Malachi eye each other. Still no love lost there. She only has to take a swing at him and this will all be on again.

'Taya and Rafa are in trouble.' Malachi's voice carries in the quiet afternoon. Now he's closer I can see a fresh bruise on his jaw, blood in his goatee. He can take punishment, I'll give him that. 'So this'—he points to his face and then hers—'has to stop.'

Mya watches him, hair disheveled, kohl smudged around her eyes. 'For now.'

Malachi nods. 'Gym?' They grip each other by the forearm and disappear.

Daisy and Jones meet halfway across the piazza, offer each other tired half-smiles. Slowly, cautiously, the Outcasts and Sanctuary Rephaim close the space between them. Jude comes over to me. His cheek is grazed and both forearms are mottled purple from blocking punches and kicks.

'You okay?'

He rubs his shoulder, squints with one eye. 'Still in one piece.'

'You want a hand with that?' Micah is a few paces away. His knuckles are bloodied and his nose a mess.

'I can't return the favor,' Jude says.

'No dramas. I'll find Daisy afterwards.' He checks me over. 'Are you all right?'

'I didn't get involved.'

'I know, that's my point.'

'Well, see, that's where I differ from Gabe. I'm happy to sit out a full-on brawl if I can.'

He shakes his head. 'Shame.' And then to Jude: 'Ready?'

I fight a pang of fear. They disappear and my heart bangs once, twice. It's all right. It's all right. It's—

They're back. Jude reaches for me to steady himself. The graze on his cheek is all but gone.

'Sorted,' Micah says to me. 'See you in the chapter-house.'

'What's in the chapterhouse?'

'There'll be a briefing at some point after this little demonstration.' He smiles, weary, and then he's gone.

Zak and Ez are back—they shifted with Rephaim I haven't met—but no sign yet of Mya. I hope she and Malachi aren't going at it again in the gym.

'So what happened out here?' I ask.

Zak surveys the piazza. The lawn is a mess, divots everywhere, torn bits of fabric littering the grass. 'We were having coffee in the rec room when Mya turned up and said Jason had brought a kid here.'

'How did she hear that?'

He looks at me sideways. 'Best guess? When she finished with Brother Stephen she stalked Daisy.'

Of course she did.

'Just the three of you came?'

'We may have brought a few friends.'

I check the window, see Dani and Jason deep in discussion on the other side. Maria's face is bleak, her arms wrapped around herself. Dani is agitated and points outside, in my direction. Jason turns, shakes his head. Is he trying to convince Dani to leave and she's refusing? He could force her—it's not like her mother would argue—but no matter how much he might want to get them both away from here I know he won't do it against Dani's wishes.

Nathaniel, Daniel, and Calista are talking quietly further along the cloister. Daisy joins them, dabbing at her ear. By the time I look inside again, Jason is gone from the window. The heavy portico door heaves open, hinges protesting. Jason steps out first, and then Maggie, pulling her suitcase. Dani is dragging Maria along, eyes only for Jude.

Dani starts as soon as she reaches him. 'That girl you were fighting alongside—who is she?'

'Which one?' Jude asks.

'The blonde one with the panda eyes.'

'That's Mya.'

'I've never seen her before.'

He shrugs. 'So?'

'There are a hundred and eighty-two Rephaim—'

'A hundred and eighty-three,' I correct, remembering Rafa's tally when we were trapped in the iron room. 'Counting Jason.'

'No, there are a hundred and eighty-*two*—counting Jason. I've seen them all in my mind. I've written down their names and what they look like. I have a book.' Her eyes shift to me. 'And I have never, ever seen that woman with the blonde hair before.'

THE GIFT THAT KEEPS ON GIVING

'Does it matter?' I ask.

Dani blinks once, twice. 'You and Jude are the only other Rephaim I can't see and that's only been since last year. Before that I could see you like everyone else.' She zips her parka to her chin, shivers against the cold.

'What does it mean?'

'I don't know,' she says. 'It's weird.' Her words hang in the air, none of us sure what to do with them.

Maggie steps around Jude to hug me. I breathe in cherry blossom and Chanel No. 5, fight an overwhelming urge to cry. Now's really not the time.

'Babe, I'm so sorry about Rafa,' she whispers. I nod against her hair, not trusting myself to speak. She holds me tight, trembles. 'Any word?'

I shake my head. 'Did you bring the pendant?'

'In my shoe.'

Thank god. Nobody here can force her to shift while she's got that iron trinket. At least something good has come out of that farmhouse.

'Is Simon okay?' Maggie asks.

'He's in the infirmary. We'll go see him in a bit, but we need to get Dani away from prying eyes.' I squeeze her and let go. She's dressed for Italy in winter: skinny jeans and tailored leather jacket, hand-knitted black and gray scarf looped loosely around her neck. Her blonde hair is tied back in a long ponytail.

'And who is this?' Ez smiles down at Dani.

'I'll explain in a minute,' I say. 'Hang on.'

Daniel and Daisy are headed in our direction. I meet them halfway, try to keep distance between them and Dani. Daisy stares at Jason and Maggie; Daniel, as usual, is interested only in me.

'What's this about Mya?'

Seriously, nothing gets past him. 'I have no idea.'

'Don't you think the time for secrets has passed?'

'Here's an idea. I'll tell you all mine when you and Nathaniel spill yours.' It's a throwaway line, meant to annoy him more than anything else and end the conversation. So I'm surprised to see uncertainty on his face. Or I think that's what it was—it's gone too quick for me to be sure.

'Have you guys made a decision about the farmhouse?'

Daniel's gaze skitters away. It's like a knife to the chest. 'You've already made up your mind, haven't you? You're not going to Iowa.'

'Nobody's made any decisions.'

'You must be leaning in one direction or another.'

'It's not that simple.'

'Make it that simple.'

His eyes search mine. For a second I can see how much he needs me to be *his* Gabe right now. Daisy waits at his side, silent.

'Daniel,' Nathaniel calls out. 'Escort the child and her mother to the spare guest room in my wing.'

I push past Daniel before he can respond. 'No way. They're staying upstairs with us.'

Nathaniel watches me, expressionless.

'I mean it. They stay with us or they're gone. You'll never see them again.'

'It is in everyone's interest that the child remain here,' Nathaniel says.

'Is that a threat?'

He doesn't answer and it takes another second before I understand.

'Are you saying you won't help us in Iowa if Dani leaves here? Are you so desperate to interrogate Dani you'd risk Taya's life over it?'

I look to Daisy. She won't meet my eyes. I don't think she was expecting the conversation to take us here.

'I hope that's a bluff, buddy,' Jude says. 'Because I don't know how your army will feel about you threatening a little girl.'

Nathaniel's lips tighten, the smallest of movements. 'You are not the only ones being pushed into a corner.' He looks from me to Jude to Jason, and then turns and walks away, signals for Daisy to join him. She shoots me a quick frown—confused—and falls into step. Daniel hesitates a split second before following, and in that moment I catch a shadow of something I've never seen in his face before.

Doubt.

CIRCLE OF TRUST

'You can't keep her safe from him,' Jason says, watching Nathaniel walk back into the library.

A breeze swirls through the piazza, drags a stray hair into my eyes. 'The sooner we get an army together, the better. People here care about Rafa and Taya. If we can tell them what's going on in that room, maybe they'll sign on whether Nathaniel approves or not.'

'Do you honestly believe that's possible?' He walks to the edge of the cloister, takes in the number of windows overlooking the piazza and comes back. 'We can't stay here. It's not safe for Dani.'

I grab his sleeve. 'Don't make this about Dani—we can protect her long enough to do what she needs to do. This is about you and your issues with the Rephaim. If I can be here after what happened in the cage—if I can stand the accusation and the tension and the churning gut—so can you.'

Jason looks to Maggie, a silent question. She nods and forces a smile. 'We can do this.'

His shoulders ease a little.

He doesn't speak as we make our way upstairs, Ez and Zak with us. The only sounds are the rumble of Maggie's suitcase wheels on the cobblestones and our hurried footfalls. Ez can't stop glancing at Dani.

Jude lets us into his room and I falter when I see Rafa's rucksack on his bed.

'Zak went back for it,' Jude says, and unzips it.

That's what they were talking about in the library. 'Why didn't you tell me?'

'You had enough on your mind.' Jude takes the laptop to the desk and turns it on. It shouldn't bother me, but there's just something about the situation: the idea he made plans without telling me. 'I assume the other stuff in there is yours.'

I check in the rucksack, see a T-shirt and cargo pants. Lacy underwear. Rafa packed them for me two days ago. Another punch in the chest. I need to keep it together.

Maria sits on the opposite side of the bed and pulls Dani into her lap, hugs her close.

'Do you have to do this right now?' Maria's voice has all the hard edges I remember from our phone call in Rafa's kitchen.

'Yes.' I sink to the carpet in front of them and take a steadying breath, look to Dani. Try not to give in to the fear and hope threatening to smother me. 'What do you need to be able to find Rafa?'

'A quiet spot, that's all.' She wriggles off Maria's lap. 'Sometimes it takes a while.'

Ez kneels on the floor next to me, looks from Dani to me and back to Dani again. 'Is someone going to tell us what's going on?'

Dani smiles almost shyly. 'You're even more beautiful in person.'

Ez's fingertips are almost to the scars on her cheek when she realizes what she's doing. 'You've seen me . . . in photos?'

'In my mind.'

Ez frowns. 'I don't understand.'

We don't have time for this, but I owe Ez and Zak an explanation. 'Dani has a connection to the Rephaim. She has visions of us—sees things that have happened and will happen. And she can tune in and find out where any of us are . . . any time.'

Ez opens her mouth. Closes it. Zak stares at me as if I've just told him I've got a unicorn in the bathroom.

'She'll be able to see inside the iron room and tell us what's going on,' I say. 'Help us plan our attack. We need her to start looking now. Right now.'

Still they stare. 'She can *see* us?' Ez asks. 'How?'

At the window, Jason is rigid, fingers clamped on the sill. Maggie is next to him, hands tucked between her knees.

'I do this meditation thing,' Dani says, as if it's the most natural thing in the world. 'I can see you whenever I want—usually.'

'Holy shit,' Zak says.

'How?' Ez says again. 'Are you part of the family from Iowa?'

'Of course she's not,' Jason snaps.

'Then how do you know her?'

Jason meets my eyes, shakes his head.

Ez turns to Jude. 'You knew about this girl?'

'As much as Gaby, which isn't much.'

'There are a few too many secrets piling up around here.' She massages her temples, looks back at me. 'You seem to be in on a lot of them for someone who didn't know who she was a week ago.'

'Not by choice, trust me.'

'How is it there's a child who can *see* us, and how is it she knows the three of you?'

Jason and I exchange a long look. Neither of us answers. Dani bites her lip, stays quiet.

'Okay, enough,' Zak says. He's standing over me now, even more intimidating when I'm on the floor. 'You either trust us or you don't.'

I wet my lips. 'There are things about Dani that will

change everything for the Rephaim. If Nathaniel knows the truth about her, that's all he'll care about. Not Rafa and Taya. And they don't have time for him to get sidetracked.' The words tumble out. 'I don't want to lie to you, but I don't want you to have to lie to everyone else.'

'Just tell us the truth,' Zak says. 'And then *we'll* decide who we will and won't tell, given we know everybody in this place better than anyone else in the room.'

I rub my eyes. I know he's right. And he's right on the other count too: either we trust him and Ez or we don't.

And I do.

'Okay.' I find a spot to sit against the wall and I tell them the truth, the whole, messy truth—in as few words as possible. About Nathaniel killing our mother and taking Jude and me. About Jason's mother surviving and raising him; having another child years later—a child who saw angels and demons. About the line of first-born girls with similar gifts. Until Dani came along and could see Rephaim.

When I finish, Zak stares at a spot above my head, peels the corner of his thumbnail. Ez is still focused on me. 'You're saying he murdered all the other women—my mother—too?'

'Unless you think it's possible he only lied about one of the women.'

For a while, nobody speaks. Zak and Ez look at each other. Seem to have an entire conversation without words.

Jude is only half-tuned in now: he's caught up in whatever he's found on the laptop. Maggie lowers herself to the floor and catches my eye. I give her a quick smile. It stretches the skin on my face, feels all wrong.

Ez finally gets up and sits on the bed, leaves space between her and Maria. 'If there's a line of gifts—'

'Curses,' Maria corrects.

'Do you have one?'

'*Had*. It stops at puberty. I had nightmares about wars between angels and demons. Horrible blood-drenched nightmares, every night of my life until I turned fourteen.'

'Past or future wars?'

'I didn't know and I didn't care. My life started when the nightmares ended. Just like Dani's will when all this goes away.'

Ez leans forward so she can see Dani. 'You must be very brave.'

'It's not like I fight demons,' Dani says. 'Not like you. All I do is watch.'

'I still don't understand how that works.'

Dani crawls around her mother so she's closer to Ez. 'I have to be really still until my breathing slows right down. Then I think hard about the person I want to find. It helps if I know roughly where they are or what they're doing. And then . . . it's hard to explain. It's like I'm inside their head. Sometimes, though, it's like I can see them through someone else's eyes. I can't explain it.'

'Inside our heads . . . ?' Ez looks at Zak, alarmed.

'Other times I see things without warning. I usually faint for those. Sometimes I know what I've seen has already happened, and other times I know it's going to happen in the future. But not always.'

'What sort of things do you see?'

Maria puts her arm between Ez and Dani. 'That's enough questions. She's risking her life to be here. That's all you need to know.'

'It's okay.' Dani scrunches her face in concentration. 'Last year I saw you holding a baby, Ez. I think it was in a market somewhere hot and sunny. There were a lot of people and donkeys and music. You got sad when you gave the baby back, but you didn't let Zak see.'

Ez blinks, and her eyes slide towards Zak. 'No, I didn't,' she says. 'But he knew anyway. Was that a vision?'

'No, I went looking for you.' She ducks her head, shy. 'Sometimes I like to see what you're doing.'

Dani climbs off the bed and goes to Zak. He sits on his heels but he's still so much bigger than her. She reaches for his thick black hair, touches a curled strand almost reverently.

'You've always been one of my favorites,' she says. 'You're a big scary bear. Except around Ez: then you're a pussy cat.'

Zak laughs—surprising himself as much Dani. 'I can see how that would be dangerous information in the wrong hands. I don't suppose you saw what happened to Jude and Gabe last year?'

She bites her lips together and shakes her head. Jude looks up from the computer and meets my gaze. We need to tell Ez and Zak about Dani's involvement, but not now; not when Dani needs to concentrate on Iowa. I give the smallest shake of my head. He goes back to his screen.

'And Rafa and Taya—you really think you can see into that room?' Zak asks.

'Yes,' she says.

'Okay.' Zak puts a hand on her head, gentle, affectionate. 'Don't worry about anything else. We'll keep you safe.'

Ez checks her watch. 'I should check on Mya. Make sure she doesn't incite another riot.'

I stand up and stretch my ankle until it cracks. I trust Ez, but I have to ask. 'What are you going to tell her?'

Ez flattens a crease in the blanket. 'We have to let her and the rest of our crew know about Dani and what she can do'—she holds up her hands—'not why or how, just *what*. It will give them hope and stop everyone getting too restless. It's going to get harder to keep them here the longer Nathaniel and the Five take to make a decision.'

Jason looks like he's about to throw up.

Zak stands and his broad shoulders block the sunlight. 'Relax, Jason. You think I'm going to let anyone hurt a twelve-year-old girl?'

Dani climbs back on the bed and crosses her legs, takes

a deep breath. My chest tightens. This is it.

'I don't think I can do this with everyone in here,' she says. 'I just need Mom and—'

'We're not leaving you unprotected.' Jason stands up, looks around for support.

'Zak could stay too, and the rest of you go away for a while?'

'Blossom—'

'It's all right, Jason. You don't have to go far.'

'But why Zak?' He sounds a little stung.

She smiles, but I can see her nerves now too. 'Because he's not freaking out as much as the rest of you. And he's so big.'

'*I'm* not freaking out,' Jude says, but he packs up the laptop and heads for the door anyway. 'Come on. We'll go next door.'

Maria places pillows around Dani. She looks tiny in the middle of the mattress. On impulse, I kneel on the blanket and give her a quick hug. She's shaking.

'Are you sure you're okay to do this?'

Dani nods.

'What is it?' I feel everyone else in the room go still.

She rubs her nose with the back of her hand—such a child-like gesture—and then meets my eyes. 'I tried to see Rafa before Jason came to get us. I only had a glimpse . . .'

'How bad was it?'

'Bad.'

Her pale face blurs, then sharpens.

'And Taya?'

'I don't know.'

'What else? Please, Dani.'

'He's afraid.'

My insides are all scooped out. 'Of course he is—'

'He's afraid you're going to try and rescue him.'

'Why?' I whisper.

She closes her eyes so she doesn't have to see me. 'He's terrified of what Bel and Zarael will do to you if you do.'

STORM ON THE HORIZON

'What are you thinking?' Jude asks as soon as he shuts my door.

I don't answer. I'm still trying to get my head around Dani's words. Maggie leaves her suitcase by the wardrobe and goes to Jason, sitting on the edge of the desk. She stands between his knees and hugs him. He puts his arms around her and she rests her cheek on his head. Talks to him quietly. Their gentle intimacy brings an ache deep in my chest.

'Gaby,' Jude says, firmer. 'Talk to me.'

'I'm not staying away from that house because Rafa doesn't want me to get hurt.' I don't look at him.

'Nobody's asking you to.'

I need to move. I walk to the bathroom and back again. Eight steps. I need eight thousand: I need to run. Rafa's been in that room now for four hours. I try not to think about him being afraid. It's like drowning: too much panic; too little air. A terrifying weight pressing down on me.

Jude blocks me on my third lap. 'Promise me you won't do anything stupid.'

I try to move around him but he grabs my arm.

'Promise me you won't go without me,' I say.

'Gaby, whatever is coming, we'll face it together.'

'And what am I supposed to do while we wait for Dani?'

He nods at the desk. 'Help me work out if there's anything useful on the computer.'

'There's nothing on there except generic research on angels and demons and a handful of bookmarked websites for surf beaches. And one photo of me, asleep in a hammock. Nothing to help us get inside that room.'

Maggie and Jason move away from the desk so Jude can set up. Maggie is watching me, worried.

'I'm okay,' I say, before she can ask. And then I remember that my best friend just met a fallen angel and involuntarily joined a dysfunctional community of half-angel bastards. 'How are *you*?'

A strained smile. 'Okay, I think.'

'I can't believe Nathaniel pulled that stunt in the library.'

Jason makes a quiet noise of disgust and turns away, looks at Jude's screen over his shoulder.

'It was amazing though, right? Those wings . . . so

beautiful.' Maggie lifts her fingers like she's drawing them.

'Yeah, and if Jason hadn't protected you, you probably wouldn't be here to admire them.'

Her hand drops to her side. 'Okay, so they're also a little terrifying.' She takes a moment to consider the room. 'This place is so not what I imagined. What's with all the beige? Would it be that hard to add a couple of throw pillows? *Any* color would work in here.'

I smile. She can't help herself. In Maggie's world, everything can be made better with color. Just having her around settles my pulse. It's selfish, but I'm glad she's here.

Maggie opens the curtains and her eyes track from the piazza to the mountains. 'I can't believe I'm in Italy.'

I give her a moment to absorb it. My thoughts automatically slip back to Rafa and Dani, and what's happening in the next room. And then I see the notebook and album from the storage room on the bedside table. Daisy must have gone back for them after the brawl.

'What are those?' Maggie asks.

I hand the album to her and she opens it to the second page, to the photo of Rafa and me. 'Oh, wow . . .'

I reposition the pillows on the bed, plump them harder than necessary. Listen to the sound of the plastic-covered pages turning. I can't bear to see Rafa smiling and cocky. What if I never see that again? What if—

'Remind me who's who again,' Maggie says. I can't tell if

she really needs the refresher or if she's trying to distract me. But I sit with her, take a steadying breath and point out everyone I know. I don't bother with Taya or Malachi: she knows them well enough after their time together in Pan Beach.

'Is that Micah?' She taps a photo of him grinning with a bottle cap stuck in the middle of his forehead. She doesn't seem traumatized to see him: further proof he looked out for her at the cabin last week. 'You guys laughed a lot back then.'

'There's not a lot of that going on these days.'

Maggie sits sideways so she's facing me. 'How are you—honestly?'

I close my eyes for a moment, try to find the words. 'Have you ever had the best and worst things in your life happen on the same day?'

'No, Gaby. I haven't. And I can't imagine how screwed up that must feel. Finding Jude, seeing Rafa hurt . . .'

'This place doesn't help. I'm trying to get everyone on the same page, but just being here is enough to almost start a brawl everywhere I go.'

'Not just you, princess,' Jude says from the desk. 'Both of us.'

'Yeah, but you've got the Outcasts on your side.'

'They're on yours too.' He says it carefully.

'As long as I make decisions they agree with.'

'You think that applies only to you? This loyalty they're

showing me, that's all about who I used to be. I don't know how far it would go if I went against them.'

'But you're not going to go against them, are you?'

'Not as long as they're supporting our plan to get Rafa and Taya.' He rests his arm on the back of his chair. 'Gaby, this isn't about them versus you. There's no contest. It's you.'

'Jude—'

'I don't care what happened a decade ago,' he says. 'Don't make me keep saying it.'

I sigh. 'Anything useful on the laptop?'

'There's research on angel and demon hierarchy. Mostly to do with archangels, especially Michael and Gabriel.'

'What's so special about those two?'

Jude turns back to the computer and rubs his jaw. He needs a shave. 'Michael is the Captain of the Angelic Garrison. If anyone's giving orders to Nathaniel about what we should or shouldn't be doing, you'd think it would be him.'

'And Gabriel?'

'One of his lieutenants. Supposedly more compassionate than the others.' He turns the laptop so I can see the screen. On it is a document with two columns. One says *Michael – retributive*. The other, *Gabriel – restorative*. Under each is a list of books, articles and documents.

'What does that mean?'

'No idea. But all these bits and pieces—there must be

a reason I kept them. They have to make sense at some point.'

God, I hope so. I'm so tired of being undone. 'What now?'

Jude stretches his neck from shoulder to shoulder. He's restless. 'You said Rafa started to teach you how to shift. Let's give it go.'

'Now?' I have a momentary stab of panic, remember the one and only time I almost shifted on my own. That terrifying sensation of being sucked into a vortex—and the sickening feeling that followed when it didn't work. 'But I didn't shift. Not really.'

'You came close, though, right? And Jase here can give us some pointers, can't you, buddy?'

Jason straightens from the desk. 'What about Dani?'

'What about her? You'll still be here.' To me: 'What happened when you tried it with Rafa?'

'I face-planted the concrete.' I touch my cheek and remember the jarring, the blood. Stars wheeling. 'But before that, I felt the pull. Rafa says I disappeared for a second . . .'

'How? What did you do?'

'We were in a park. Rafa got me to think about everything I could see and hear and smell where I was standing. Then I walked down the hill and he told me to imagine myself back at that exact spot.'

'That's it?'

'Ah, no. That didn't work, which is when he told me the Rephaim actually pass into another dimension when they shift.'

Jude blinks. 'They what?'

'It kind of makes sense. We're not *flying* when we travel—otherwise we'd be smashing into stuff all the time. We disappear from one place and appear in another. We have to still exist somewhere.'

'Fuck.'

'Rafa said nobody's ever been stuck there, wherever "there" is. We used to do this all the time, so maybe it will be like it is with fighting: our bodies will remember what to do.'

'You don't look convinced.'

'Yeah, well, that first attempt scared the shit out of me.'

Jason rubs the back of his neck. 'Rafa had the right idea. Your first shift needs to be short, and to somewhere you're familiar with. This blind shifting everyone else does . . . it's beyond my skills.'

Jude moves away from the desk, flexes his fingers. 'Why's it so intense?'

'Wherever we go—whatever that place is—it's like being sucked into a tornado,' Jason says. 'When you taught me, you told me to stay on the edges of it. It took a bit of practice, but I got there. I didn't realize there were other ways to do it until I shifted here with Rafa last week to get Gaby. He doesn't protect himself from whatever is on the other side.' Jason glances from Jude to me. 'Maybe you two didn't either.'

'Like, extreme shifting?' Jude asks.

A shrug. 'Possibly. But that's not what you're going to try now. Whose room is next door?'

'Zak and Ez's.'

'Right. You're going to shift from there back to here, and you're going to stay out of the chaos.'

We spend a minute taking in the sounds, smell, and layout of my room and walk next door. Maggie stays behind and pulls out wool and knitting needles from her suitcase. Jason positions himself in the hallway so he can see inside both rooms.

'When you feel the pull you have to give in to it and then take control again almost immediately,' he says. 'It's like being swept down a river with a safety rail within reach: you have to get in the river before you can reach the rail. Your mind's the rail. Stay focused on where you want to get to.'

Jude and I stand about a meter apart in the middle of Ez and Zak's room, side by side.

'Same time?' Jude says to me.

'You worried I might go first and throw you off your game? You are so competitive.'

I get a quick grin. We both take a moment to ground ourselves and then Jude turns back to me. 'If we can do this, nobody else needs to know.' I nod. The idea of Jude and me keeping something from the rest of the Rephaim is oddly comforting.

'We're going to your room. Nowhere else.'

'*Okay.*' I close my eyes. Take a slow, calming breath. Hear Jude do the same. What if he goes first?

You're thinking too much.

My heart squeezes at the memory of Rafa's words in the park. It's an effort but I push away thoughts of Jude and Jason. Of Dani and Maggie. Even Rafa. I picture the room next door. The window, the desk, the bed. The smell of Maggie's Chanel No. 5. Then I imagine the curtain I need to step behind to get into that icy chaos.

I feel the drag almost immediately. It's even more ferocious than in the park, as if whatever is on the other side knows it's got me this time. Pressure builds in my head, in my chest. My heart is about to explode. It's freezing. I'm stretching, compressing, turning inside out. Shit, shit . . . Focus on the room. The room. The—

COLORS BLEED TOGETHER

The pressure is gone so suddenly and so completely it leaves me dizzy. I'm swamped with new sensations: warmth, the sound of a guitar, the smell of woodsy aftershave.

The guitar stops abruptly.

'It's polite to knock.'

I spin around and have to reach out to keep my balance, find a wall. I'm still inside out. Micah is sitting on the edge of a bed with an acoustic guitar. His blond hair spikes in all directions.

I'm disoriented, drunk. 'Where am I?'

He gives me a pointed look.

It's a room like others I've been in here, but this one is well and truly lived in. A desk covered in loose sheet music; a chest with two drawers half open, socks and T-shirts hanging over the ends; two electric guitars propped in stands either side of a small amplifier; a bedside table with an empty beer bottle. Stray guitar picks on the floor, along with an assortment of boots and runners. The bathroom door is open, wet towel on the floor; two katanas and a poleax against the wall near the door. The only thing that doesn't quite fit is the painting over his bed: a woman with mocha hair, her soft watercolors leaching into each other.

'Your room?'

'Bingo.' Micah rests his arm on the top of the guitar. 'You want to take a seat before you fall down?'

I nod, crumple to the carpet. 'First proper shift on my own.' I cross my legs, lean back against the drawers sticking out from the chest. Smell fabric softener. 'Holy shit. I did it.'

'Congratulations.' He shoves clothes from his bed to the carpet to make room for me but I'm not ready to get off the floor. 'Were you aiming for my room?'

I shake my head, ride a wave of nausea.

My phone rings and I fumble with it before my fingers work. 'I'm okay, I'm okay. Did you—'

'Yes!' Jude's buzzing. Of course he could shift properly first time. I hear him grinning through the phone.

'Where are you?'

'Where I'm meant to be. Where the hell are you?'

I shoot Micah an embarrassed look. 'Micah's room.'

'What's that about?'

'No idea.' I glance at Micah, still watching me from

the bed. 'Everyone okay there?'

'Yeah, we're good.'

'Okay. Give me a minute and I'll head back.' I pause. 'On foot.'

I hang up and take another look around, slower this time. There's an ordered chaos to the stacks of CDs, books, and clothes. 'Why do you think I ended up here?'

Micah shrugs. 'You used to hang out here a bit, listen to me butcher songs.' He runs his palm over the worn guitar. 'Especially after you hooked up with Daniel.'

'That was Gabe, not me.'

I still can't imagine being that person; being with Daniel. But I can picture myself sitting on Micah's carpet listening to him play, so I guess Gabe and I have that in common.

'Did you and Jude get along . . . you know, before he left?'

'Yeah, of course. Although we had some epic arguments over music.' Micah smiles at the memory. 'He was always banging on about bone-crunching rock. He didn't care about musicianship, only that a wall of noise hit him in the chest. I, on the other hand, appreciate technical skill, even if I have none myself.'

'Were you surprised when he walked away from'—I catch myself before I say *me*—'the Sanctuary?'

'Like I said, he had to in the end: he pushed Nathaniel too far.' Micah lifts the guitar from his lap, rests it against the bed. 'That's when everything turned to crap. Nobody knew how to deal with him and the others being gone, including you. Especially you. It was like you didn't know how to relax without Jude and Rafa. And it wasn't just about them: you were tight with Ez and Zak and Jones. We all were. Daisy was a mess for a year.'

There's so much history between the Rephaim and me. Maybe Mya's right to be angry that I don't remember any of it.

'Everyone kept waiting for you to go too,' Micah says, when I don't speak. 'I think that's half the reason you hooked up with Daniel in the end—to reassure the rest of us you were staying. Don't look at me like that, he's not a total tool. You would never have been with him if he was—you didn't care about us *that* much.' He gives me a crooked smile. 'Daniel's straight down the line. He takes everything seriously, but he's the smartest guy here and you liked that he saw you as more than a soldier.'

'Then why did I hang out in here so much?'

Micah stretches out his long legs, crosses them at the ankles. 'You still needed to laugh occasionally.' He studies me. *Reads* me. 'For what it's worth, I think he was in love with you, or as close to it as Daniel can be. I'm not saying he was the love of your life, but you were happy enough with him.'

'I told you that, did I?'

'As a matter of fact you did. We had a lot of deep and meaningful chats in this room. Me sitting here with a guitar, you down there keeping the wine topped up. Once we started to have serious run-ins with the Outcasts, it was obvious you were never joining them. Some of the fights you had with Rafa . . .' Micah checks my reaction, lets it drop. 'You were doing okay for a while. And then the Rhythm Palace happened, and Ez's injuries. When you heard the news . . . I've never seen you like it. You tore the gym apart. You couldn't go to Ez. You thought Mya was going to get them all killed and that Jude couldn't see the danger. Nobody could get near you. Not Daisy. Not me. Certainly not Daniel. Everything you'd been repressing for all those years came out: you blamed yourself for letting Jude go, blamed yourself for what happened to Ez. That was the start of the downward slide with Daniel, even if it took another year or so before you finally ended it.'

'And then what?'

'And then last year you started talking to Jude again. Daniel acted like it was no big deal but it was eating him up big time. He was prickly whenever you left to see Jude and then pretended he didn't notice how distracted you were when you came back.'

I lean back on my elbows. I'm adrift again. Unmade. It's always same when I hear the Rephaim talk about this other life I don't remember. 'Was I planning to join the Outcasts by that point?'

He shakes his head. 'I doubt it. Reconnecting with

Jude and turning against the Sanctuary—that's two very different things.'

'But you just said—'

'You were still with us, even if your head wasn't. You volunteered to go with Taya and Malachi when we got a tip about the Gatekeepers sniffing around in Iceland. The three of you ended up in a brawl with Bel and Leon. You took a blade to the leg.' He brushes his finger across his thigh on a spot that matches one of my old scars. 'But you guys still came back with a hellion.'

Something cold and dry stirs in the back of my mind. Like sawdust on the floor of the cage. 'What happened to it?'

'We lost it.'

'When?'

'Around the time you disappeared. Daniel tried to shift with it and the filthy hell-turd took him to a horde of Gatekeepers.'

I reposition myself on the carpet. I can't get comfortable. There's not enough space in my body to carry all this. It's big, it's important. And it's too much right now. I close my eyes, let my attention drift. Thoughts scatter, diffuse.

Micah starts to play again, a slow blues tune. When I look up, I find the watercolor painting. All pinks and purples and oranges. Huge brown eyes stare out from under a thick fringe. Melancholic, heartbreaking, beautiful.

'Who is she?'

He doesn't lift his eyes. 'Adeline. '

'Is she Rephaite?'

'No. Perfectly, fragilely human.'

'It's a stunning painting.'

'Self-portrait. She was gifted.'

'Was?'

He keeps strumming. 'Probably still is.'

I sit up straighter. The room doesn't spin. I need to get back to Jude, but there's something in Micah's voice that holds me here.

'What happened?'

'I remembered I wasn't human.'

'What does that mean?'

A few more bars. 'I couldn't give her what she wanted— a husband, fat happy babies—so I walked away while she still had time to have them.'

'Were you in love with her?'

He changes from strumming to picking. 'Yes.'

'Shit, Micah, I'm sorry.'

'Nathaniel warned us against forming attachments. I thought I knew better.'

'How long ago?'

'Fifteen years, four months . . . I'll pretend I don't know the weeks and days.'

'Have you seen her since?'

'From a distance. With kids.' He smiles, but it doesn't

quite reach his eyes. 'She got married, and I'm back to "wham-bam-thank-you-ma'am" for the rest of eternity. Could be worse.'

I watch him focus on the strings. 'So Nathaniel prefers you screw around rather than form meaningful relationships if it means you have to explain who you really are?'

'You still catch on quick.'

'How does that fit with the lecture Daniel gave me about Nathaniel teaching the Rephaim to "control the lustful desires" of our fathers?'

'Ah now, see, there's doctrine and then there's reality. And it's not realistic to think a bunch of supernatural beings eternally trapped in adolescent bodies with adolescent urges are going to keep their pants on.'

'So he just turns a blind eye.'

'If we're discreet he can delude himself into thinking it's not happening. Plus we can't procreate, so that makes it less of an issue for him. Or the Garrison.'

Micah changes his tune to something lighter, faster. 'So what's going on with you and Rafa?'

I scuff the sole of my shoe over the carpet, notice a wine stain half hidden under his bedside table. 'It's complicated.'

'I don't doubt that. Not much of a surprise, though. All that brawling and sledging had to be compensating for something.'

I look away. His words aren't all that different from

Mya's theory on my past with Rafa.

'What?' he asks.

'Mya says I threw myself at Rafa and he turned me down. She thinks that's what he and I fought over before they all left.'

Micah's fingers stall on the strings. 'Firstly, you wouldn't throw yourself at anyone. And secondly, if you did and it was Rafa? There's no way he'd knock you back. I don't know what happened between you two, but it was bigger than that.'

I try to imagine that other life with Rafa in it. But which version? The Rafa I fought in the training room in Dubai, the one who forgot I wasn't Gabe and needed to pin me to the mat? Or the Rafa I was wrapped around at the beach two days ago, whose lips and hands set my skin on fire? I'd take either version right now, as long as he's standing in front of me, alive and in one piece.

'Then what was it?'

Micah's door swings open before he can answer and Daisy steps in. 'Nathaniel has—' She stops when she sees me. 'Oh, hey.'

'Doesn't anybody knock anymore?' Micah says, but he's already set the guitar aside. 'What's going on?'

'Nathaniel's called everyone to the chapterhouse. He and the Five must have made a decision about going to Iowa.'

WATCH FOR THE SPIN

I want to ask. I can't.

I follow Daisy and Micah downstairs and along a hallway, realize we're at my door. I'm vaguely aware of Daisy telling Jude what's happening and then the four of us going down more stairs. Jude takes my hand as we walk. He gives a quick squeeze and lets go.

We move beyond the main buildings, out into the open compound between the main piazza and the chapterhouse, past the angel statue. Gravel crunches under our boots. Dull clouds drift down the mountain, making it impossible to know what time of day it is. My best guess is mid-afternoon. Muffled voices carry from the ancient building ahead of us.

The chapterhouse is packed. Conversation is low, whispered. Jude stands on his toes to do a quick headcount.

'There's at least a hundred and fifty Rephaim in here. Maybe more.'

It's still not enough to hide the blood and vomit stains on the stones. I hear Mick's grunts, Joffa's screams. Mya's words: *That's it. No one else survived.*

Nathaniel is on the dais. Daniel is on his right—of course—Calista and Uriel behind him. Ez, Mya, and Jones push through the crowd to us. 'Zak's stayed with Dani,' Ez whispers to me. Malachi hovers on his own at the back of the chapterhouse near the main doors. Everyone is tidier now: fresh clothes, blood gone, bruises and cuts healed.

Nathaniel's attention skims over the faces of the Rephaim. He seems to linger on Jude or me—it's hard to tell from this distance—and then raises a hand for quiet. A hush falls immediately. 'Thank you.' His voice rolls from the walls and ceiling like the ocean. All movement ceases. It's so quiet I can hear chirping outside. I have no idea what kind of bird makes that sound. It's as foreign to me as everything else here.

'As you are all aware, Zarael has Taya and Rafael prisoner in a room that inhibits them from shifting beyond its walls. Most of you also now know that the woman responsible for that room is in our custody.' He doesn't look at us. 'We have also now become aware of a child, a girl, who claims to have a psychic connection to all of you. She too is in our custody.'

Mya shifts her weight beside Jude. She's paler than

usual. She clicks her fingernails against each other. The sound is loud in the chapterhouse. Jones glances at her, nudges her shoulder. She scowls at him, leaves her nails alone.

'Who is this child?' someone closer to the front asks.

'A prophet,' Nathaniel says. 'Sent to us at our time of need.'

Jude turns to me, mouths: 'Seriously?'

The Rephaim are silent, and then: 'How does the trap work?'

'Did you know about it?'

The questions come from opposite sides of the chapterhouse, meet in the hollow of the domed ceiling.

'There are forces working against us,' Nathaniel says. 'Things in the dark that even I cannot see. I believe our enemy has found a way to harness them in this realm.'

Is this a story to keep his Rephaim under control, or does Nathaniel really believe it? Either way, there are massive gaps in the information he's sharing.

'When are we going after Taya and Rafa?' Malachi calls out from the back.

I hold my breath. This is it.

Nathaniel scans the faces of the Rephaim, slowly. Controlled. 'When I receive a sign from the archangels.'

It's like someone stomps on my chest in steel-cap boots, crushes all the air out of me. He's not sending Rephaim to Iowa.

There's movement in the chapterhouse now, shuffling, murmuring. Whispered questions. My head pounds. When did the archangels enter the equation? Daniel seems composed but his eyes are fixed on a spot somewhere above my head. Did he know that's what Nathaniel was going to say?

A storm builds behind my ribs. Accusations tumble over each other in my mind, fight to be given voice. I draw breath, ready to launch them at Nathaniel. Ready to—

The doors behind me crack open. Cold air hits the back of my legs. I turn, annoyed, and see Brother Ferro from the infirmary. He's carrying something, a wooden box. The strangeness of it cuts through the haze of anger.

Malachi reaches him before the monk has a chance to close the doors. Someone's asked Nathaniel another question—about how he found Dani—but I'm not really listening now because there's an intense whispered exchange between Malachi and Brother Ferro. Malachi wants to see what the monk is holding; the monk doesn't want to show him. Malachi takes him by the elbow and leads him outside. Jude catches my eye and we follow them. The air is bracing on the chapterhouse steps. It sharpens my focus.

'Show me,' Malachi says, using his height advantage to stand over the middle-aged monk. He notices Jude and me; doesn't care.

'Is addressed to Nat'aniel,' Brother Ferro says in his thick Italian accent.

'From who?'

'I don't know. It was left at the front entrance.'

'Give it to me.' Malachi puts his hand on the box. Brother Ferro looks to us, realizes we haven't come to help him. His shoulders slump and Malachi takes the box. It's made of carved timber, like an old-fashioned cigar box, held shut by a clasp at the front. Malachi flicks the catch and his hand goes still. Our eyes meet, my pulse hammers. And then he opens it.

Jude sucks in his breath.

It's a finger.

FLESH AND BONE

A slender index finger with dried blood under the nail. Flesh still pink. Sitting on a pile of tissues.

'Motherfucker,' Malachi spits. 'That's Taya's.'

'How can you tell?' The words are wet cement in my mouth.

'The scar.'

I force myself to look closer. There's a tiny white line running across the middle knuckle. My first reaction is overwhelming relief it's not Rafa's; the second, guilt. Even if Rafa can heal Taya, this finger's never getting reattached to her body. And if he can't heal her, she must be in unspeakable pain.

'Why Taya?' Jude asks, strained.

'Because she's loyal to Nathaniel.' Malachi stares at the bloodied digit, his chest rising and falling. 'Zarael thinks she's worth more to Nathaniel. She's bait for him. Rafa is bait for you two.'

I reach for the box. My fingers shake. Malachi lets me close the lid and hand it back to Brother Ferro. 'Show Nathaniel. Maybe it'll put a rocket up his arse.'

The monk flinches at my language and then slips through the chapterhouse door.

Malachi walks down the steps, kicks out at the gravel. Stones and dirt rain down on the path. 'We're running out of time.'

'When was the last time Nathaniel heard from any of the archangels?' Jude asks.

Malachi doesn't answer.

'So it's an excuse to do nothing?'

'Nathaniel won't risk our lives unless he thinks he's meant to.' There's no bitterness in Malachi's words, only resignation. 'Maybe this really is big enough for the archangels to get involved.'

'Bullshit.' I grind out the word. 'He's stalling. And while he's making excuses, Zarael's cutting off body parts.'

Mya and Ez slip out the door. We don't have much time: Nathaniel will send someone out here soon to check on us.

'What's in the box Brother Ferro just delivered?' Mya is washed out but she's sharp. 'Nathaniel handed it to Daniel and kept talking. He didn't open it.'

'It's Taya's finger,' Malachi says.

Ez closes her eyes. 'Oh my god.'

Jude walks a few steps, turns, comes back to us. 'Dani can tell us what's going on in the room but we still need to know how to get them out.'

'This Dani . . .' Mya is clicking her fingernails again, watching me. 'What exactly can she see?'

'Where we are, what we're doing. Sometimes even what we're thinking.' I don't tell Mya that Dani can't see her, and nobody else volunteers that information. 'She's upstairs right now trying to see what's happening to Rafa.'

And what *is* she seeing? Rafa lying in his own blood, in agony, forced to watch Taya lose a finger? They might have been enemies for the past decade but he would have tried to protect her. And he would have been outnumbered.

'What are you thinking?' Malachi asks Jude.

My brother points in the direction of Nathaniel's private wing. 'We need to get to Virginia. Now. We know where she is, but we need to shift in there.'

A pause. Malachi is torn between obedience to Nathaniel and his need to do something.

'We have to go while everyone's still inside,' I say.

'What if someone sees us?'

'Isn't it worth the risk? Or would you rather wait until Zarael delivers a head?' I'm getting louder; I can't help it. 'You can shift us in there right now—straight to her room.'

Malachi draws a slow breath. Nods.

'Wait,' Mya says. 'Debra's a better option.'

Malachi frowns. 'Who?'

'Virginia's daughter. She designed the room. I know where she is in LA.'

'How the hell—?'

'It doesn't matter,' Mya snaps.

'And you didn't think to mention that before?'

I get between them. 'For fuck's sake, can you two stop antagonizing each other for thirty seconds?'

They glare at me and then each other, but the sting has already gone.

'I'll go to LA,' Mya says. 'I guarantee there are eyes on the rest of you—especially Jude and Gabe—but Nathaniel won't miss me.' She turns to Malachi. 'Unless you tell him I'm gone.'

'Get back here quickly and I won't have to.'

She shifts without bothering with a comeback.

'You sure you want to wait?' Malachi asks Jude.

He nods. 'Let's give her a chance. Debra's likely to know more than her mother.'

We go back inside in time to hear Nathaniel say: 'We shall convene here again in an hour.'

An hour? What will be left in that room in another hour?

He sees us come in. 'Gabriella, Judah: a moment please.'

Jude and I hang back while everyone files out. Ez and Malachi wait with us. Jones raises his eyebrows as he passes and Ez nods for him to leave with the others. Daisy lingers inside the door.

'The rest of you may leave,' Nathaniel says from the dais.

'They may as well stay,' I say. 'We'll tell them whatever happens in here, just like we'll tell them what's in that box if you don't.'

'Gabe, think,' Daniel says.

'That's all I've done since we got here. I'm over it. Go on, look in the box,' I say to Nathaniel. 'See what your patient approach has delivered.'

Nathaniel holds out his hand without looking away from me. Daniel hesitates and then places it in his palm. Nathaniel opens it, looks down, closes it. No reaction.

'It belongs to Taya,' I say.

Silence.

'Don't you have anything to say?'

Nathaniel hands the box back to Daniel. 'This is a ploy to draw us into a fight,' he says.

'It's not a ploy, it's a fucking finger!'

'Oh god.' Daisy turns away.

Nathaniel is interested only in me. 'Gabriella—'

'Why didn't you tell everyone you had a message from Zarael before you let them leave? You knew it was from him.'

'I did not desire to have a hundred and fifty-six Rephaim reacting as you are at this moment. It serves no purpose—'

'What *does* serve a purpose?'

'You know the answer to that: waiting for a sign from the archangels.'

'Since when?'

'Since you brought a human child within my walls with the ability to see the offspring of the Fallen.'

'A minute ago you said Dani was a prophet sent in your hour of need—isn't that a sign?'

'Gabriella, I have spent a hundred and thirty-nine years protecting each of you. Readying you for your destiny. Giving you the chance to win favor with the Angelic Garrison and earn a place in the battle that will decide the fate of the world. I will not risk your lives without knowing what the Garrison wants of me.'

'What if they say nothing?'

'Then we do nothing.'

Pressure builds in my head. Malachi steps forward before I can form a coherent sentence.

'We need eyes on the ground outside the farmhouse. Let me go and check it out.'

'Nobody is going near that house,' Daniel says. 'I was there yesterday, Malachi. I know what we're dealing with.'

'Then let us speak to Virginia,' Jude says.

'No.' Nathaniel's tone is razor sharp. 'Your time would be better served demonstrating to me that you are capable of obedience.' His irises flare. And then he's gone.

Uri and Calista flinch at his disappearance. Daniel seems less surprised.

'What a fucking joke,' Jude says.

'What is wrong with you two?' Calista comes down the dais stairs two at a time. Uri catches her before she reaches us, but she shakes off his grip. 'You think you're the only people who care about Taya and Rafa?' She stops in front of me and I shift my weight, ready for her to take a swing.

'We seem to be the only people willing to do something about it,' I say.

'There's more than one way to get them back. Why can't you trust us?'

'If you have to ask that after what you just heard, you're beyond delusional.'

My stomach drops. Daniel is beside us. Did he just shift ten meters?

'That's enough. Calista, you and Uriel should go back to the library. I'll be there shortly.'

Calista opens her mouth as if to argue but then thinks better of it. Daniel waits in silence until the chapterhouse door latches behind them. Then he turns to me.

'We need to talk.'

POT. KETTLE. BLACK.

I start to turn away—I want to get back to Dani—but
then I remember what Micah said about the hellion from
Iceland. The one that disappeared around the same time
I did. The shadow of it has been lurking in the back of my
mind, finding form.

'I'll give you three minutes.'

If Daniel is surprised I've agreed so easily, he hides it.

'Gaby?'

'It's fine,' I say to Jude. 'This won't take long.'

Daniel disappears through the back door and leaves
it open for me. Cold air surges in. I start to follow and
then go back to Jude. 'Make sure Dani's well protected. I
don't trust Nathaniel.'

'I've briefed Jones,' Ez says. 'He's upstairs with Zak as
we speak.'

Daniel is waiting in a breezeway between the back of the chapterhouse and the wall surrounding this end of the Sanctuary. I leave the door open so Jude can see I'm okay. Manicured bushes stand guard, neat, regimented. Daniel waits at the bottom of the steps. He pushes down the sleeves on his woolen sweater, watches me closely.

'I need to know you're not going to do anything foolish,' he says. His breath comes out as a cloud of vapor.

'Define foolish.'

'Taking Zarael's bait and going after Rafa and Taya.'

I wrap my jacket around me tighter, drum chilled fingers on my arms. Already my nose stings and my ears ache. It's hard to stand still out here. 'You think we should wait for a bigger body part?'

'Gabe—'

'Tell me about the hell-beast I brought back from Iceland.'

He falters. 'What's that got to do with—'

'What happened to it?'

Daniel watches me, dark eyes framed by long lashes. Searching mine. Weighing the question.

'You want me to trust you, but you still haven't given me a reason to.'

He runs his fingers through his hair, smiles at me, grim. 'The hellion isn't the place to start.'

'Why not?'

'Because your view of the world is skewed.'

'Try me.' I tuck my fingers under my arms to warm them. 'You're the one who keeps banging on about truth, about me needing to understand who I was. Why did I bring you a hellion?'

A pause. 'We had a theory we wanted to test.'

'Who's "we"?'

'You and me. The Five. We've always known about the psychic bond hellions have with their Gatekeepers. We thought the same might be true for Nathaniel, that we could use that link to our advantage.' He looks away and I see it again—a shadow of uncertainty. Guilt.

'And the first experiment was after I went missing?'

Daniel picks at his sleeve. He drags his teeth over his lower lip. 'When you and Jude reconciled, it took us all by surprise. I asked you what had changed, and you withdrew even further from me. I had no idea what Jude was planning, but I knew it had to be dangerous for him to have made contact with you after a decade.'

I'd love to tell him that Jude reached out because he missed me, but I know enough now to understand it was more complicated than that.

'Right before you disappeared, you were badly injured.'

'Fighting with Bel and Leon when we captured the hellion—Micah told me.'

Daniel glances at my leg. 'The laceration was deep. Brother Ferro stitched it up when you got back.'

'And?'

Daniel touches the sleeves on his sweater again, first one then the other. He's uncharacteristically fidgety. 'I had him keep the bandages he used to clean you up. I knew you were going to see Jude again and wanted to be prepared. So when you went to see him for a third time in under two weeks, when you'd started avoiding me . . . I thought you had joined the Outcasts.'

He doesn't want to spell it out, but I know. I can see it in his eyes. 'You gave the bandages to the hell-beast so it could track me.'

He's completely still. That would be a yes.

'You let it taste my blood and then you set it loose after me?' I feel sick. 'What the fuck were you thinking?'

'I was thinking I could find you and stop you before it was too late.'

'How?' I snap. 'Hellions are mindless killing machines.'

Daniel lifts his hands to his lips, blows on them, and rubs his palms together to warm them. I take in his clipped nails, his perfect hair, his beautiful face. His hypocrisy. I want to hurt him so badly.

'We sedated it so Nathaniel could search its mind the moment it caught your scent. And it worked—the hell-beast reacted to the blood. It was enough for Nathaniel to know it had found you, but not where. We gambled that its need to track would be so strong it would take me to you.'

'And what went wrong? The fact I'm standing here with a demon blade scar on my neck and no memory of the life you keep talking about is pretty damning evidence it didn't go as planned.'

'I had the hellion shackled and muzzled. Nathaniel and I agreed I would go alone; if you had betrayed us we wanted to understand why, before others became involved—'

'You didn't tell the rest of the Five?'

'I was trying to protect you.'

'And what happened?'

'The hellion took me to a room filled with Gatekeepers. They weren't expecting me so I had time to shift before their blades connected with my neck.'

'And the hellion?'

He shakes his head. 'Bel got a grip on it before I could bring it back.'

'You handed them a demon that had tasted my blood and knew where I was. They came straight for me. And Jude.'

'We don't know that for sure. For all we know you planned to meet them.'

'Are you kidding me?' My voice ricochets between the wall and the chapterhouse. Inside, Jude looks our way. I hold up a hand, let him know I'm okay. 'Bel said he and Leon attacked us. He put a blade through my neck, Daniel. I think it's fair to say we were ambushed.'

Daniel can't meet my eyes. No wonder he had so little to say when Bel and Leon turned up on the mountain on Tuesday night, bragging about killing me.

'For what it's worth, we recaptured the hellion a few months later when Leon attacked Micah's unit in Pakistan. At the time, I thought it was a sign, but Nathaniel found no trace in its memories of you or Jude.'

'Did you try again?'

'No. It had lost your scent, and your bandages were long gone.'

The realization hits. 'The hellion you had here last week, that was the same one wasn't it?'

'Yes.'

'The one you let savage me and drink my blood. Get a taste of me again.' I shake my head. 'All that bullshit about putting me in danger in the hope it would jolt my memories. Rafa was right—you wanted it to get a taste of me because you thought I was lying about the Fallen. That if you could track me, I'd lead you straight to them. Of course this time, you would've taken an army with you. Am I on the right track?'

'I'm not going to apologize for going to extremes. I thought it could work. But yes, the plan B was to have a way to track you. If you remembered who you were, you'd understand why—'

'I get it,' I snap. 'I've heard it enough times. The fate of the Fallen and the destiny of the Rephaim is more important than me being torn apart by a hell-beast.' I wish I had something hard and heavy to slam into his head.

'I would never have let it kill you.'

'Well it's heartening to know you were okay with the tearing apart bit.'

The cold finally gets the best of me and I have to rub my arms. We stand in strained silence.

'I'm sorry,' he says. It comes out soft. 'I never wanted to hurt you.'

I tuck my hands back under my arms. 'But you wouldn't do things differently, would you? You honestly think you're on the higher ground in all this.'

He shakes his head, but it's not a denial. More a way of avoiding answering. 'I want to help you now.'

The clouds are lower, darker. I lift my face as the drizzle starts again. How would the rest of the Sanctuary feel about what he's just told me? I have every excuse to use it against him: another bombshell to rock the Rephaim. But what good would it do? This place is in a big enough mess as it is. And I need to get back to Dani.

'The only help I want is to get Rafa and Taya.'

'What do you think I've been doing?'

'It's not enough, Daniel. You want to help me? Then be on my side.'

'I am on your side, Gabe. That's why we're having this conversation.'

'No, I mean if I end up "doing something foolish" I want to know you're not going to hang me out to dry to Nathaniel and the rest of the Five. That you'll back my decisions.'

'I can't do that if I don't know what those decisions are.'

'And if there happen to be others involved, don't use it as another wedge to drive between the Sanctuary and the Outcasts. Promise me.' I hold his gaze, challenge him to show me proof of all this respect he says he and I once shared.

'I won't make promises I may not be able to keep.'

'Then this conversation is over.'

I head for the warmth of the chapterhouse.

'Will you tell me what you're planning, even if you know I won't approve?'

I stop on the third step. 'I won't make promises I may not be able to keep.'

Daniel gives me a steady look. 'You need to meet me halfway. I want your word you'll tell me what's going on before you and the Outcasts take matters into your own hands.'

After what he's just told me, I can't believe he has the gall to make demands. But I know now that we have to disobey Nathaniel. Having Daniel in the loop might be the only way to stop the Rephaim tearing themselves apart. Again.

'I'm not giving you my word, Daniel.' I put my hand on the door. 'But I'll do what I can.'

THE STUFF OF NIGHTMARES

'Could an angel change our memories?' Jude asks Ez as I walk back inside. They're in a huddle with Daisy and Malachi.

'I've never heard of it,' Ez says.

I close the door behind me. 'Nathaniel said Semyaza didn't have the power to change memories.'

'I'm not talking about fallen angels.' Jude looks over at me. 'I'm talking about an archangel. A member of the Angelic Garrison. Could they do it?'

'No way,' Daisy says. 'They'd never get involved in our lives.'

'I didn't say *would*, I asked *could* they do it.'

Nobody answers. Ez's fingers brush her scars and settle over her throat, protective. I cross the chapterhouse, suddenly aware of the ancient space around me; of the stones and marble stained with blood and lies.

'Let's get back to Dani.' I keep moving towards the front door.

'What did Daniel say?' Malachi asks when he reaches me.

'He asked me to tell him before I do anything stupid.'

'And you agreed?'

'For the sake of keeping the peace.'

'But that's good,' Daisy says. 'Running around behind everyone's back is only going to aggravate the situation. So you told him about Mya going to LA?'

I guess I missed more than one topic of conversation while I was outside.

'No, and you need to keep that information to yourself.'

Daisy's lips flatten. As always, her taste for rebellion only goes so far—especially where Mya's involved.

We cross the compound in silence. This place doesn't feel right: the birds, the smell of the trees, even the light— it's too muted. All of it is wrong. I need bright sunshine and thundering waves. Magpies. Eucalyptus. My house, with the front door that sticks, the faulty stove and the dodgy water pressure. My home.

Jones is waiting in the hallway outside Jude's room. 'They won't let me in. I thought I'd hang here anyway.'

Jude taps lightly. 'It's us.'

The door cracks open a fraction and Jason appears, face bleak. He takes in all of us. 'Let's talk out here.'

I look over his shoulder and my heart lurches. Dani is curled up on the bed, Maria stroking her hair. Zak stands sentry by the window. Maggie comes to the door, guides Jason through and closes it behind her.

'She's okay, just exhausted,' Maggie says.

'What did she see?'

'She hasn't told us.'

I think about Taya, give Maggie an impulsive hug. She hangs on tight. Neither of us speaks. Everyone shuffles around until they find their own space in the hallway.

'When can I talk to her?' I ask and step back from Maggie.

'When she's ready,' Jason says.

Malachi bends down and stretches his calves. Rolls his wrists until one of them cracks. 'What else do we know about that iron room?'

I tell him about the journal with photos of burning corpses and instructions for sacrificial rites written in German; about Jason discovering the family was excommunicated from the Lutheran Church around the time the Fallen broke out of hell. That the family knew about the Rephaim and warned Jason away from the rest of us. I describe the floor plans and the photos of the Rephaim; Rafa's theory about a mole at the Sanctuary.

'No way. None of us would betray Nathaniel.' Malachi raises his eyebrows at Ez.

'Come on,' she says. 'We've had our differences, but

we'd never put anyone here in danger.'

I give a short laugh. 'An hour ago you were all pounding the crap out of each other with your bare hands.'

Ez and Malachi share an ironic smile. 'Yeah,' Malachi concedes, 'but we'd never let anyone else do it.'

'So how did the women get the photos and floor plans?'

'What about the monks?' Jude asks.

Daisy shakes her head. 'They've been with us for years, some from the same family. They give up everything to be here: friends, family, money. Sex. They totally believe in Nathaniel's mission to find the Fallen. There's no way any of the brothers would put him or us at risk.'

'What if they found out Nathaniel had lied about something?' I ask the question carefully.

'Like what?' Malachi asks.

'Doesn't matter what.'

Malachi holds my gaze. 'Nathaniel has no reason to lie.' But he knows that's not true. He just watched the fallen angel lie to a roomful of Rephaim.

'Were you aware this place is protected from demons by wards made from Nathaniel's blood?' I ask.

'Rubbish.' Malachi looks at Ez. 'Right?'

'I didn't know about the blood,' Ez says. 'But Nathaniel told us about the wards this morning. Why do you think we're still here?'

'Who told you there was blood involved?'

'Nathaniel.' I don't mention the significance of the

wings in the room. That seems like too big a piece of news right now.

'So the wards in the iron room . . .'

'Could only trap Rephaim if Rephaite blood created the ward.'

All eyes turn to Jason. Color creeps into his cheeks. 'I did *not* give them blood.'

'You're the only one who's had contact with them all these years,' Ez says. She's not accusing, just stating a fact. 'You could have cut yourself around them. Maybe they only needed a drop or two—'

'I'm telling you, there is no way they could've taken blood from me, accident or otherwise.'

Maggie puts herself between Jason and the rest of us. 'Don't take this out on him.' She looks around at each of us. 'If he says he didn't give them blood, he didn't. Back off.'

There's silence for a few seconds, and then: 'Way to let your woman fight your battles, blondie.'

I turn my head so fast it hurts my neck.

'What?' Jones says. 'What did I say?'

I let my breath out, feel the emptiness in its wake. 'You sounded like Rafa.'

Jason leans back against the wall, takes Maggie's hand in his. Some of the tightness leaves his jaw. 'If it was Rafa, I'd be slammed against furniture by now with a hand around my throat. He tends to throttle first, ask questions later.'

Maggie bumps Jason's shoulder. 'And he'd call you Goldilocks.' She smiles at me, sad, hopeful. The door to Jude's room clicks open and the tension snaps back. Zak fills the doorway.

'She wants to—'

Dani ducks under his arm and runs to me, buries her face in my chest.

Malachi stares at me. 'You're kidding—you know this kid too?' But when I meet his eyes I see the more important question. *How bad is this going to be?*

My lungs burn for a second until I remember to breathe. Then I take Dani back into the room and we sit on the bed.

Her face is streaked. I'm numb, blank. Everyone else crowds inside. She brings her slender knees up to her chest and I vaguely notice her jeans are threadbare at the knees.

'They're alive.'

I close my eyes and warmth washes over me like a sun-baked sea. *Alive.*

When I open them, Malachi has sunk to the floor. Zak pats his shoulder. Maria is on Dani's other side, eyes only on her daughter.

'But . . . ?' My voice cracks.

'They're hurt bad.'

'We know about Taya's finger . . .' Ez says.

Dani wipes her cheek on her sleeve. 'It took me so

long to see through the noise. I've never been so close to so many of you before. And everyone is right here, all around me.'

I try to follow Dani's words. Keep them in order so they make sense.

'And when I did'—her eyes meet mine, wounded, frightened—'it was so intense. I was *there*, Gaby. I was *right there*.'

I reach for her hand, slide her fingers between mine. I want to tell her it's okay, but it's not. I put a twelve-year-old girl in a room with violence and demons—or I may as well have. Maria takes Dani's other hand. 'It's all right, baby. Take your time.' She meets my eyes, all storm and fury.

Dani chews on her bottom lip, thinks for a moment. 'Some of it was going on in Rafa's head because it had already happened, but other things happened while I was there.' She swallows. 'At the start, there were twenty Gatekeepers in the room. They all had needles. Rafa and Taya kept shifting—I felt sick from it, even in Rafa's memory— but the demons got them in the end. Whatever they gave them didn't knock them out totally, but they weren't awake enough to shift.'

Her lower lip trembles and her fingers tighten on mine. 'Rafa tried to stop them hurting Taya. Bel stabbed him again and did other things . . . There was so much blood, Gaby, but they kept fighting.'

Of course they did. Rafa and Taya are soldiers. It wouldn't have crossed their minds to give up, even facing impossible odds.

'You're all he thinks about.'

I close my eyes, feel a tear slip out.

'Rafa was stabbed clean through the stomach on the mountain,' Jude says. 'There's no way he could've put up a fight if that wound was still open. They must be able to heal each other.'

'They did, at first. Now Zarael doesn't leave them awake long enough.' Dani lets go of my fingers to take the tissue Maria offers. 'I think being here changes what happens when I meditate. Or maybe it was because Rafa was drugged—'

She stops to blow her nose, then scrunches the tissue and tucks it in her jeans pocket.

'What?' I ask.

Her blue eyes find me again. 'Rafa could sense me.'

'How do you know?' I whisper.

'He said my name.'

'Could you talk to him?'

'No, but he was shouting at me in his head. He doesn't want anyone to try and rescue them.'

'Why not?'

Her mouth turns down and she hiccups. 'Rafa and Taya know they're going to die.'

All the warmth leaves me.

Zak grunts. 'Come on, that's—'

'He wants you to end it.'

I open my mouth but nothing comes out. Zak looks at me, and then Dani. 'End it how?' he asks.

A tear slips down her pale cheek. 'He wants you to make sure the demons are all there. And then he wants you to destroy the house with him and Taya inside.'

WHEN IN DOUBT, GET A BAZOOKA

I spring up from the bed. 'That's not happening.' I look around and dare someone to contradict me. Maria pulls Dani close, protective.

'Of course it's not,' Zak says. 'I'm ready to raze that place flat but Rafa and Taya won't be inside when it happens.'

I nod, but my hands are still shaking. I flex my fingers, try to force out the tension. Maria is giving me a filthy look and it takes me a moment to realize I've been swearing under my breath.

'Oh. Sorry.'

Dani manages a small smile. 'I've heard worse.' Of course she has. She's seen Rafa with demons.

I sit down again. My pulse is slowing but my chest burns from the burst of adrenaline.

'What are you thinking, Mal?' Zak asks.

Malachi drags his fingers through his hair. 'I want to rip every limb from Bel's putrid body and build a bonfire with them.'

'Count me in.' Zak holds out his fist. Malachi bumps it without hesitation. 'What now?'

Everyone looks to me.

'We're going in.'

Daisy shifts position in the doorway. 'You're going to disobey Nathaniel?'

'Yes.'

She clenches her jaw. I know how hard the idea is for her, no matter how high the stakes. She left me alone in a cage with a hellion because Daniel ordered her to. She's not afraid of much, but bringing on the wrath of Nathaniel and the Five is high on the list.

'Daisy,' Jude says. 'We can obey Nathaniel and hope Taya and Rafa are still in one piece by the time he hears from the Garrison—*if* he hears from them. Or we can go in now and wear the consequences. Worst-case scenario, we all end up dead. Best case, we get them back and hope that's enough to placate Nathaniel. What's that old saying? It's easier to beg forgiveness than ask permission.'

'I'm in,' Zak says.

'Me too,' Malachi says, and then to Daisy: 'You saw Taya's finger. You know that's not where it will end. We don't have time to wait.'

'We should at least tell Nathaniel they're still alive,' Daisy says.

'You can't tell him Rafa's willing to sacrifice himself and Taya to keep the rest of us safe.' The thought of him making that decision . . . it's like someone's scraping out my heart with a butter knife.

'I won't.'

'I mean it, Daisy.'

'Seriously, I won't. Just that they're alive.'

Malachi rubs a knuckle along his jaw. 'You know Nathaniel won't do anything until he gets whatever sign he's waiting on, no matter what you tell him.'

'We still have to give him the chance. Maybe he's found out something about the room from Virginia. Maybe that will count as a sign. And anyway, you still need to know how to get in and out if you don't want to end up in there with them.'

'Daisy's right. How did you get in last time?'

'We used a ram,' Zak says. 'But it took about twenty hits to disengage the lock. We won't have that much time.'

Jude picks up his katana, absently checks the blade in the dull afternoon light. 'Where was the keypad?'

'I didn't see it,' Jason says. 'Sophie shut the door when I was on my way over there.' He rubs the back of his neck. 'She wouldn't tell me how to open it, and I didn't push her because she was terrified. She was still on the far side of the room, so it had to have been done remotely.'

Jude nods. 'The architect will know.'

'Let's say we find a way to get Taya and Rafa out,' Malachi says. 'How are we going to destroy the place afterwards?'

I notice he says 'we'. Malachi's signing on for more than a rescue attempt.

'The Butlers have plenty of fire power,' Zak says. 'That rocket launcher would do some serious damage.'

'Do you know how to use one?'

'No. But we know a couple of lads who do.'

I shake my head. 'You can't go back to that camp. Zarael will have Gatekeepers sweeping through Pan Beach waiting for us to make a move.'

'I know where the launcher is. All I need is to find out where the rockets are. Me and Ez will be in and out in less than five seconds.'

I check with Ez. She nods. And like that, my skin is warm again. Buzzing. We have a plan. 'Mags, what time is it in Pan Beach?'

Maggie checks her watch. 'Nearly two in the morning.'

'At least it's dark.'

Ez picks up an empty cup on the bedside table. 'You must be hungry,' she says to Dani. And then to Zak: 'Give me a couple of minutes to organize something for Dani and Maria to eat.'

'Someone else can do that,' Zak says.

'I realize that, but I'd like to.'

He nods, understanding. 'I'll meet you in the infirmary.'

Maria helps Dani up from the floor. 'Come on, sweetie, go and wash your face.' She waits until the water is running in the bathroom. 'When is this going to be over for us?'

'When Rafa and Taya are safe,' I say.

Maria keeps her hand on the doorknob. 'She won't go until you tell her you don't need her anymore. She doesn't want to let you down after—' The tap turns off and Maria stops.

'It means a lot, you being here.'

'That means nothing if she's in danger.'

Jude pats Zak on the shoulder. 'Right then. Let's have a chat with our munitions experts.'

'You're not touching my weapons.'

'You make it sound so dirty,' Jude says.

Mick pulls on a pair of jeans one-handed. They're not a great fit. Mick's stocky, and these belong to someone with a slightly longer leg. He winces with each movement but refuses to let anyone help him.

Simon is hugging Maggie with one arm. She sniffs at the poultice between them, screws up her nose, kisses his cheek again. The circles under his eyes are darker, like slow-spreading bruises. A pencil and sketchbook lie abandoned on the bed; Maggie tries to see the drawing but Simon leans over and closes it. The rest of Mick's guys are on their beds, watching us.

'Do you know how hard it was to get my hands on that launcher?' Mick says, panting as he struggles with the zipper.

'I don't want you to give it to me, Mick, I want to borrow it.'

'To do what?'

Jude glances at Jones, who takes yet another quick look into the treatment room, nods that Brother Ferro is out of earshot. 'Once we've got Rafa and Taya clear, we're going to blow the shit out of that farmhouse.'

'Not without me you're not.'

Mick doesn't have an issue with the blowing-up part, just with being excluded from the action. No surprises there, really. He bends to put on his boots and Rusty steadies him. The younger Butler is showered and wearing grass-stained jeans, traces of color back in his bearded face. He fiddles with the bandage on his chest.

'Nobody touches our stuff but us,' he says.

'Remember the demons who killed your mates?' I say carefully. 'There are maybe fifty of them at that farmhouse. Probably hellions too.'

'Perfect,' Mick says. 'We'll blast all those fuckers back to hell.'

'Wake up, Mick,' Simon says. 'How many more guys you want to lose?'

'Just because you left your balls back in town doesn't mean we're ready to bend over for these pricks,' Mick says.

Zak steps closer, towers over Mick. 'Who are you calling a prick?'

Mick glares up at him. He's like a pit bull; not much intimidates him. 'Not you, sunshine, the cocksuckers who did this to us.'

'We'll get the hardware, then we'll discuss who is and isn't blowing up shit,' Zak says.

Jude raises his eyebrows at him and Zak shrugs.

'We might need a hand. Especially if it's just us and not a whole army.'

Simon repositions himself on his bed. 'Any news?' He doesn't ask anyone in particular but his eyes find me.

He doesn't know. How could he?

'Zarael delivered Taya's finger half an hour ago,' Malachi says, his voice flat.

'Is she—'

'She's alive,' I say quickly. 'So is Rafa, and we plan on keeping it that way. That's why we're here.'

Simon focuses to my right, goes somewhere else for a moment, and then squeezes Maggie's shoulder. 'Can you ask Jason to take us home?'

'Yeah,' Mick says. 'I'm over this greaseball food. Hasn't anybody heard of a bloody T-bone in this country?'

'Simon,' Maggie says gently, 'we can't go home, not yet.'

'Why not?'

'Because it's not safe in Pan Beach for us.' She gestures to Mick and Rusty, Woosha and Joffa, the other guys in the ward; to Simon and herself: the only people in Pan Beach who know about the Rephaim and the Gatekeepers.

'What about the rest of the town? Who's protecting them?'

'Nobody else in town matters to them,' Zak says.

'What if that changes?'

'Then we'll deal with it. Right now, we've got enough on our hands.'

Maggie rubs Simon's arm. 'It's okay.'

'It's not okay, Mags. It's a frigging mess and we shouldn't be in the middle of it. *You* shouldn't be in the middle of it.' His eyes flick to me, his meaning clear: this is my mess and I'm the only one who should be tangled in it. And I get it. He and Maggie have been friends since kindergarten. I'm just the backpacker who blew into town nine months ago and turned out to be more trouble than I'm worth.

'So.' Mick looks like he's decided to lift the mood. 'You want standard RPG rounds or armor-piercing?'

Zak and Jude glance at each other and say, simultaneously: 'Armor-piercing.'

Mick hassles Simon for his pencil and a piece of paper. He scribbles out a mud map of the camp and where to find what Zak needs. Malachi offers to go with him.

'You sure?'

'No, but I can't sit here doing nothing.'

They grab wrists and disappear.

I sit on a spare bed without making eye contact with

Simon. Jude joins me. Maggie finally gets her hands on the sketchbook. She studies Simon's drawing for a moment and then holds it around for us to see. It's the stretch of sand north of Pan Beach, where the headland meets the water. Simon might be a dud at drawing crude maps but he has some skill when it comes to something with more texture.

'That's really good,' I say.

Simon shrugs but takes the compliment.

'Have you guys always lived in Pan Beach?' Jude asks.

Maggie nods. 'Simon, Rusty, and I were in the same class all through school. Mick and his mates were two grades above us.'

'You guys surf much?'

'Nah, mate,' Mick says, dropping into a metal chair by Rusty's bed. 'Not all of us are board jockeys. Place is crawling with 'em these days. Bloody surfers and backpackers and rich pricks with more money than brains. The Imperial's the only place left in town that's not full of wankers.'

'I assume anyone who doesn't drink at your pub is a wanker?'

'Bang on.'

'So it's more of a philosophical choice to avoid the beach than any aversion to sand?'

Mick narrows his eyes. 'You and your sister think you're fucking clever, don't you?'

I bump my knee against Jude's. 'Don't rattle his cage too hard. He's actually sharper than he looks.'

'Fuck you,' Mick says, but I think I catch a shadow of a smirk under his half-beard.

'Maybe you should come down to Rick's one weekend,' Maggie says to Mick.

'What, and drink that imported shit he keeps on tap?'

Simon gives a short laugh. 'I think Rick's happy with the current arrangements as well.'

I think about turquoise water rolling onto the beach, set after set. The palms along the boardwalk and how they shake when the breeze picks up. The stillness of the rainforest. The ancient fig trees that blot out the light. The smell of fish and chips and sunblock on the esplanade.

'You're coming back, aren't you?' Maggie asks me. 'When this is all over, you're coming home?'

I almost look to Jude but stop myself, afraid of what I might see. The brother I remember—the one from my fake life—wouldn't hesitate to hang out in Pan Beach. But the real Jude, the one beside me, may not want to go back to a surfer lifestyle when this is over. He might want to try on his old life with the Outcasts for a while.

'That's the plan.' I force a smile. It's probably impossible—hell, I might not even be alive—but right now I need the promise of something real.

Maggie sees my doubt and opens her mouth to say something else, when Zak and Malachi materialize, almost on the exact spot where they left. Maggie and Simon flinch, bump shoulders. Zak has the launcher and Malachi carries a tube-like bag, straining at the handles. He puts it on the end of Simon's bed and the mattress sags.

'Man,' Rusty says to Zak, 'that teleporting thing . . . that's fucking mind-blowing.'

Mick's more interested in the bag than the fact the Rephaim can defy the laws of physics. 'Let me see.' He hobbles over, pops the studs at one end of the bag and pulls out a rocket. 'These two are all I've got left, so we better make 'em count.'

'Left?' Simon says. 'What did you do with the rest?'

The brothers grin at each other. 'Had some fun up the mountain during the big thunderstorms before Christmas.'

'Yeah.' Woosha lifts himself up on his elbows in bed. 'We nearly turned the western gully into a gravel quarry.'

The main doors to the infirmary open and close, footsteps echo on the lino floor. Mick shoves the rocket back in the bag and Zak hides the launcher behind his back.

It's Ez. She looks from Zak to Mick, raises her eyebrows. 'You went without me.'

Zak smiles, guilty. 'Mal had my back.'

She turns to Malachi. 'You want to be careful, I might start to like you again.'

'Keep dreaming,' he says.

Ez's phone vibrates. 'It's Mya,' she says. 'She's back.'

*

We meet her in the gym, along with the rest of the Outcasts. The dank cocktail of sweat, sawdust, and centuries-old mortar still permeates the place. Mick and Rusty are with us, carrying their small arsenal between them. Mya is in the middle of the practice mats and waits for us to reach her and the others before she speaks. Maggie is back upstairs, safe with Maria and Dani. Jason's ready to shift with them at the first sign of trouble.

'I can get around the lock on the door.' Mya pulls a small pair of pliers from her back pocket. 'I know where the keypad is.'

'We won't have time,' I say. 'We need the code.'

'Debra doesn't know it.'

'She's lying.'

'She says Louise was the only one who knew.'

'Who's Louise?'

'Virginia's other daughter—Sophie's mother. They'd never locked the room before. They weren't intending to use it anytime soon.'

'But they had a panic button and a silent alarm.'

'Not specifically for the room. That iron trap is a proto-type. They didn't even know if it would work.'

'Sophie was in a hell of a hurry to trap Rafa and me in a room that may or may not have worked.'

'It doesn't matter.' Mya waves away my doubt. 'Debra told me where the keypad's hidden and the type of electronic lock—I can get around it, but I need cover for the time it takes to cut the wires.'

Jude raises his eyebrows at me.

'She's good,' I concede, remembering her quick work at the nightclub in LA. 'How did you get Debra to talk?'

'I threatened to bring her here.'

Jude rolls his shoulders. Mine are tight again too. I think about Sophie. How long did Zarael keep her and her mother alive to learn the secrets of the iron room? What else did they find out?

'Did she tell you anything about the trap itself?' Ez asks. 'Anything about Rephaite blood being used to create the ward?'

Mya scowls. 'Rephaite blood? Who said that?'

'Nathaniel.'

'Nathaniel thinks one of us is involved with them? Who?'

'It might not be anyone—who knows what they used to make the room work. Once we crack the door it won't matter. The ward will be broken and Taya and Rafa can shift straight out. And then we'll let these guys loose.' I gesture at Mick and the rocket launcher.

Mick nods, all business.

'Let's do this,' Zak says. 'We'll need teams outside the house to create a distraction, a team to protect Mya while she gets the door open, and at least two of us to go in and get Rafa and Taya.'

'I'm going in the room,' Malachi says.

Adrenaline fires through me. 'Me too.'

'No way,' Jude says. 'What if they can't shift on their own? How are you going to get Rafa out of there?'

'Malachi or Mya can help. What are you going to do?'

'I'll help these guys.' He gestures to Ez, Zak, and Jones.

'You're going to fight Gatekeepers? You think that's safer than going in the iron room?'

'No, but at least I'll have your back.' His eyes are bright, his fingers already flexing. He's feeling the adrenaline too.

I've fought Gatekeepers twice. Come off second best twice. Jude's never fought them—not outside of his dreams, anyway. But he doesn't care, he trusts his body. Trusts that he can do all the things Rafa's told him he can do. Right now I need to find that place too. A nest of Gatekeepers and hellions is no place for doubt and second-guesses.

'We'll need at least one of us to keep an eye on these guys.' Zak points to Mick and Rusty. 'Just in case they get trigger happy and think it might be fun to blow the place while we're still in it.'

Mick gives Zak a dirty look, but it's quite clear the thought has crossed his mind. Seth volunteers. He goes over to the Butlers, stands head and shoulders over them. Rusty looks nervous; Mick ignores him.

Zak sorts the rest of the Outcasts into teams and then calls us all in together. He arranges barbells and weights on the mat to create a map of the farm.

'We'll shift into the corn, get our bearings.' He stabs at a spot on the mat outside the barbells. 'Then we'll shift into the clearing, draw as many demons away from the house as we can. We're going to be seriously outnumbered, so don't think twice about shifting to stay safe.' He looks around the group. 'I mean it. There's no shame in keeping your head on your shoulders.'

It's a point of pride with the Rephaim—even the Outcasts—not to shift in the middle of a fight. I'd put money on the Gatekeepers not having a similar code of honor.

'As soon as Rafa and Taya are safe, we'll clear out of the farmhouse. I'll give the sign and our friends here can bring the place down. We need to be well away by then.'

'The usual signal?' someone asks.

'Yes.'

I don't know what the usual signal is, but I don't need to. When Zak gives it, I'll be long gone from the farm-house. We take a moment to absorb the weight of what we're about to do, the danger of it. My body burns with the need to get moving, to get this done. To get Rafa back. My stomach drops.

'Please tell me you're not going to that farmhouse.' It's Daisy. She and Micah have shifted into the gym.

I break away from the group. 'We've got enough infor-mation to do what we need to.'

'You can't go now. Nathaniel's only just heard that Dani

saw into the room and knows they're both badly injured. You need to give him time—'

'We don't have time, you know that.'

'Then tell him what you're planning. Maybe he'll send some of us with you.'

'Come on, Daisy,' Ez says. 'You know that's not how it works. You heard what Dani said. Rafa and Taya are a mess and Bel will keep using sharp objects on them until we either hand over Jude and Gabe or take them on.'

'So you're taking Jude and Gabe right into their trap? This is exactly what Zarael wants—a reckless renegade group to charge in outnumbered.' She spots Malachi beside Zak. 'God, Mal, tell me you're not serious. You want to end up roaming the globe with this lot? And you—' She turns back to me. 'You do this, and there's no doubt which side you're on.'

'I don't give a shit what side anyone thinks I'm on as long as Rafa and Taya are alive and safe.'

Daisy's scorching gaze scans the crowd until she finds Mya. 'How do you know that what she's told you is true?'

'Why would she lie?'

'It's *Mya*! You've never trusted her. You didn't trust her enough to follow her out of here a decade ago; why would you trust her now?'

'Because she's risking her life too.'

Micah steps between us. 'Gabe, I get why you're doing this. But Daisy's right: this is exactly what Zarael's been playing for. The visit here, the severed finger, this is all to draw the Outcasts into a fight and fragment the Rephaim.'

'You sound like Daniel.'

He frowns at me, annoyed. 'He's not always wrong.'

'Ah fuck,' Jude says behind me, and I turn to see Daniel standing on the other side of the boxing ring.

'How long have you been there?' I ask.

'Long enough.' He looks tired, drained, and totally pissed off. 'We just got everyone settled down after that debacle in the piazza, and you want to tear it all apart again?'

'This isn't an exclusive outing; anyone who wants can join,' I say. 'And I'm not tearing anyone apart—Nathaniel is, with his excuses about the Garrison. You knew this was coming.'

'Not this quick. Think.' Daniel's trademark control has dipped below the waterline. 'You need a full-strength army. That's the only hope of successfully taking that farmhouse, not whatever you've got planned.' His eyes snag on the Butlers. 'You're taking humans along? You're determined to get them eaten, aren't you? And I don't even want to know what that's for.' He gestures to the rocket launcher. 'But it better not be for what I think because Nathaniel needs to inspect that room.'

'We have to have control of it first,' Jude says.

Daniel's lips press into a thin line. 'You ripped this place in half once before, Jude. It doesn't surprise me you'd do it again, but don't drag your sister down with you.'

Jude steps up to Daniel, gets in his face. 'My sister and I don't answer to you or anyone else. And if you cared about her at all, she wouldn't have that hellion scar on her neck. So back the fuck off.'

Daniel's nostrils twitch. He looks across at Malachi. 'Step away.'

'I don't want to defy you, but you give me no choice if you order me to stay.'

'This isn't a discussion.'

'Give him permission,' Micah says, urgent. 'Send him to spy on them, who cares what you call it.'

Zak pulls a katana out of his weapons bag. 'This conversation is going nowhere. We've got places to be. Jude?'

Jude takes out his phone and makes a call, not taking his eyes from Daniel. 'Has she—' He stops, listens, nods. 'Yep. Yep. Okay.' He hangs up.

'Dani says Rafa and Taya are alone right now.'

'Let's go.'

The Outcasts fall into formation and Jude and I find a place between Ez and Zak. I take one last look at Daniel. He's pensive, watching me, wrestling with the situation.

'Malachi,' he says as I reach for Ez. 'Be my eyes and ears.'

ON THE WINGS OF AN ANGEL

The sun hasn't been up long over the cornfield. The air is still and frigid, cold enough for snow. I shiver in my jacket, my breath misting between the papery leaves of dead corn.

We don't have long. There are demons keeping watch from the farmhouse roof. If we stay here for more than a few seconds, they'll see our collective breath rising from the plants.

Zak leads us along the cornrow, gives Jude and the others a chance to see the house and the clearing, get their bearings. The house was always eerie, but it looks sinister in the early morning light—the gleaming super-sized shipping container jutting from the side of the hill perched on a concrete base. At least a dozen Gatekeepers are on the roof, prowling back and forth.

Rafa is in there. Hurt, bleeding. Ready to die. My heart leaps into my throat, beats so hard I think I might never swallow again. Jude touches my arm.

'Ready?' The pulse in his neck keeps time with my own. I nod.

Mick and Rusty kneel down in the corn. Rusty quietly slides the first rocket from the bag, ready to load. Seth positions himself behind them, nods that he's got the brothers covered.

Ez and Zak reach for Jude and me; Zak checks with Mya and then signals to the other Outcasts. They're coiled, ready to shift into the open: more than a dozen of them taking on a horde of Gatekeepers and hellions to buy us time. I have a second to see them ready themselves—resolute, weapons raised—before the ground drops out beneath me in a rush.

We arrive upstairs outside the iron room. My head swims from the shift, and blood pounds in my ears. I brace for attack, scan the room for threats, but the place is empty. The pot-belly stove by the wall is black, lifeless. The couches we sat on only a few nights ago are overturned like discarded toys, a lampshade smashed across the scuffed timber floor. From our place at the back of the room, all I can see through the floor-to-ceiling glass is cold blue sky.

Sounds of shouting and ringing steel carry up from outside. It's started.

Mya races to the wall near the stairs. She pushes aside a painting of cheery yellow flowers smeared with blood. A keypad is recessed into the plasterboard behind it. She swaps her sword for pliers. The others fan out in front of her, ready for attack. Malachi and I take up positions in front of the iron door. It's been beaten back into shape; enough at least for a tight seal. Mya pulls the cover from the keypad, yanks out wires. The seconds pass slowly.

Three loud beeps and something clicks. The door grinds open behind us. I turn, rush in—

My heart stops.

I can't feel my legs.

Rafa.

Blood everywhere.

Rafa.

He's slumped on the floor against the filing cabinet, chin on his chest. T-shirt soaked crimson, knuckles raw. The left side of his face is so swollen I can't see his eye. Hair matted.

My legs give out. My knees hit the timber with a jolt; the katana clatters to the floor. A movement to my right. Malachi is bent over Taya. I'm assuming it's her: it's hard to tell from here. She's propped against the wall, the etched angel wings stretching out either side of her. One hand wrapped around the other. Unconscious.

Malachi scoops her up and they're gone before he's

straightened. In the void, I vaguely register that the plasterboard has been ripped from the room and all the photos of the Rephaim are gone. All that's left are giant wings on all four walls.

A groan.

Rafa.

I crawl over to him. I have no words for this moment. I push his hair back from his forehead, wipe blood from his good eye as gently as I can with my thumb. I need to get him out of here. I look around for someone, anyone. There's shouting outside the room now, sounds of fighting. I have a stab of fear for Jude, which shifts to panic: Malachi is gone and everyone else is creating a distraction. It's up to me to get Rafa out of here.

But I can barely shift on my own. How the hell can I do it with someone else?

I bite down on my lip, try to concentrate.

'Gaby?' Rafa's voice is raw, scratchy. He opens his good eye, tries to focus on me. 'Ah fuck, no.' He reaches for me, grimaces. Has to shut his eye to deal with the pain.

'Rafa, how do I—'

But he's out again.

What do I do? Where can I touch that won't hurt him? I'm running out of time. I suck in my breath and hook his arm over my shoulder. He leans into me. My head reels from the smell of sweat and fear.

I can do this.

I try to reconstruct the infirmary in my mind: the fluorescent lights, the tang of disinfectant, the squeaky lino floor.

Before I can get it set in my mind, the iron door thuds shut.

BEHIND CLOSED DOORS

The walls press in, black spots bleed together. My heart thunders now, reckless with panic.

I couldn't save Rafa. And now we're both trapped. And Jude's out there fighting Gatekeepers and possibly hellions. Daniel was right: this is what Zarael planned all along. We should have waited. We should have listened. We should have—

I finally draw breath before my lungs collapse. The blackness dissolves but my head keeps pounding. I unwrap myself from Rafa. I have to protect him. I crawl over to my sword, hold it out in front of me as I inch my way back to him. My hands are shaking. *Shit*. How could I be so stupid? Jude will be beside himself. Why didn't we just wait? Why—

Mya materializes inside the room.

I blink twice. 'How did you—?'

'Shut up.' She paces the room, strangling her katana. Her steps are urgent, panicked. 'I don't . . . I can't . . .' She stops, shuts her eyes and steadies herself. Then she opens them, lifts her palm and calmly slices it open.

'What the fuck?'

'I need blood.'

My mind scrambles for traction. Blood. Rephaite blood. That's what Nathaniel said created the ward. Does that mean it can break it?

'There's enough in here without you mutilating yourself.' It comes out raspy.

She ignores me, squeezing her hand into a fist until blood drips out onto the floor. She walks over to the nearest corner, stands on her toes and smears her palm over the tip of the wing. Then she does the same on the next corner.

'Did Debra tell you to do that?'

She heads for the third corner without answering.

I'm about to ask again when my view of her is blocked by a towering figure in a trench coat. Long white hair. Flickering orange eyes. I have a second to register the sword flashing down before I dive sideways and bring my blade up to protect my face.

'Gabriella.'

Bel.

I roll to my feet, block another blow—jarring—then

another. I get my balance, back away, feel that familiar rush of whatever it is that makes me Rephaim. I try not to look for Mya. He doesn't know she's in here. How could he? No Rephaite should be able to shift into this room. But she's gone already.

Bel swings again, and again I block him. 'Zarael has given me a few moments with you,' he says, grinning. 'Let's not waste them.' He aims his next strike for my head and I manage to block it and move back, try to keep my bearings. Look for—

Thunk.

I back into the wall. I try to duck sideways but Bel slams me against the solid iron, his hand around my throat. His blade is on mine, pressed against my chest. It's like LA all over again, when he had me pinned outside the nightclub, but this time I don't have a knife tucked in my jeans. His eyes flare burnt orange under the insipid fluorescent lights.

'Rafael will watch you beg for mercy. And then you can watch me take his head and give it to my hellion to pick clean.' His breath is hot, rotting. He's close enough that I can see puckered skin around the bullet scars on his forehead. 'And then I shall peel your flesh from your bones until you remember what happened with the Fallen last year.'

Where is Mya? Why isn't she helping?

Rafa is on the floor bleeding. Jude is outside fighting

god knows how many demons. The Outcasts are outnumbered. I'm trapped in here with Bel. *Me.* Not backpacker Gaby and not Gabe, the Rephaim's best fighter: someone in between.

I push against Bel. He leans in harder.

Nobody's coming to save me. Another surge of adrenaline washes through me, clears my mind. Fires my limbs. I am Rephaite: I'm stronger than this. My whole body hums and I shove Bel as hard as I can.

His weight is immediately gone and it takes me a second to realize I've launched him about three meters away. I rush him while he's still off-balance. He blocks my strike, grunts with the effort. I'm quicker now; it's taken him by surprise.

'There is no happy ending for any of you,' he says, slightly breathless between strikes and blocks. I ignore him, looking for an opening to do serious damage. My boots slide around on the slick floor but I refuse to look down.

'The Garrison doesn't want you.'

Swing, block.

'The Fallen don't care about you.'

Another swing, block.

'Even the humans who built this room want to kill you. Why do you all keep—'

I kick out his knee and risk a quick look at Rafa. I can't tell if he's conscious again or not. It costs me my fleeting advantage because Bel is already up again. It takes everything I have to defend the onslaught of blows that follows. I keep moving, keep breathing. Bel keeps talking between breaths.

'One way or another . . . you're going to end up . . . in hell with your fathers. You think I can hurt you here? You have no idea . . . what I can do to you down—' He howls and drops to his knees.

Mya is behind him. She wasn't there a second ago. Her blade flashes up, shining with his blood. She's hamstrung him. Bel swivels from his waist, tries to strike out behind him.

Don't think.

I change the grip on my sword, draw all my energy to my shoulders and swipe at his neck. Hard and fast. The blade is sharp: there's almost no resistance. Bel's head leaves his body and hits the floor with a soft thud. His torso stays in place, as if confused about what happens next. I stare at it. Blank. Not processing the horror of it. Mya puts her boot between his shoulderblades and pushes his body forward. I step sideways as it topples towards me.

I shake. Gag. Lean against the wall to steady myself. Don't lose it now, we're not out of this yet.

'We need to go,' Mya says and wipes her palm on her jeans. 'Leon found the override for the door. It's not opening again without a ram.'

Override?

Dazed, I look around at the corners of the room, all four smeared with her blood. There's no time to work out what she's done in here, but if she could get in, then she can get us out.

I drop back on the floor next to Rafa. My arms ache, my lungs burn. He's watching me with his good eye. So fierce, it almost undoes me. Mya kneels on his other side and we each take an arm to support his weight. He grunts as we lift him. 'Just to the cornfield,' she says. I nod. I have a split second to visualize the spot where we left the Butlers before Mya's taken control and the room is gone.

The shift is like nothing I've experienced before. It's as if we're in a protective bubble: I can feel the press of the wind but it doesn't touch me. And then we're in the cornrow. Both Butlers flinch at our arrival. It's cold out here, but a cleaner, sharper cold. Seth falters when he sees Rafa, recovers, and rushes to help us lower him to the ground.

'Help Jude,' I say and catch my breath.

Mya disappears.

I sit cross-legged in the dirt, holding Rafa to me. 'Hang on,' I whisper to him. I can't stop touching his face. He's battling to stay conscious. 'Where's Taya?' he rasps.

'Malachi's got her.'

He swallows, closes his eyes.

Through the cornstalks, I make out flickering movement. Rephaim striking and then shifting, frustrating their demon opponents. Dust kicks up next to me. Ez and Jones. Flushed and panting. Where's Jude? Panic crushes me. And then I see him behind Jones. He's bleeding above his ear and cradling his left arm but he's intact. He searches for me and our eyes meet. Relief surges between us.

Rafa opens his good eye, spots Ez. 'Love your work,' he manages.

Ez lifts her hand up to cover a tiny sob, and then she kneels down and gives him an awkward hug. Jude limps over and squeezes my shoulder, says so much without words.

'Get ready, boys,' Seth says, and Rusty hoists the launcher onto Mick's good shoulder.

'Where's Mya?' I ask.

Ez stands up. 'She's clear of the house.'

'You sure?'

'She left with us.'

Zak appears on the roof of the farmhouse. He lifts his fingers to his lips and lets out a piercing whistle, then he disappears . . . and he's next to Ez. He takes one look at Rafa. Turns to Mick and says, 'Aim for the back of the house.'

Mick doesn't need to be told twice.

There's a muffled *whompf*, a puff of smoke, and a second later the rocket punches through the side of the farmhouse. Glass explodes: a shower of concrete. The corn shakes. I lean forward to protect Rafa but we're too far away to get hit with debris.

'Again,' Zak says.

Rusty fumbles to load the second rocket. There's a gaping hole in the side of the farmhouse now, the outer galvanized iron torn and jagged. Plumes of plaster dust roll out from inside. Mick sends the next missile into the belly of the house. Another ear-cracking explosion and the roof folds in. No way is that iron room still in one piece. A howl of rage inside confirms it. Or maybe Zarael just found Bel.

'Nice shot.' Zak says. He rests a hand lightly on my head to get my attention. 'Let's get out of here.'

SKIN DEEP

Brother Ferro is waiting, latex gloves, surgical instruments laid out on the infirmary bench. Taya is on a bed across the room, either unconscious or sedated. Another monk, at least two decades younger than Brother Ferro, tends to her injured hand. Brother Benigno.

Rafa gasps as Zak lowers him onto the gurney. He doesn't look any different after the shift. Why doesn't he look any different? His breathing is ragged, his eye still swollen shut. Blood still seeps through his shirt.

He spots Jude with his good eye, relaxes a little.

'I don't understand,' Zak says to the older monk. 'He shouldn't still be bleeding.'

Brother Ferro waves him out of the away. 'What are his worst injuries?'

'Two stab wounds to the stomach, possibly more,' I say.

'Chest and thigh,' Rafa croaks.

I glance down, see that his jeans are torn and stained dark too.

'Gabriella, your help please.' Brother Ferro's Italian accent is even thicker under pressure. He shoves Rafa's shirt up and places gauze over the wound on his stomach. He gestures for me to keep pressure on it while he cuts Rafa's jeans. Rafa's leg is still bleeding. Everything is still bleeding. It's like he hasn't even shifted. Rafa fumbles for my wrist, misses. Why is he so weak?

'Out, out!' Brother Ferro snaps at the others. Zak, Ez, and Jude take a few steps back but nobody leaves.

Ez is holding the swords—hers and mine—all stained dark. Jones stands with the Butlers, blood dripping from his blade onto the floor. Mick's still got the rocket launcher on his shoulder. Zak notices and takes it with one hand, puts it on the bench. He nods to Jones. 'Can you check everyone made it back okay and then look in on Dani?'

Jones glances at Rafa, swallows. 'Okay.'

I check Taya. Malachi is in a chair next to her bed, holding her good hand in both of his. His eyes meet mine, totally exposed.

Brother Ferro is trying to stop the bleeding from Rafa's leg. 'Here,' he says to me, and I take over, putting pressure on that wound so the monk can get back to Rafa's stomach. He cuts Rafa's T-shirt and peels the fabric away from his sticky flesh. I can take it. I can—Oh my god. I turn away.

My eyes lock on Ez. Her face crumples, but she nods at me to keep it together. The smell of antiseptic burns in the back of my throat.

'That one I can stitch,' Brother Ferro says, nodding at the gauze on Rafa's lower stomach. 'But this one has already closed over.' The monk points to the older wound a little higher, where the demon sword went through him at the Butlers' camp. But it's not the stab wounds or the dark purple bruises across Rafa's ribs that turns my stomach. Or even the thought of what that blade must have done to his organs. It's the huge crescent moon carved into his chest with a thick, ugly line through it.

Rafa winces as Brother Ferro jabs him with a local anaesthetic.

'Did Bel do that?' I whisper. Was this Bel's response to my taunt about his bullet wounds? Did I goad him into doing that to Rafa?

Rafa opens his good eye. 'Yeah.' He coughs, recovers. 'And now he doesn't have a head.'

All movement stops. Even Brother Ferro pauses, surgical needle in one hand, suture thread in the other.

'How?' Zak asks.

It takes a bit of effort, but Rafa turns his head to see him. 'Gaby.'

Jude stares at me. The cut over his ear has stopped bleeding, but he still needs it dressed.

'Mya hamstrung him,' I say. 'I finished him off.'

'Mya? How did she get in there?' Jude asks.

I jerk my chin in Brother Ferro's direction, hope he takes the hint. I don't want to talk about what happened in front of the monks; they'll take the news straight to Daniel or Nathaniel. But whatever just happened with Mya is big. So big she hasn't come to the infirmary yet—not even to see Rafa.

The door into the ward swings open and Micah's head pops through.

'Holy shit. What hap—'

'Out!' Brother Ferro snaps. 'This is not the commissary.' Micah disappears.

'Keep that pressure strong, Gabriella.'

I do. With my free hand, I stroke Rafa's cheek with the back of my fingers. His stubbled skin is hot and clammy. He lets out a deep sigh and my chest aches. He passes out again. Brother Ferro has me hold gauze on Rafa's chest now too.

The monk is trimming the last suture on Rafa's stomach wound when the main door opens again. The monk's head comes up but the rebuke dies on his lips when he sees who it is.

Daniel takes in Rafa and then Taya. It's a moment before he can speak. 'How are they?' The question is for Brother Ferro, not me.

'Brother Benigno is working to stave off infection in Taya's hand. She has a number of lacerations and bruises, and I suspect she had cracked a rib before Malachi healed her. She has also taken several heavy bumps to the head, but she will be awake again soon.' The monk keeps working while he talks, unwrapping an antiseptic wipe. He nods for me to take the pressure off the chest dressing, and cleans the crescent moon gouged into Rafa's flesh. Blood immediately pools.

'And Rafa?'

Brother Ferro pauses. Sweat beads on his neck. 'He didn't heal in the shift.'

Daniel stares at him. 'How is that possible?'

'He's lost a lot of blood. The first wounds were partially healed, but these others . . .' He tosses the bloodied wipe aside, unwraps another. 'I've never seen anything like this. Not even when Calista was hurt. It's drained his strength. It's made him, I don't know'—he shakes his head—'more human than Rephaite.'

I watch Brother Ferro carefully trace the outer arc of the crescent room with another wipe. 'What does that mean?'

'I don't know, Gabriella. The trauma of these injuries would have killed a human long since.' The monk wipes his forehead with the back of a latexed hand. 'I don't fully understand how your physiology works. If he can't heal during a shift, then I don't know if he will heal at all. And if there is internal bleeding . . .'

'That's not good enough,' Ez says, stricken. 'You have

to do more than patch him up. You have to fix him. We *need* him.'

'If he were human, I would give him a blood transfusion but we don't have—' Brother Ferro stops.

'What?' Ez and I say together.

'We could try Rephaite blood.'

'How?' Daniel asks.

'It would have to be person-to-person. It's archaic, but we don't have time for anything else—unless you want to shift to a hospital? I didn't think so.'

Blood continues to seep from Rafa's chest. The monk wipes it again. And again. The gauze I'm holding on Rafa's leg is soaked through.

'We'd need a match.'

Daniel goes to the computer next to the sterilizing unit.

'You know Rafa's blood type?' Ez asks.

'The brothers have medical information on all of you.' Daniel clicks through files. 'Okay, Rafa is Type B. So is Malachi and—'

A chair scrapes over the lino. Malachi is on his feet. 'Tell me what to do.'

'Malachi, there are others with your blood type.'

Malachi places Taya's hand at her side. 'Rafa kept Taya alive in that house. Tell me what to do.'

BLOOD IS THICKER THAN ANGER

Malachi is propped on pillows on a gurney next to Rafa, tubes and bags hooked up between them. Rafa is out again, each breath short and labored.

We stand there, impotent, watching dark red blood flow from Malachi into Rafa, while Brother Ferro stitches Rafa's leg. The infirmary is quiet except for the muted voices from the ward next door: Mick and Rusty reliving the farmhouse attack.

'All we can do is wait,' Daniel says.

I'm still keeping pressure on Rafa's bandages, my fingers sticky with his blood. His face is puffy and discolored. Lips cracked and bleeding. Dark blond hair damp with sweat. God, he's a mess.

A hand touches my elbow, tentative. 'Gabriella.' It's

Brother Ferro. 'I don't know how long this will take. You should clean yourselves up and get some rest. I promise I will get word to you if there's any change. Brother Benigno can take over with these wounds.'

I don't want to leave Rafa. I can't. I—

'Come on.' Jude is beside me. He puts an arm around my shoulders. I can't look away from Rafa, even while Jude wipes my hands clean. And then he's steering me towards the door and out into the hallway. I put one foot in front of the other, numb.

When we're outside in the cloister, he grabs me in a rough hug. 'Fuck, Gaby, I thought I'd lost you again.' I cling to his shirt. I don't remember when I started shaking.

Jude walks me to the bench and I slump beside him. Light drizzle wets the grass in the piazza. The sandstone bleeds dark brown and the late afternoon sky hangs low; everything is close, quiet. I close my eyes and listen to the sound of rain.

'Are you hurt?'

I open my eyes to find Daniel standing in front of us. Ez and Zak are behind him. Ez still has my sword.

'No.' It's not really true: I'm sore and bruised from my fight with Bel, but what is that compared with Rafa and Taya's pain?

Daniel studies me, his jaw working. 'That was the most reckless thing you have ever done and the fact everyone came out alive owes more to good luck than—'

'She killed Bel.'

Daniel's head snaps in Zak's direction. 'Bel is dead?'

'That's what Rafa said.'

I bring my knees to my chest, lean against the wall. Exhaustion creeps up on me like warm water in a bath. Daniel is about to say something else when another thought strikes him. 'Tell me you didn't use the rocket launcher.' I don't answer and he rests his hands on his hips, focuses on the pavement. His shirtsleeves are rolled up; tendons stand out on his forearms. He's strung tight, even with Taya and Rafa back.

'Would you rather we'd left that room intact?' I ask. 'Do you want Zarael to come after us again?'

'No, Gaby, I don't. What I'd rather—' He cuts himself off.

'What?' Anger flares. Faithful, reliable.

He gives me an impatient look. 'I'd rather you weren't still behaving so much like your brother.'

Jude gives a rough laugh. 'One day, pal, you and I are going to have a long chat about this bug you've got up your arse about me. And about some of your decision-making regarding my sister.'

Daniel's shoulders tighten. He's standing with his back to the piazza, framed by falling rain.

'The room's gone,' I say. 'Deal with it.' I think about those angel wings on the wall, Mya smearing blood over them. I touch my shirt, stained with Rafa's blood. 'Did

Nathaniel tell you he's seen the winged symbol before?'

'He told you that?' I know Daniel well enough to see this is news to him: the fact Nathaniel shared something with us that he hasn't told the Five. 'He said the symbol was used to confine Semyaza and the Two Hundred before they were sent to hell.'

Daniel watches me for a long moment, not blinking. Not seeing. Then he walks a few paces, shifts his attention somewhere towards the other side of the piazza. None of us speaks.

'And the hits keep coming,' Ez says eventually. 'What does any of that mean?'

'I don't know.' Zak holds out his hand for the swords she's carrying. 'I'm going to clean these. Do you want to check on Dani while I do that?'

I want to tell them to stay—they need to know about Mya—but I can't tell them in front of Daniel. They walk off in opposite directions.

Daniel turns back to me. 'Can I see the photo again?' I hand him my phone and he enlarges the image.

'He hasn't said anything to you about any of this, has he?' Jude says. 'I guess he doesn't want too many people thinking those women might really be getting messages from heaven.'

'That's impossible.'

'Then how is it they have the exact same symbol on their wall as the one used by the Garrison?'

Daniel is still fixated on the screen. 'This is an angel trap?'

'No,' Jude says. 'Apparently angels can only be trapped using the blood of an archangel.'

'If you're so sure an archangel gave them instructions to create that room, why couldn't they have given blood as well?' There's a brittle edge to him now.

'Nathaniel says they're forbidden from shedding their blood on Earth.'

'Why would you believe him if you doubt everything else he says?'

'Because by telling us, he's admitting he broke the no-angel-bloodshed rule when he created the wards here. Why lie if all it does is put himself in the shit?' Usually it's the opposite for Nathaniel: he lies to keep himself out of it.

Daniel's nostrils give a telltale flare. 'Nathaniel explained the role of the blood in the wards to us this morning. That's not a secret.'

'*Us* being the Five, not the rest of the Rephaim, even though he had every chance to do that at the chapter-house.'

'It's about free will—'

'It's about controlling information,' Jude snaps.

Daniel's chest expands as he takes a slow, steadying breath. Straightens his shoulders. 'I trust Nathaniel will tell us what we need to know when we need to know it.'

'Mate, there's a point when loyalty becomes naïvety. I think you just crossed it.'

'It's uncanny'—Daniel's lips barely move—'how easily you've slipped back into your old skin. It won't be long now and you'll be shouting down the chapterhouse, turning more Rephaim against Nathaniel.'

'Hey, Daniel.' It's Micah. His hair is damp from the rain. Daniel moves away from us, runs a palm over the front of his shirt. 'You're wanted in the library. Nathaniel has reconvened the Council.'

Daniel glances at me, barely meeting my eyes. 'We'll finish this later.' He leaves without looking at Jude.

'How's Rafa?' Micah asks. 'Jones says he's not healing?'

I walk to the edge of the cloister and let Jude give him the update. The afternoon is darkening, the clouds lower now. I scan the shadows across the piazza, try not to think about Rafa lying a few meters way, his life—his *immortal* life—leaking away.

Something moves in the other cloister. Someone. Shuffling towards the bronze doors into Nathaniel's private garden. Why the secrecy? They're closer now, robes whispering on the cobblestones. A monk, then. I slip behind a column and peer through the gloom.

It's Brother Stephen, cradling his arm. Something quivers in my stomach. Why is he so cautious about going into Nathaniel's compound?

I click my fingers to get Jude's attention. Hold my finger to my lips.

'What?' he mouths.

I point to Nathaniel's quarters as the door closes behind the monk. I set off after him and Jude and Micah catch me in a couple of steps. 'What are you doing?' Micah whispers.

'Brother Stephen just snuck through those doors.'

'It can't be him: he's in bed with a broken arm. And he wouldn't be sneaking.' We reach the lion and the lambs and I put my hand on the bronze latch. 'Gabe, no.'

'You don't have to come, Micah.'

He follows Jude and me inside.

It's darker in the passage now. Like last time, we pause at the entrance to the garden and stick our heads out for a quick look.

'What the—'

Micah doesn't finish his sentence. He's too busy staring at Brother Stephen in the middle of the garden, hugging Virginia.

OUT IN THE OPEN

Virginia gasps at Micah's voice. The monk's eyes fly open. He lets her go and his good arm hangs in the air for a moment, trembling. I think how old he looks, his skin thin and papery, marked with liver spots. He and Virginia stand beside a wrought-iron table under a garden umbrella, in a sea of mint and tomato bushes. His right arm is wrapped tight in a sling across his chest.

Micah heads straight for them. Jude and I stick to the cover of the blueberry bushes. I'm trying to make sense of it: the monk and the matriarch of Iowa, embracing. The drizzle soaks through my hoodie.

'What are you doing?' Micah demands.

The monk's chin quivers. His face is ashen. 'Micah . . .' Brother Stephen can't hold his gaze. He barely resembles the monk who faced down Zarael in the car park.

'Leave him be.' Virginia's voice is rough, her face pinched and tired. The fight is draining from her. Unraveling her. She's still dressed in her tailored black suit but all traces of makeup are gone and her gray bob is no longer neat. Wisps of hair float around her face. Something's happened since we saw her through the window a few hours ago. Her blue eyes flick to Brother Stephen. She's afraid—for him.

'Brother, do you *know* her?' Micah asks.

Silence.

'Do. You. Know. This woman.' I've never seen Micah this angry. It changes his features, sharpens them.

'Yes.'

There's a long moment while we absorb this piece of information. Holy shit . . .

The monk reaches a gnarled hand for one of the wrought-iron chairs. He drags it out from under the table and Virginia holds his good arm so he can lower himself onto it. I slide into an empty chair opposite them. Jude comes in under the umbrella but Micah stays out in the rain.

'How long?' Micah is stunned. Devastated. 'How long have you been working against us?'

Brother Stephen's good hand grips the edge of the table, his knuckles bloodless. Scraps of information fall around me like confetti, start to take form.

'The blueprints, the photos . . . that was you?'

His lips tremble. 'Please, no.' Pale eyes meet mine.

'Stephen . . .' Virginia warns.

'How do you know Virginia?'

A long pause. 'She is my niece.'

I blink. That can't possibly be right.

'I am a member of the prophetic family.'

Virginia grabs his wrist.

I'm still stuck on the first bit. A monk at the Sanctuary is related to the people who built that iron room. The people who hate us.

'You mean the family who believes that if the Rephaim find the Fallen, we'll release them, and Semyaza and the Two Hundred will make war on heaven?'

He nods, weary. 'Yes, Gabriella, but that is not the entire prophecy.'

Virginia digs her fingers into his papery flesh. 'You have taken a blood oath.'

'And I have lived with Nathaniel and the offspring for sixty-five years. As I have told you many times, they are not all as you believe.'

'Sacrilege.' She clutches at him. 'How can you betray us in our darkest hour?'

'Our time has passed, Virginia. It may be that our role is complete—'

'It will never be complete while these abominations walk the earth.'

'Ease up, lady,' Jude says. He taps his knuckles on the

table in front of Brother Stephen to get his attention. 'Keep going.'

Brother Stephen fumbles inside his robe and pulls out a thin chain with a crucifix. He closes his eyes and holds it against his forehead for a moment, murmurs a prayer only he can hear. And then he opens his eyes, kisses the crucifix and drops it back under his robe. He's shaking. Cold or fear? The monk draws a shallow breath, keeps his eyes on the twisted iron under his fingers.

'The first revelation was that the Fallen were trapped in another realm after they escaped from hell and again lay down with human women.'

'That's not news: it's the Sanctuary's number one theory,' I say.

'How?' Jude asks. 'Who trapped them?'

'We do not know. But what our ancestor was shown— what Nathaniel does not know—is what is required to free the Fallen. Or at least, what must occur before the Fallen can be freed.'

'Stephen, if you do this—'

'Let him speak.' Micah glares at her. Virginia sits back in her chair.

'The Fallen can only be released by their bastard offspring, and only if the Rephaim are united in the cause to do so.'

Virginia sags. 'God save us all.'

It takes a second for me to understand the significance

of his words. 'But . . . that means Jude and I couldn't have released them last year.' A tiny flare of hope. 'Maybe it's not as bad as we think.'

'Maybe,' Jude says. 'That doesn't mean we didn't try.'

Oh.

'Do you know where they are? *How* to release them?' Micah asks.

The monk looks up, desperate for Micah to understand. 'Our family was ordained to prevent the Rephaim ever being unified, nothing more.'

I rest my forearms on the table. The wrought-iron swirls dig into my skin. The rain patters around us, kissing petals and leaves and soil. The smell of mint is sharper now.

Only the Rephaim can release the Fallen. And only if they all agree to it.

'That's why your family went to Jason and fed him the lie about keeping separate from the others—why those women told him he could avoid being sent to hell with the rest of the Rephaim if he stayed away from Nathaniel.'

'It was the truth.'

'Did you build that room for him—in case he changed his mind?'

'No.' Virginia straightens her spine. 'It was not for Jason. We do not know for whom it was intended. We received instruction and we obeyed. It had not been fully tested—'

'Sophie said it was a prototype. Were you planning

on building one big enough to hold all of the Rephaim?'

'That is not your concern.'

'Who received that vision?'

Virginia squeezes her eyes shut. 'My daughter, Louise.' Her mouth pulls down. Her dead daughter.

I have a sudden image of Zarael threatening Brother Stephen in the car park, enjoying the monk's fear and then disappearing without him. Maybe that wasn't the plan. My eyes drop to the neckline of his robe. 'That crucifix is made of iron, isn't it, like Virginia's pendant?'

Stiff fingers involuntarily find the shape through the fabric. 'It is all the protection I have ever had. That, and my faith.'

Jude drags a chair over the concrete and sits down. His hair is damp and starting to form ringlets to his shoulders. He used to hate that when we were kids and then he discovered how much the girls loved it. Our fake life was so much simpler.

'How do you know the revelations come from heaven and not somewhere else?' He directs the question to Brother Stephen.

Silence.

'Brother,' Micah says. 'You can tell us, or I can shift you to Nathaniel and the Five right now and you can explain it to them.'

He touches his broken arm and winces. 'It was my great-grandmother who first dreamed of the Fallen, of their children and what would become of them. An angel presented her with a set of scales—a sign that our family would be the balance. She heard battle horns and when she woke from her reverie she was holding a feather.'

'Which means . . . ?'

'It means that Michael spoke to her.'

The Captain of the Angelic Garrison. I expect Micah to scoff at the story but he doesn't and his silence makes me uneasy.

'When was this?' Jude asks.

'The year the hybrids were born.'

'And there have been other visions?'

The monk's eyes flit to Virginia and away. 'Irregular, but yes.'

It's not as consistent as the seer line in Dani's family, but close enough to sound plausible. Does that mean Dani's visions come from an archangel—maybe even the same one?

'Whose blood did you use to create the wards?'

The monk's eyes drop to the table.

'Did you help yourself to blood-soaked bandages in the infirmary?'

'Of course I didn't.' The monk seems genuinely repulsed by the idea. And even if he did, he still had to get them to the other side of the world before the blood dried.

'Jason gave us his blood,' Virginia says.

I click my tongue. 'Micah, can you get Jason, please?'

Micah is still fixated on Brother Stephen, as if the elderly monk's betrayal will start to make sense if he stares at him long enough.

'Micah.'

Micah gives me an impatient sigh. 'Don't let them out of your sight.' He disappears.

Virginia fiddles with her charm bracelet even though Daniel has the protective iron pendant that used to hang there. 'Nathaniel knows about Jason? He's here?'

'Yeah,' I say. 'Even after all those decades of manipulation, he still ended up at the Sanctuary.' She doesn't need to know the circumstances, and Micah and Jason appear before she can ask.

'Are you all right? Have they hurt you?' Jason's concern for Virginia is genuine and she has the decency to appear uncomfortable. Jason glances at Jude and me. 'I'm glad you're both okay.' He scans the courtyard. 'Is it safe to be in here?'

'For the moment.' I press my fingertips into my eyelids. God, I need to sleep. 'Did you know Virginia's related to the good brother here?'

Jason opens his mouth, closes it. Frowns.

'He's the one who provided the collection of photos at the farmhouse. It turns out Nathaniel's had Virginia's uncle here helping out for about sixty years. And Virginia just told us your blood sealed the trap.'

'She what?' Jason's surprise shifts to something

stronger. He stares at Virginia. 'How is that possible, given I didn't know that room existed until two days ago and I've never given you a drop of my blood?'

Virginia turns her face away.

'It wasn't me,' he says. 'There has to be someone else. Another Rephaite.'

Virginia stands up so fast she bumps her leg against the table, making her grimace. 'Why am I still here? The house is gone, the room is destroyed—' She stops.

'Hang on,' I say. 'How do you know about the house?'

She looks to the monk again, but he doesn't meet her gaze.

'Brother Stephen didn't tell you. He didn't know.'

Virginia's nostrils flare. She stays on her feet, fists clenched at her side.

'Oh fuck . . .' I spring to my feet. I move too quick and the tomato bushes blur together for a second. I reach for the table.

'What?' Jude steadies me.

There's only one answer: 'Mya.'

TWISTED FAMILY TREE

'What's Mya?' Jude asks.

'She shifted into the room after the door was locked.'

'So?'

'You think it's a coincidence she's the only Rephaite not restricted by the iron?'

'But you got out—'

'After she smeared her blood over every point the wings touched.'

'Oh. Shit.' Jude frowns. 'Maybe Debra told her how to do it when she questioned her?'

'Then why not tell us?' I turn to Virginia. 'Debra used Mya's blood to activate the ward.' It's not a question and she doesn't answer. 'And Mya's already been here to see you since we got back from Iowa to tell you about the farmhouse. Hasn't she?'

With so much shifting going on here at the moment, she could've easily shifted in and out undetected. All she had to do was make sure Virginia was alone first.

'Why would Mya do that? I know she doesn't respect Nathaniel, but—'

'She is our cousin.'

Wait. What?

Brother Stephen clears his throat, swallows. 'She has been a part of this from the beginning.'

I sink back onto the hard seat. The iron women of Iowa are Mya's family—her human family. Just like Dani and Maria are mine, Jude's and Jason's. Bloody hell.

We sit with the news in silence. And, slowly, a few more things make sense.

The fact Mya was such a mess in the cornfield after the attack. She wasn't hung over, she was grieving for Sophie and Louise.

The fact she could snatch up Debra, even though Virginia's daughter must have had an iron trinket. Debra left of her own free will because she *knew* Mya. Trusted her.

The fact she knew what to do in the iron room.

And then there's the fact she stayed at the Sanctuary today even though she hates the place. It was because Virginia was a prisoner here.

Jason wanders into the rain. He stands there, dazed, his blond curls turning dark. 'All this time, you had a member of the Rephaim in your family?' He waits for Virginia to look at him, but she's focused somewhere to his left. 'Did Mya know about me?'

'No,' Brother Stephen says.

That explains her reaction to Jason in Pan Beach—and her obsession with his connection to the farmhouse. 'And keeping them in the dark about each other—was that another failsafe in your plan to prevent the Rephaim uniting?' I ask.

The monk glances at Virginia, nods once.

Micah links his fingers behind his neck. 'I don't know what Nathaniel's going to do when he hears about this.'

'Micah.' Jude gets up from the table. 'We need to talk to Mya before we do anything that puts her at risk. And the Outcasts should hear about this before Nathaniel and the Five.'

'You're kidding, you want me to sit on this?' He lets his hands drop.

'Nobody's at risk.'

'You don't know that. And given you don't remember what it's like to be a part of this circus, you don't know what you're asking. Mya and Brother Stephen are *spies*.'

I catch his eye. 'Micah—'

'Don't, Gabe, it's too much to ask. You don't owe Mya anything.'

Aside from the fact she's saved my life. Twice. And Ez and Zak definitely need to be in the loop on this before

Nathaniel and the Five. I owe them at least that. 'I know what it's like to have everyone here treat you like a traitor.'

'She *is* a traitor.'

'Just give us time to tell her crew and get her side of the story,' Jude says.

'No way.'

'Come on, Micah,' I say. 'Please.'

He looks at me, levelly.

'I thought you trusted my judgment.'

'Not fair, Gabe.'

I wait.

Micah takes a breath and lets it out impatiently. 'Fine. One hour.'

'Can't you at least wait until we know if Rafa's okay?' It comes out flayed, raw.

He rubs his neck, calculates something. 'Okay, you've got three hours. And then I have to take this to Daniel.'

BRUISES AND SPONGE BATHS

The drizzle is heavier now. Water runs along the gutters and drips onto the cobblestones in a steady rhythm. I stop outside the infirmary.

'Do you want to check on Rafa?' Jude asks.

Do I? What if nothing's changed? What if he's worse? I'm still standing there in damp clothes, shivering, when Jude puts his hand on my back and guides me through the doors. Our boots squeak on the lino in the hallway. My legs are jerky: they don't feel like they belong to me. The smell of antiseptic grows stronger.

The infirmary door opens just before we reach it and Zak steps into the hallway. He stops abruptly. 'Hey, I was on my way to find you.'

'What's happened?' Jude asks. His grip tightens on my hoodie.

Zak doesn't answer, he simply holds the door open. I step through first and my heart stumbles. Rafa is sitting on the side of the bed. His sliced shirt hangs open, his chest and abdomen still caked in dried blood. *Dried* blood.

'Gaby...' His voice is ragged. I reach him in three steps and put my arms around him, careful not to hurt him. He leans into me. He manages to lift one hand to my hip. It slides off. He's still so weak.

'Careful,' Brother Ferro says. 'The transfusion has stopped the bleeding but he still needs to heal. That's the next test.'

Rafa mumbles something into my shoulder. Possibly my name again. I slide my fingers through his hair, soaked with sweat. There's so much I want to say to him, but not in here and not in front of anyone else.

'Gabriella, you need to let Zachariah heal him now.'

I nod at Brother Ferro, give Rafa's wrist a gentle squeeze, and step back. Malachi is sitting up now too, watching Brother Benigno take the IV needle from his arm. It's an effort, but Rafa twists so he can see him. 'I owe you one.'

Malachi glances back at Taya. 'No, *compagno*, we're square.'

I realize Daniel has been standing by Taya's bed all this time. He doesn't speak.

'We'll shift around the compound,' Zak says to me. 'Straight back, I promise.'

They disappear. I close my eyes, breathe in antiseptic

and bleach, start to count to ten to calm myself. Cold air stirs against my skin before I get to five. They're back. Rafa keeps his arm around Zak for support. He gives me a tired half-smile. His face looks better, less shiny and purple, and his left eye is no longer swollen shut. Brother Ferro is straight in to check his wounds, probing, prodding. 'Praise the saints, they've closed over.' The monk leans over the bed and pats Malachi on the knee. 'Good job.'

Rafa looks around for Jude. 'You intact?'

Jude gives a short laugh, touches the dried blood above his ear. 'Yeah, buddy. I'm fine.'

'You hold your own?'

'I did okay.'

Brother Ferro waves Jude and me away. 'Rafael needs a shot of antibiotics and a sedative.'

'I don't need sleep,' Rafa mutters, struggling to keep his eyes open.

'That's exactly what you need.' Brother Ferro pulls off his latex gloves and tosses them into the bin. 'But first we'll clean you up and dress those wounds properly. Zachariah, could I trouble you for some help there too?'

A tired laugh rumbles out of Rafa. 'A sponge bath from you two? Shit, this makes it all worthwhile.'

'The rest of you can go now,' Brother Ferro says. 'You too, Gabriella. Rafael needs rest. His body has taken a lot of punishment.'

I think about arguing, decide not to. I move closer to

Rafa, fiddle with a corner of his torn shirt. 'See you when you wake up.'

Rafa runs his fingers along my forearm. 'We're staying here?'

'For now.'

His eyes stray to my lips. 'Okay.'

'Come on buddy, let's get you to the washroom.' Zak changes his grip on Rafa.

'Put him in my room when he's ready to rest.'

Zak looks at me over his shoulder. 'You want me to leave him in your bed?'

I nod, conscious that Daniel is watching. Brother Ferro hustles them along before I can see Rafa's reaction. The door clicks shut and there's an awkward silence.

'How's Taya?' I ask.

'Doing better.' Malachi holds cotton wool inside his elbow where his IV was. 'She was awake a few minutes ago. Brother Benigno gave her something so she'd keep sleeping. I'll shift with her again in a while.'

'But she's healing okay?'

'Yeah. She didn't lose anywhere near as much blood as Rafa.'

'Thank you.' I say it quietly.

A shrug. 'What's a bit more blood out of me today?' He looks exhausted. 'So what are you going to do now?'

'That's a good question,' Daniel says, crossing the room. 'What happens when the Outcasts are ready to leave?'

'I don't know, Daniel. It depends on what Rafa and Jude want to do.'

'You need to think about who you trust.'

Jude blocks his path, stops him from reaching me. 'How the fuck can you talk to Gaby about trust after what you did to her?' Everything about Jude is a challenge: his posture, his tone. The way he eyeballs Daniel.

I catch a shadow of something in Daniel's face—guilt? Regret? But it's already gone. He keeps his eyes on me. 'You've been so quick to decide who to put your faith in—'

'Don't you dare make this about Rafa,' I say. 'Not now.'

'I'm talking about *before*. I wouldn't wish what happened to Rafa on anyone, but that doesn't change the fact that you didn't trust him a year ago. Before you disappeared, you'd spent a decade looking for any opportunity to meet him in a fight so you could hurt him. Really hurt him. You should at least trust that, if nothing else.'

I reach for the gurney, touch the sheet Rafa was bleeding on only moments ago. 'I trust Rafa with my life.'

'And that's going to be your downfall. You've thrown your lot in with him. You've aligned yourself with the Outcasts.'

'I haven't aligned myself with anyone.' But that's not true anymore. Not after Iowa.

Jude looks from me to Daniel and back again. 'Okay, what's going on here? Why's he so obsessed with you and Rafa?'

I really don't want to talk about this with Jude. 'It doesn't—'

'Gabe and I were lovers.'

Oh my god. Could he be any more of a tool about it? I meet Jude's eyes and recognize what I find there: disappointment. It stings. 'I don't remember it,' I remind him. Malachi finds something interesting on his shoe, leans down to get a closer look.

Jude's gaze shifts back to Daniel. 'Then how the fuck could you put her in a cage with a monster and watch it suck the life out of her? What sort of prick does that to someone he's shared a bed with?'

He's talking about me having sex. Shoot me now.

'We're not having this conversation,' I say. I walk over to the stainless steel bench, pick up a clean scalpel. Think about throwing it at Daniel.

'No, I think we need to. This arsehole thinks he has some claim on your loyalty. Let's explore this.'

'Let's not.'

'No, Gabe, he needs to hear the truth.' Daniel faces Jude. 'Your sister was smart enough not to follow you and Rafa a decade ago. She remained loyal to the Sanctuary, to the Rephaite cause. You were running around with Mya, risking human lives, risking the lives of your friends—letting Esther be torn to shreds by a hellion—all for the sake of money and ego. Gabe stayed here and kept our forces strong, kept searching for the Fallen. She never forgot the truth: that we are nothing until we deliver the Fallen to the Garrison.' Daniel is breathing quicker now, his neck tense. 'Then she started talking to you again last year and in less than two weeks she was gone. She left without telling anyone what she was doing, which means she was doing something she didn't want us to know about—something you talked her into. She disappeared without a trace. The Gatekeepers started a rumor they'd caught you tracking the Fallen . . .' His eyes slide to me. 'As far as I knew she was dead. Gone. Forever.'

'Don't dump your guilt trip on him. You don't know who influenced who,' I say. 'Or what we did.'

'And then she turns up alive, with no memory of who or what she is or what happened,' Daniel says, as if I haven't spoken. 'Because of you, we had no choice but to try to jolt her memory back. Because of you—'

'We found the Fallen?' Jude prompts. 'Then where are they now? And why did that arsehole Bel think he killed Gaby?'

'Only the two of you know the answer to that.'

I want to punch Daniel to make him shut up. His accusations are so much worse now they're aimed at Jude because I can see my brother is quick to carry them, repositioning the rest of his baggage to make room.

'It's been a big day, Daniel. Any chance you could save the witch-hunt until we've caught up on some sleep?'

He pushes a shirtsleeve down and rolls it up again,

each fold precise. 'If that's what you want.' I get the feeling he's talking about more than me sleeping.

'It is.'

'Fine.' And he's gone. Shifted. Again.

Malachi shakes his head. 'You really have a gift, Gabe. Nobody winds him up like you do.'

The infirmary door bangs shut and I turn to see Jude's gone. I find him out in the hallway, sitting on the floor with his back to the wall. He rests a forearm on one knee and stares at the black marks on the lino, decades' worth of gurney wheels and boots.

'It's not your fault,' I say.

'Everyone here seems to think it is.'

'Daniel's not everyone. And he was laying all that blame on me not so many days ago.' As was Taya, but I'm not sledging her while she's lying unconscious and missing a finger.

Jude rubs his jaw. 'These people we're supposed to have been . . . You were with *him*, we didn't speak for a decade, I nearly got us both killed last year . . . I don't want to be those people again.'

'Me neither.' I sink to the floor next to him.

'But if we're going to work out what happened last year, we have to know who we were.'

'I know,' I say. 'And it scares the shit out of me.'

SANDALWOOD, CINNAMON, AND HONEY

I stand outside my door, feel weirdly nervous.

Jude has gone to his room to talk to Ez. I argued for all of ten seconds about going with him to break the news about Mya. My need to see Rafa is stronger. Maggie, Maria, and Dani are safe—Dani's sleeping—so they don't need me right now.

I take a breath and open my door.

Rafa is in my bed.

He's on his back, head turned to one side, mouth slightly open. His chest rises and falls with the slow rhythm of sleep—or, actually, sedation. There's a pile of clothes stacked on the carpet—jeans, track pants, T-shirts, and sweaters—probably out of the supply Mya brought for Jude. I lock the door behind me and stand there for a moment, watching him. Try to order the thoughts crashing around in my head.

Mya is not who she says she is.

A family in Iowa is most likely receiving signs from an archangel who wants the Rephaim to stay divided.

I beheaded a Gatekeeper demon.

I still don't know what happened a year ago. Or a decade ago. Or anything before that.

But Rafa is here in one piece, sleeping soundly. And Jude is close by—banged up but alive—trying to figure it all out. My throat closes over. God, I am shattered. I pick at my shirt. And I'm filthy.

I grab clean undies and a fresh shirt from my pile on the floor and head for the shower. The water is warm and strong, comforting. I scrub myself clean and wash my hair.

A waft of steam follows me out of the bathroom, wraps around my bare legs. It's dark gray outside. Titanium clouds hug the mountain ridges beyond the Sanctuary. Rafa is on his side now, still breathing deeply. The lamp on the desk throws a soft pool of light over the bed.

I stand for a few seconds and watch him sleep. Then I lift the blanket, ready to climb under. Rafa's chest and stomach are wrapped tight with bandages but the rest of his torso is bare, and that trail of hair . . . Wait—is he naked? Is this Zak's idea of a joke: leave Rafa in my bed unclothed and unconscious? My pulse skitters. I lift the blanket a little higher. Am I still going to get in if—but no. He's wearing low-rise fitted boxers. I let out my breath and slip under the covers. The sheets are cool. The blanket floats down slowly and then I'm wrapped in smells that are all Rafa: sandalwood, cinnamon, honey. I lie facing him, breathing him in. I'm tired, but I don't want to close my eyes. I want to look at him for a while. This volatile, smartarse half-angel I can't live without. I know we have a complicated history, but whatever's going on between us feels simple right now.

His hair sticks up in odd directions like it always does after a shower. His lips are slightly apart, the lower one almost back to its normal size. The stubble on his jaw is darker than his hair. I let my gaze wander to his throat and along his collarbone, to the strong line of his shoulder and then his chest. Tufts of hair poke out from the top of his bandage. I glance at his face and my heart falters: his eyes are open.

We lie there, watching each other. Breathing each other's air. Not touching.

'You're supposed to be sleeping,' I whisper.

'No chance.' His voice is rough from sleep. His eyes roam my face, linger on my mouth. 'Why did you come to Iowa? Why risk it?'

I don't answer; I don't have the words right now. I reach for him, feel the contours of his shoulder and gently roll him onto his back. He lets me. I push the blanket aside and sit up in the bed beside him, take a few more seconds to soak in the reality that he's here, alive, with me. I lean down and kiss his forehead. He slides his fingers into my wet hair, tucks it behind my ears. Watches me with an intensity that steals my breath.

'Close your eyes,' I say.

He does, and I kiss one eyelid, then the other. My lips graze over his stubble. I kiss his cheek, his chin, his throat. His fingers trail down my neck and over my shoulders. He smells amazing, all traces of the infirmary rinsed away. I taste his neck, the spot right under his ear. He runs his fingers down my waist, over my hip to my legs. Fingertips on bare skin.

'I thought I was going to lose you,' I say, my lips on his collarbone. 'And I can't lose you, Rafa. I can't—'

He sits up—stronger than he should be—and pulls me onto his lap. I hook my legs around him. He holds me close, tight. Inhales me. Trembles. He almost feels more vulnerable than when I found him slumped in the iron room. We stay like that for a moment, bodies molded together.

'I thought I'd never touch you again,' he says, and his hand slips under my shirt, makes small circles on my lower back. I'm aware of every place my skin touches his. Aware of the heat in his body. In mine. He kisses my jaw, my throat; his tongue leaves a trail of warmth. His breathing is quicker now. 'God, I love being with you.'

His mouth covers mine. This kiss is deep, demanding.

It's like it was on the beach, except there's less fabric between us. He lifts the hem of my T-shirt and I raise my arms, let him pull it over my head. His eyes drop to my bare skin and for a second, I feel exposed, vulnerable. But then he kisses the hellion scar, runs his thumb over the claw marks in my side. Brushes his fingers across my breasts. I move against him without thought, responding to his touch. He makes a low noise in the back of his throat. And then his hands go still.

'Gaby . . .' His voice is thick, husky. He draws back so he can look at me. 'One of us needs to stop, and I'm telling you now: I'm not a good enough man for it to be me.'

My heart beats hard against my ribs. My skin raw from his stubble. Every part of me aches for him. It's not that the past doesn't matter—it does. But not here. Not in this moment.

'Gaby—'

'This is me, Rafa. *Me*. Nobody else.'

I tighten my legs around him and pull him with me down to the mattress. I roll my hips so he has to reposition himself between my thighs. I feel his heart now against my ribs, strong, insistent. The other part of him responding to me.

Rafa searches my eyes, sees what he needs there. His lips find mine again. We kiss until my tongue aches. And then his lips trail down my neck again, my collarbone, under my arm, along my ribs to my abdomen. He slides my underwear down so he can kiss my hip. He keeps sliding the fabric as his lips work down to my thigh, my knee, my ankle. He kisses the tender skin on the sole of my foot, distracting me from the fact I'm now naked.

He works his way back up my body, and I reach for his boxers. He watches me through heavy lids as I help him out of them. And then he's naked too, except for the bandaging around his chest and thigh. The dressing taped over his stomach.

Rafa draws me to him again, his tongue and fingertips teasing until my entire body is on fire. I wrap my legs around his hips, draw him closer. Finally, he positions himself above me, weight on his arms.

'Are you sure?' He's breathless, full of need. But he watches, waits for my response.

This is it. I run my hands up his forearms, over taut biceps. My entire body hums. I'm sure. 'Be gentle.'

He smiles and everything inside me dissolves.

'You too.'

NO PARACHUTE

Afterwards, we lie together.

'You all right?'

I nod. 'Are you?'

He laughs, deep in his chest. 'That wasn't my first time.'

I press my thumb into his bandaged side, gently. 'No, but you're pretty banged up.'

'Trust me, I'm not feeling any pain right now. You?'

'No. It's . . . weird. That didn't feel like my first time.'

He gives me a pointed look.

'Yeah, I know, technically it wasn't.'

'Was it okay?' He's looking at me seriously.

I close my eyes, remember the sounds that escaped me. My *enthusiasm* for him. I put my face back against his chest so he can't see the heat there. 'It was okay.'

His hand slides down my back, lower. 'Just okay?

Wait until I'm full strength again.'

A thrill runs through me at the thought.

'You should sleep,' he says.

'Look who's talking. You staying in here?'

'You're naked in my bed—I'm not going anywhere.'

'Actually, it's my bed.'

'*Actually*, it's some random bed in the Sanctuary.' He pauses. 'Why are we at the Sanctuary?'

'Long story. Can we sleep first? I'm wrecked.'

He draws me closer, slides his fingers through my still-damp hair. 'Gaby, we can do whatever you want, as long as you stay within arm's reach.'

I dream of demons and hellions. Of a terrifying darkness punctuated by flickering light and the stench of wet leaves. There's dirt in my mouth, blood on my face, pounding in my head.

Pounding.

It comes again. I surface from the suffocating darkness, taste soil and blood. Someone is knocking on the door. Rafa is already on his way over, stops to pull on track pants. They hang low on his hips. The room is shrouded in early evening gloom. He looks back at me, hand on the doorknob.

'Hang on,' I say, still groggy. I grab my undies and T-shirt from the floor. He watches me put them on, a half-smile playing on his lips. I look around for my spare clothes. The bathroom. The knock comes again. I get back into the bed and pull the covers over my legs.

Rafa cracks the door open. 'Hey,' he says, and blocks the view into the room.

'Shit, man, you look much better.' It's Jude. I grip the blanket tighter. Wish I had on more clothes. I'm not game to make a run for the bathroom in case Rafa opens the door wider.

'I feel better.' Rafa shifts his weight. 'Zak says you really stepped up in Iowa. Did some damage. I'm sorry I missed it.'

'I don't know about doing damage. I took some big hits.' Jude clears his throat. 'My sister still in there?'

'Yeah.' Rafa pauses. 'That okay?'

'I'm guessing it's a bit late if it's not.' Another pause, more awkward. I bring my knees up to my chest. 'Anyway, I'm not here about that. We've got a problem.'

'What?' Rafa hasn't moved.

'Mya just took Virginia.'

I rest my head on my knees. Shit. And I haven't explained any of this to Rafa yet.

Rafa looks over his shoulder at me, the tangled sheet. 'Can you give us a minute? We'll come to you.'

'Dani's still sleeping in my room. I want to check out a book in Gaby's stuff downstairs so I'll meet you in the garage.'

The door closes.

I dash for the bathroom before Rafa can ask what's going on. I want to be freshened up and fully clothed for this conversation. I catch a glimpse of myself in the mirror. Still me. Everyone besides Maggie still sees Gabe when they look at me. Well, maybe not everyone. I'm pretty sure when Rafa looked at me in that bed, he saw *me*.

I had sex with Rafa.

I grin. My reflection grins back.

I finally notice my crazy bird's-nest hair. What was I thinking going to sleep with it damp? I manage to wrestle it into a ponytail, finish getting myself sorted. Wonder how Rafa feels about everything (me) now he's had a sleep—and seen Jude.

By the time I come out, Rafa's put on jeans, a T-shirt, and hoodie. He meets me halfway across the room, boot-laces still undone.

'About that stuff I need to tell you,' I start.

'In a minute.' His fingers find my hips, draw me close. 'I'm not done with this conversation yet.' His lips brush mine. He's tentative, as if he half expects me to push him away. I grip his hoodie, lean in. We kiss, slow and tender. Heat flares in all the right places. And then I remember all the things Rafa needs to hear about. I break contact first.

'Seriously,' I say. 'We need to go.'

'Okay.' But he doesn't move away. Instead he leans his forehead on mine. 'Thanks for coming for me.'

'You would've done the same.'

'Yeah, but you're meant to be smarter than me.'

I touch the new scar through his eyebrow. 'Not when it comes to you, apparently.'

His lips curve. 'I like the sound of that.'

I kiss him again and wish we didn't have to be somewhere else. 'You know this thing we've got going on? It only works if we both have our heads. Literally. I can't believe you thought the solution was to die in there.'

He jerks his head back. 'Dani really got that? Shit— Dani. Jude said . . . She's here?'

'Yeah. She went searching for you and heard what you were thinking.'

He rubs the back of his neck. 'I could *feel* her there, but I had no idea she could hear me.'

I want to know more, but Jude's waiting. And the Mya situation. 'Come on. Let's go.'

'Shift?'

I answer by sliding my arms around him.

'You've been practicing.'

'How—'

'I felt you when we left the cornfield. Not strong, but your energy was definitely in the mix.' He squeezes my hip. 'Are you up for a quick detour on the way to the garage?'

'Where?'

'Still in the Sanctuary. I want to show you something. It'll only take a minute.'

There's something about the quietness in his voice.

'Okay. Just a minute.'

Our shift is the calmest I've experienced with Rafa, as if even he's had enough chaos for a while. It's actually colder when we stop. When my eyes adjust I see we're standing under a huge tree. It hulks over us, stretches out in all directions. But we're not in a park, we're in a tiny courtyard. Icy wind shakes the branches and dried leaves rasp along the footpath. I smell damp earth and something sweet. This must be the tree I saw from the roof. Blinds are drawn in the windows around us, casting outlines of muted light. Everything smells of rain.

'Where are we?' I whisper.

'Nathaniel's original courtyard.' Rafa takes my hand and leads me further under the canopy. The trunk is as wide as a wine barrel. Thick, gnarled arms reach out and gouge sandstone walls; smaller branches spike upwards, dressed in pale blossoms. Rafa sits on a twisted limb and guides me onto his lap. I steady myself on the trunk: the bark is tough, hardy.

'This apple tree's older than us. It was half this size when Nathaniel transplanted it the year he moved into the monastery.' I shiver and Rafa rubs my arms through my hoodie. 'The monks didn't have the balls to tell him the courtyard wasn't big enough for it. So it outgrew the space and they've been pruning it for a century, trying to stop it busting through the walls. The roots must be playing hell with the foundations.'

I pick at a piece of bark. It comes away more easily than I expect. 'I didn't realize you were a closet tree hugger.'

I feel the laughter in his chest. 'When we were kids, we used to sneak in here every summer. You, me, and Jude. Sometimes Micah and Daisy. We'd dare each other to climb to the top. The real challenge was not getting sprung by Nathaniel or the monks.'

'And how successful were we?'

'We scrubbed a lot of floors in those years.' He draws me closer. 'Even back then you were fearless, before we really had an idea of what we were capable of.'

'Yeah?'

'One time when we were fifteen, you and me were racing to the top. There may have been some heckling and wrestling and I got ahead of you. And then my branch broke and I lost my grip. I was a goner.'

'What happened?'

'You caught me.'

'I did not.'

'No, it's true. You grabbed me as I went past. Gutsy move.' He leans in until his lips are against my ears. 'I may have started having inappropriate thoughts about you around then.'

I laugh and nudge him away with my elbow—gently—and try to imagine being a fifteen-year-old in this ancient place, hanging out with fifteen-year-old versions of Rafa and Jude. It's like the last time Rafa told me a story about the childhood I don't remember: strangely comforting. And it reminds me this place, so foreign to me, was once my home.

'I thought you might like to see it.'

I turn my face and kiss his cheek. 'Thank you.' I wish I could see his eyes, but it's too dark out here. 'Sorry to bring you back here.'

'Ah, it's not all bad.'

'I thought you hated this place?'

He shrugs. 'Only since we walked out. Before that, it was okay.' He looks around, even though there's nothing to see except the tree and the walls and patches of cloudy night sky. 'We made a lot of memories here. It's hard not to get attached to a place you've lived in most of your life, even with all the crap that comes with it.' There's a strange note in his voice I can't quite place. Nostalgia?

It makes me wonder . . . did his aversion to the Sanctuary stem from the falling-out with Nathaniel? Or the falling-out with me? I breathe in cool air, picture living here as one of the Rephaim. All of us, eating, drinking, sleeping, training, and fighting together. Laughing together. Backing each other. In the life I remember—the life of hostels and campgrounds—I missed having a place to call home. Is it the same for Rafa? Does he miss being a part of the fabric here, even with its flaws?

'I bet Ez has been happy to be back,' he says. 'She still misses the brothers, not that she'd admit it.'

I think about her conversation with Brother Ferro and his concern over her scars. 'I doubt she's missed the antagonism with everyone else.'

'I can imagine the warm reception the crew got.' Whatever was in his voice before has gone.

'Come on, we need to go. Jude's waiting and there's a lot to tell you.' I shiver again and Rafa laughs.

'Seriously, Gaby, living in the tropics has made you soft.' He wraps me up in a bear hug. 'I kind of like it, though.'

OH, AND BY THE WAY . . .

We shift to the garage.

'Is that my Ninja?' Rafa's arms leave me before I open my eyes. I smell concrete, grease, fuel. He half-jogs over to the far corner and rips off the blanket. He runs a hand lovingly over the fairing. Swings a leg over the bike and grins at me. 'We're taking this for a ride.' He looks past me. 'You see this?'

Jude is in the doorway to the storage room, holding a hardcover book. 'I did. Impressive. But we need to sort a few things before you start up that bad boy.'

Rafa sighs, climbs off the bike.

'Good sleep?' Jude says to me. I feel the flush creep up my neck. He looks from me to Rafa and back again, as if he's still making up his mind how he feels about us being together. Oh god, I really don't want him thinking about it.

'What's that?' I point to the book.

He shows me the cover. It's in Italian but there's a photo of what looks like the Sanctuary on the cover. 'Nathaniel picked it up when he was down here. I thought it was worth another look.'

'So,' Rafa says. 'When did Mya take the old girl?'

'About twenty minutes ago.'

We follow Jude into the storage room. It's still cold and stale, but more private than the garage. The boxes are packed away on the shelves and the floor's been swept clean. Dust still hangs in the air.

'Did she take Brother Stephen too?' I ask.

'No.'

'Why not?'

'Because—'

'Hold up,' Rafa interrupts. 'Why would Mya take Brother Stephen?'

Jude raises his eyebrows at me. 'He doesn't know?'

'Not yet—hey,' I say in response to the look he gives me. 'We've been sleeping.'

The eyebrows stay up.

Rafa leans against the cinderblock wall. 'Okay. Fill me in.'

Jude looks to me. I spot a tennis ball wedged in the metal bracket holding the shelves to the wall. I pry it free, roll it between my palms while I get my thoughts together.

I give Rafa the run-down: retreating to the Sanctuary

after he and Taya were taken; Nathaniel's confession about the wards at the Sanctuary; the Outcasts coming here and the violent fall out; Zarael's visit and the delivery of Taya's finger; the significance of the symbols in the iron room, and where Nathaniel last saw them. And then the biggest news: Mya's connection to the women and Brother Stephen's six-decade side career.

Rafa blinks, as if he's waiting for the punchline. 'No way . . . seriously?' We give him a moment for it to sink in. 'Fuck.'

'Exactly,' Jude says.

'Who else knows about this?'

'Micah and Jason,' I say.

'And Ez and Zak. They'll be here in a sec.'

'Nathaniel?' Rafa asks.

Jude shrugs. 'Only if Micah's talked.'

'He said he'd give us three hours—'

'That was before Mya stole Nathaniel's prized prisoner. He's pretty pissed off.'

I frown. 'Why didn't Brother Stephen go with them?'

'It would have raised more questions. Now it just looks like Mya is playing games with the Five.'

'Yeah, but Micah knows the truth.'

Rafa shakes his head. 'Micah's no idiot. He'll keep quiet. He has to now if he doesn't want to wear some of the shit hitting the fan.'

'I asked him to trust me. He must hate me for this.'

'It's Micah,' Rafa says to me. 'He couldn't hate you if his life depended on it.' He pats the pockets of his jeans. 'Shit, I have no idea where my phone is. Don't suppose either of you have Mya's number?'

'I do,' Jude says, not looking at me.

When did that happen? Jude must have been with Mya at some point when I wasn't around. I feel a faint sting. Still.

There's a knock. 'Just us.' Ez and Zak let themselves in. They're carrying their swords—and ours.

Ez hands hers to Zak and hugs Rafa. The embrace is silent, intense. Ez steps back, wipes her eyes. 'You've heard about Mya?'

'Yeah,' Rafa says. 'Unbelievable. She's been playing us for a decade.'

'We don't know that. I'd like to hear what she's got to say before we burn her at the stake.'

'Have you called her?'

Ez nods. 'She's not answering.'

'That should tell you something.'

'It tells me she's gone to ground. Do you blame her?'

'Mya didn't have to come into that room today when the door slid shut.' I say it quietly. 'That's what gave her away in the end: saving you and me.'

Rafa stares at me. '*You're* defending her?'

'Just stating a fact.'

He cracks a knuckle. God, I've missed that sound. 'How

widely known is it that Virginia's gone?' he asks.

'It's not,' Zak says. He's in the doorway, keeping an eye on the garage. 'The Five won't be in a hurry to admit they've lost her.'

'We need to talk to the crew, get in front of this.'

Jude slips his phone from his pocket. 'Let me try Mya first.' He looks to me, waits for my nod of support. He dials. She's not going to answer, not now that she knows we know—

'Mya—are you okay?' Jude half-turns away. 'We're still at the Sanctuary . . . Gaby, and Rafa. Ez and Zak . . . Yeah, he's okay. Taya's good too.'

Rafa waves to get Jude's attention. 'I want to talk to her,' he says.

'I'm putting you on speaker. Don't hang up.' Jude taps the screen. 'You still there?'

Silence.

Rafa leans over the phone. 'What the fuck, Mya?'

She doesn't answer.

'That's it. That's all you've got? After all these years. After everything we've gone through. Fucking unbeliev-able.' The telltale muscle in Rafa's jaw twitches. 'Was anything out of your mouth the truth?'

Jude pulls the phone away. 'Rafa . . .'

Ez moves closer. 'Mya, please come and talk to us.'

'I can't, Ez.' There's a note in Mya's voice I've never heard before. Regret.

'Where are you?'

'It doesn't matter.'

'Are you with Jess?'

'Forget about Jess.'

'What about Virginia?'

'She's with her daughters. They're no threat now.'

Daughters.

It's a few seconds before it hits me. 'Oh my god.'

Jude frowns at me. 'What?'

'Jess is part of the family.'

More silence on the other end of the phone.

'Is that true?' Ez asks.

A long pause, and then a loud sigh. 'Jess, Louise, and Debra are sisters. *Were* sisters.'

I *knew* the detective reminded me of someone: Jess looks like Sophie, her niece in Iowa.

The LA situation makes a lot more sense. It was no accident Jess was in the Rhythm Palace when Gatekeepers and hellions terrorized the club the first time around. And no accident she formed an alliance with the Outcasts. My mind spins—and then abruptly finds traction.

'Did Jess go to the farm yesterday? Fly out there to give Virginia a report?'

'Why?' Mya's wary now.

'Bel saw us out the back of the club. He knows she was working with us. He could've followed her after we left, and if she went to Iowa—'

'Gatekeepers can't track humans.'

'No,' Rafa says, catching on, 'but Immundi could have shadowed her to the airport, boarded her plane in LA, and followed her to the farm. Those monkey pricks can almost pass as human if they clip their nails and keep their mouths shut.'

'I have to go.'

'Mya,' Jude says. There's nothing for a few seconds and I think maybe she's hung up.

'What?'

'Don't let your crew hear about this from anyone but you.'

She laughs, cold and short. 'It doesn't matter, nobody will trust me now. Outcast from the Outcasts.'

The phone disconnects.

A QUICK TRIP

Rafa slams his palm into the nearest shelf and the metal rattles. He winces and puts his hand against his bandaged torso. 'That still hurts.'

'You need to cut her some slack,' Jude says and slides his phone back into his pocket. 'Let her explain herself.'

'She's had twelve years to explain herself. And the crap she's given Gabe over that time . . . the hypocrisy is mind-blowing. If either of you remembered, you wouldn't be so understanding. You've always had a soft spot for her, but even you'd be losing your shit over this.'

'Given that Gaby and I possibly found the Fallen behind everyone's backs, I'd say we're not in much of a position to throw stones.'

He waits to see if I've got anything to say. I don't—as much as I'd like to. I've been wearing bile from Mya since the moment she walked into that iron room the first time. And the whole time she's been part of a family hell-bent on destroying the Rephaim. I pull my hoodie tighter around me. How has that worked for her, given she's one of us?

'Her family is part of everything we've ever touched,' Rafa says. 'The Sanctuary, Iowa, even LA. That's no accident—it's a fucking conspiracy. And she's been up to her neck in it.'

Ez straightens a box on the shelf—the one with the stuffed dog in it. 'What do you think about the family's claim they receive instruction from Michael?'

'More bullshit. You seriously believe the Captain of the Garrison is dispensing divine wisdom to a cult in a cornfield?'

'Someone's giving them information. And someone's giving Dani visions,' she says.

Jude absently traces the old scars on his knuckles with his thumb. 'We need to understand more about how archangels communicate with humans. *If* they communicate. I skimmed through the files on the laptop—not much there. But there were a heap of books about angels on Patmos.'

I stare at him. 'You want to go back to Greece?'

'Only if you come with me.'

'Zarael knows about that place, Jude. The iron room might be gone, but he can still attack us. He can still hurt us.'

'Zarael thinks we're all here. He's got no reason to look anywhere else right now.'

I check Rafa. He's up for it. Unbelievable.

'We'll come,' Zak says. 'Just in case.'

'What about Maggie and Jason?' I say. 'What about Dani? We can't leave them here unprotected.'

'We'll be five minutes. Ten tops. Nobody will miss us. Face it: Nathaniel can't be any more pissed off at us than he already is.'

'But—'

'You four go,' Ez says. 'I'll keep an eye out upstairs. Go. I'll call if there are any dramas.'

I zip my hoodie. My fingers are shaky so I shove them in my pockets. I don't want to risk facing Gatekeepers again, but I can't let Jude and Rafa go to Greece without me, not even for five minutes.

'Okay.'

The cottage is in darkness when we arrive. I smell the fireplace instantly, charcoal and ash.

Rafa digs out a camp light and flashlight from a cupboard and gives me a guilty grin. One of those would have been handy when I was stumbling around in the dark here last week. He turns on the lantern and the lounge room comes into focus in stark white. Blankets are strewn around the antique couch, a reminder of the night Rafa and Jason brought me here after my first encounter at the Sanctuary. Light bobs across the plaster and the school of copper fish shimmers over the mantel.

We follow Jude down the hallway. Shadows creep up the walls and along the floor. The house is quiet, a cold shell. It seems like forever since I've felt sunshine on my face. Jude goes straight to the bookcase in the room that was his in another life. He hands the lamp to Zak and starts pulling out books and flicking through them, tossing the ones he wants to take with us on the bed.

I hear Rafa moving about in the room next door. Light sweeps the hallway, disappears. I make my way into his room, find him poking around in the top drawer of a dresser. There's enough light in here to see his bed—still made—and a bookcase jammed with motorbike parts. The bedside table is cluttered with a half-full bottle of Jack Daniels, an empty glass, a tattered paperback, and a pile of coins in an old glass ashtray.

'I knew this was still here somewhere.' He pulls a knife from the back of the drawer, takes it out of its sheath, and shines the flashlight on it. I move closer until our shoulders touch.

'That's beautiful,' I whisper.

It's no ordinary knife. The long blade and handle are made from curved steel, and both are engraved with elaborate patterns. I lean closer, realize the markings on the blade are rudimentary tigers. The steel is old and worn. It looks antique, valuable. Not something you'd leave lying around in a drawer of an abandoned cottage.

'You gave this to me.'

I take the knife. It's heavier than I expect. 'Please tell me it was a gift and not something I stabbed you with.'

He laughs. 'It's a Damascus dagger—a collector's item. Even you wouldn't stick that in someone. Not even in me.' He glances at me over the knife, knows he's brought up the one thing neither of us wants to think about just yet.

'Twenty-first gift?' I say, trying for humor.

'Christmas. The last one before it all went to shit.'

I stand there with the dagger in one hand and in the other the katana Rafa gave me before we stormed the Butlers' camp. 'Have we ever exchanged gifts that weren't designed to kill?'

A wry smile. Shadows dance on his face as he leans in. 'It's never too late to start a new tradition.' For a second I think he's going to kiss me, and then more light spills into the room and he pulls back.

Jude's in the doorway with a stack of books tucked under his chin. 'Can I have a minute with Gaby before we go back?'

'Sure.' Rafa shuts the drawer behind him without looking. He takes the dagger from me, tucks it in the back of his jeans and gives me the flashlight.

Jude waits until Rafa and Zak are moving down the hallway. He puts the books on Rafa's bed in a neat stack, studies me in the light. 'Are you okay still being at the Sanctuary?'

I shrug. 'Honestly? I'd rather take our chances in Pan Beach. But we may as well find out as much as we can at the Sanctuary now, because when Nathaniel realizes we're not coming back into the fold, he won't keep the door open for us.'

'Gaby, we can go to Pan Beach if that's what you want. We're not staying in Italy if you don't want to.'

For a second, I nearly tell him I *don't* want to stay in Italy—I want time alone with him, with Rafa, far away from the complications of Nathaniel and the rest of the Rephaim. But it's not all about me. 'We need more time with Dani. I doubt Maria will agree to come to Pan Beach when we can't offer protection from demons. Plus there's no guarantee the Outcasts would follow us and Rafa needs them right now, and . . .' I hesitate but I have to say it. 'So do you.'

'Gaby . . .'

'Jude, I get it.' I sit on the mattress and his books spill over onto the blanket with a soft thump. 'Micah's told me things about who I used to be—given me hope I wasn't a complete idiot in that other life. The Outcasts are the only ones who can give you the reassurances you want.'

Jude lowers himself next to me. It's a moment before he speaks. 'I want to know the truth about the past, about who I was. But I don't want to be the guy who walked away from you.'

I bite my lip. 'And I don't want to be the girl who let it happen.'

'Then no matter what happens next—no matter what we find out—we're never becoming those people again. I meant what I said at Rafa's place: nothing is tearing us apart. I don't care what happened before or how we treated each other . . . if it all comes back, we're going to get our heads around it and move on. Deal?'

He knows as well as I do we can't make that sort of promise. We don't know who we were or what we did. Or why. But he wants it to be true and so do I—more than anything—and maybe that's enough. So I nod.

'Deal.'

PARENTAL GUIDANCE
RECOMMENDED

The four of us arrive in the hallway. Ez opens the door before we knock.

'Dani's in the bathroom.' She glances at our swords. 'No trouble?'

Zak brushes her arm with the back of his knuckles. 'We're good.'

Maggie and Jason stand up when we come in.

'Hello Margaret.'

'Rafael.' She beams at him.

'Good to see you, Rafa,' Jason says.

'Bet you never thought you'd say that, Goldilocks. I suppose you're angling for an apology now?'

'I don't want an apology. I want to take Dani and Maria away from here.'

Rafa looks at him. Really looks at him. 'I still don't get you—why all the freaking secrets?'

'All I've ever wanted to do is protect the people I care about. Keep them away from Nathaniel.'

'Even the iron bitches?'

'I didn't know what they were planning—'

'Yeah, I get that. I don't get why you cared so much about them.'

I can see he's not the only one who doesn't get it: Ez and Zak are curious, so is Jude. But when Jason talks about grief and loneliness, it feels familiar. It tugs at me. His choices about the family in Iowa weren't always smart, but I think I understand them.

Jason glances at the bathroom door. Water still runs in the sink on the other side. 'Apart from the seers in my family, the women in Iowa have been the only people who know what I am. Who I could talk to without pretending to be something I'm not. You've always lived with Rephaim. You have no idea what it's like to have to lie to everyone you meet.'

'They lied to you,' Rafa says. 'Fed you nothing but horror stories about us.' He digs his thumb into his shoulder, stretches his neck. He's stronger again since the shift from the storeroom.

'I'm not naïve, Rafa. I knew they had an agenda, I just didn't understand what it was. And I knew the Rephaim weren't all bad: I'd met Gabe and Jude.'

Ez goes to the bed and Maggie slides across so she can sit down. 'So, everything you learned about us came from Iowa, and they got their information from Brother Stephen . . . and then Mya,' Ez says and sits down. 'But how did Brother Stephen end up here in the first place?'

The bathroom door opens. Dani comes out, her cheeks pink and eyes clear. A waft of fruity soap follows her. She falters when she sees Rafa.

'Hi,' she says.

'Hi yourself.'

She crosses the room. Maria waits in the doorway, drying her hands. Dani stops right in front of him, tilts her face. The top of her curly head reaches his chest.

'You know, normally I'd be a little unhappy at having someone poking around in my brain.' He's curious, soft. 'I wouldn't recommend making a habit out of it. My head really isn't the place for impressionable girls.' He lowers himself to the floor. I do the same and Dani squeezes in between us.

'Is your chest okay?' she asks him.

'You saw that?'

She nods, solemn.

Rafa looks away, closes his eyes for a moment. 'What else?'

'What happened to Taya.' Her lip trembles. 'And I heard Bel say what he was going to do to Gaby if she went there. I didn't understand most of it . . .'

All the air is dragged out of me. Rafa leans back against the wall. For a second he's back in that room, or the room is in him. His eyes are distant; he won't look at me. And in his avoidance, I understand: Bel's taunting was explicit, horrific. Rafa's willingness to die in that farmhouse wasn't only to protect the Rephaim. He was willing to die there to make sure Bel could never get me in that room and do the things he planned.

Dani takes Rafa's hand—twice the size of hers—grips it tight. Brings him back from Iowa. 'Does it hurt?' She's focused on his T-shirt again, on the spot where Bel left his mark.

'It's not that bad. Here.' He lets go of her and pulls his T-shirt over his head. His chest is still bandaged. I lean around Dani and help Rafa unwind it. I peel away the dressing, aware everyone is watching. I'm trying not to think about touching his bare skin. The sight of his puckered flesh is like a bucket of cold water: the crescent moon, red and angry. The line slashing through it. Cruel punctuation. Maggie makes a strangled sound.

'Yeah, that's looking great,' Zak says.

Dani bites her lip. 'I'm glad that demon is dead.'

'Only fifty or so to go.' Rafa meets my eyes over the top of her head.

'Was Bel the worst?' she asks.

'No, kid. Zarael is. He makes Bel look house-trained.' Rafa puts his shirt back on.

I lean forward to pick up the bandage and my ponytail falls to one side. I feel something touch the scar on my neck—my old scar, from the accident. I flinch from habit.

'What happened to your Rephaim mark?' Dani's fingers are still in the air.

I roll up the bandage, wishing I hadn't recoiled at her touch. 'Bel put his blade through my neck last year. Apparently.'

'Oh.' She starts to sink into that guilty place she keeps for thoughts about Jude and me and last year, but then rebounds almost immediately. 'Jude, did your mark get scarred too?'

His fingers instinctively find the crescent moon on the nape on his neck. He kneels down and lifts his hair. Dani runs her fingertip over his mark, also scarred, but less hideous than mine.

'Huh.'

Jude lets his hair fall back into place. 'What are you thinking?'

'When you didn't come back last year and I couldn't feel you, I thought you were both dead. But you were alive, I just couldn't see you. So then I thought that whoever changed our memories must have hidden you from me. But now . . .' She chews on her thumbnail, looks older than her twelve years.

I glance at Ez. She didn't miss the significance of any of that. *Whoever changed our memories.*

'You think it might have something to do with our marks being defaced?' Jude asks. 'But what about Mya? You've never been able to see her.'

'She has a tattoo over hers. I saw it when she was fighting.'

'A tattoo would pierce the skin, so I guess that changes it.' Jude turns to Jason. 'Did the family encourage you to do anything to your mark?'

'No,' Jason says. 'But I saw that Celtic cross on Mya in Pan Beach and it's old. Dani's only twelve. There was nobody to hide from before she came along. It could just be a coincidence.'

I hate to say it, but someone has to. 'Unless the family received a revelation telling them to do it.'

Nobody answers. My bad knee is starting to ache. I get up and go over to the window. It's dark outside now. The cloister is bathed in faint pools of light. Two monks hurry along, heads turned towards each other in conversation.

'Out of curiosity,' Jude says to Dani, 'have you ever found a feather after one of your sessions? Or heard horns?'

Dani winds a curl around a finger while she thinks. 'Sometimes I smell incense.'

'It's time Dani and I left,' Maria says. She reaches for Dani, lifts her from the floor.

Jason is already nodding. 'Yes, she's done more than enough.'

'No, Jason, I want to stay with you.' Dani pulls away from her mother.

'You can, blossom, just not here. Maggie and I will take you and your mum wherever you want to go.'

'I want to stay with *all* of you.' She casts a meaningful glance at Rafa, Jude, and me. At Ez and Zak.

'Why?'

'I need to be where you all are. I feel it, here.' She puts her hand over her heart, looks at her mum. 'You know what I'm talking about.'

'Baby, you need to be sure you feel it and not just *want* to feel it,' Maria says. She and Dani exchange a long look.

'Mom, I promise this is where we're meant to be.'

Maria sighs, sits at the desk.

'Right then,' Jude says. 'We need to find out more about Michael.'

I grab the books from the desk and hand them around. 'This will be quicker if we all take one.' Maria is surprised when I offer her *Angels Through the Ages*. 'It'll give you something to do other than be annoyed at me.' I get a tight smile in return.

'Gaby,' Maggie says. 'Got a sec?'

I glance at Jude, but he's already lost in his book, and Rafa is listening to Dani explain about the time she saw him stalking me in the Pan Beach rainforest. 'Next door?'

We go into my room. Lamplight spills over the unmade

bed: the blanket scrunched up, mattress not quite straight, pillows scattered.

'Well, that answers one question,' Maggie says and I hear the smile in her voice as she closes the door behind us.

I start to straighten the bedding, feel heat in my cheeks. 'Which question would that be?'

'Whether or not you're any tidier away from home.'

I laugh and throw a pillow at her. She helps me make the bed and then we sit on it, face each other.

'So?' she asks gently. 'Did you two . . . ?'

I let my breath out, nod.

'And?'

'It was . . . intense.'

'In a good way?'

'Mind-blowing.' Just thinking about it makes me ache for him.

'Did he tell you what happened between you two . . . you know, before?'

I can't meet her eyes. 'I know I should've found all that out before jumping into bed with him but, Mags, I nearly lost him tonight.'

'Babe, I'm not judging you.' She touches my arm. 'It's between the two of you, nobody else.'

I nod, but like everything else in my life, it's not that simple.

'And have you seen the way he's looking at you now?

It's exactly how you want a guy to be after you've had sex: besotted.'

I choke-laugh. 'I think you're confusing Rafa with Jason.'

'Don't underestimate the effect you have on Rafa. We're talking about the guy who was willing to die tonight to keep you safe.'

I push away the memory of him bloodied and crumpled. The thought of it wrings me out. 'Have you spoken to your mum?'

'Yeah, I told her Jason and I were staying in the city for an extra night. She wasn't ecstatic about having to find someone for tomorrow's shift but she was okay. She likes Jason, so that helps.'

'How's he doing?'

'He keeps forgetting to breathe.' She reaches up and slides out the tie holding her ponytail in place. Blonde hair fans out around her shoulders. 'I've never seen him so uptight.'

'He's worried about Dani.'

'I know, but I keep telling him that Dani's got you guys looking out for her.'

'You honestly think that makes Jason feel she's safe?'

'It works for me.'

I stare at her. 'Mags, if it wasn't for us you'd be safe in Pan Beach, oblivious to the existence of demons and hellions and half-angel bastards. You wouldn't be hiding out in a medieval monastery in freezing mountains, worrying where the next threat's coming from.'

'True, but then I wouldn't have Jason in my life. Or you. And I wouldn't be in *Italy*.' She gives me a brave smile and that's when it hits me: she's the most courageous person here. Well, after Dani.

'Mags . . .'

'Shush.' She leans in and hugs me. I try to resist—I need to talk sense into her—but there's something so comforting about a Maggie hug. My throat closes over. And then, without warning, the last twelve hours catch up with me. Finding Jude. The attack. Rescuing Rafa. I honestly thought I was cried out . . . It takes a good thirty seconds to pull myself together, and even then I feel raw, wind-blasted.

'You know, before I met you I didn't hug and I didn't cry, and I didn't have deep and meaningful conversations about my *feelings*.'

She smiles, and this one is all warmth. 'Now you do all three—and kill creatures from hell with a shiny sword. You're like the poster child for paranormal self-development.'

My face is hot and my eyes sting but I laugh anyway.

'When was the last time you read the Book of Enoch?' Jude asks Ez as Maggie and I walk back in.

'Not for a couple of decades,' she says.

'It says it was the Archangel Michael who bound Semyaza and the Two Hundred.'

Rafa watches me sit down next to him, studies my face. He glances at Maggie and she gives him a reassuring smile.

'So,' Jude goes on, 'it must have been Michael's blood that confined them.'

'And if anyone was going to give humans instructions about blood wards . . .'

'It's just a theory.'

'What else did you find?' Ez asks.

Jude scans the page. 'The Archangel Gabriel was the one ordered to kill the bastards left behind—the Nephilim—and the women who gave birth to them.'

I clear my throat, check I'm together again. 'I thought he was the merciful one?'

'Not that day. This also says Semyaza taught the women charms and enchantments.'

'For what?'

'Doesn't say.'

Rafa shuts his book and tosses it aside. 'None of this is news. You knew that book inside out and it didn't answer any of your questions then.'

'We talked about this stuff?' Jude asks.

'Yeah, right. You had your existential debates with Mya, not me.'

A phone buzzes with a message. Ez checks her screen, smiles. 'Rafa, the crew is in the commissary waiting for you.'

'Excellent,' he says and stands up, holds a hand out for me. 'I could definitely go for a beer.'

A HARD-EARNED THIRST

The Outcasts cheer and whistle when we walk in. Jones reaches Rafa first.

'Looking good, dude.' They bump fists. 'Did you get any sleep?' He winks at me. Awesome. Everyone knows Rafa was in my room. In my bed.

'Yeah, some.' Rafa's eyes slide in my direction, check my reaction.

Jones is elbowed aside by Seth, who drags Rafa into a man hug. The Outcasts mill about, waiting to shake his hand or hug him. I catch a few glances in my direction from the girls—curious—and I can't help thinking about Daniel's jibe that I was the only Rephaite girl Rafa hadn't slept with. That turned out to be an exaggeration—at least in part. Still, in the last century or so there's a good chance he's been with most of the girls here, and of course there's Mya. But he's been away from all of them for the past year—I stop, remember to breathe. Let it go. None of that part of Rafa's past is news to me. I wish it didn't feel like such a big deal.

I move away to give everyone room. The only other people in the commissary aside from us are the kitchen staff. The chefs are preoccupied sautéing and steaming, banging and chopping. The smell of garlic and pancetta hangs in the air. It's dark outside, so I can't see anything beyond the windows. I could be facing sky, trees, or the mountains, it's impossible to tell. All I can see is my own reflection—and Ez walking my way.

'How are you?' she asks.

'Starving. When's dinner?' She tilts her head and I know the question wasn't about my appetite. I sigh. 'Are you going to tell me it's a bad idea—me and Rafa?'

'By my calculation it's about three decades overdue.' She smiles at my surprise. 'Oh, it's going to be messy, but you'll sort yourselves out.'

I shouldn't need her approval but I like having it. 'How long did it take you and Zak?'

Her face softens, a private smile. 'We've been *together* together for about twenty-five years, but it took us a good part of a century to figure out that's what we wanted. Or, more to the point, to have the courage to try something permanent.'

My eyes skim over the other Outcasts. They're all so

comfortable with each other, so at ease. 'Are there other couples like you guys?'

'No, we're the benchmark for longevity by at least two decades.'

Rafa is sitting on the edge of a table with Jude, surrounded by Outcasts. He's waiting for me to look at him and when I do, he widens his eyes like he needs rescuing.

'Come on,' Ez says and we move back into the throng. Jude makes room so I can sit between him and Rafa. I feel exposed, conspicuous.

'Any truth to the rumor Mya grabbed the old girl?' Jones asks.

'Yeah, Mya took Virginia,' Rafa says. 'We're waiting to hear from her.'

Not quite true, but close enough.

'What now?'

Rafa absently probes his chest through his T-shirt, around the tip of the crescent moon. 'Zarael's not going to roll over and take what happened in Iowa without retaliating. I wouldn't mind hanging around here for another hour or so, see how it plays out.'

'Are you staying?' Seth asks Jude.

Jude tips his head at me. 'We're here as long as Rafa is.'

'So now we've got both the women from that farmhouse,' Jones says. 'Do we know any more about them?'

'We know a bit.' It's Ez who answers. 'We know they've been tracking all of us from day one, and believe the

Archangel Michael is giving them instructions.'

The commissary is instantly still. It's like the archangel's name alone is enough to incapacitate the Outcasts. For a few long seconds, the only sound is the clatter from the kitchen.

Rafa rubs his jaw. 'It's probably a load of shit—'

'Were they involved with what happened to Jude and Gabe last year?'

'Doubtful,' Jude says. 'The family's more interested in keeping the Rephaim dysfunctional. They think we're the key to releasing the Fallen.'

'"We" as in us?' Jones asks, and gestures to the Outcasts.

'As in all of the Rephaim. United. They believe it's their sacred mission to keep us separated.'

'So storming out of here a decade ago was playing right into their hands?'

I look to the doorway. Taya stands there with Micah and Malachi. Her arm is in a sling, her hand heavily bandaged. The bruising on her face has faded, but now a scar follows her hairline from her temple to her jaw.

'Pretty much,' Jude says.

Taya walks towards us, slightly favoring her left leg. Deep shadows under her eyes stand out against translucent skin. She's delicate, almost see-through. 'How's the chest?' she asks Rafa.

'I won't make this year's Rephaite calendar. How's the hand?'

'Missing a finger.'

The Outcasts are wary, but there's no threat here from either side. Taya puts her good hand over the bandages covering her knuckles. 'Brother Ferro wants to get me a glove with a prosthetic finger. I'd rather learn to swing a sword better with four.'

'Of course,' Rafa says. 'That would be the hard way.' They smile at each other. Not glare. Not taunt. *Smile.* 'How much did you overhear?'

'Enough to know Virginia's gone.'

I finally look Micah in the eye. He's not happy, but he gives a tiny shake of his head, which I hope means he still hasn't mentioned to anyone *why* Mya took Virginia. I seriously owe that guy a beer. Maybe a keg.

'You might want to avoid Nathaniel,' Malachi says to me. 'He's not happy.'

'And Daniel?'

Malachi's lips twitch into a small smile. 'He scored points for sending me along to keep an eye on you.'

Micah tilts his head, gives me a look that says, *See—I know what I'm doing.*

'Did you catch up with Simon before you left the infirmary?' I ask Taya.

'Yeah. He needs to get home. All those boys do.'

I nod, but I can't see how it's any safer for them to be back in Pan Beach now. Especially not if Zarael's looking for payback.

'How's your shoulder?' Jude asks Taya. With all the trauma over her missing finger, I'd almost forgotten one of the Gatekeepers buried a sword in her shoulderblade at the Butlers' camp.

'So-so.' She heads over to our table and sits between Jude and me, as if it's the most natural thing in the world. 'I hear I missed a good brawl.'

Jones smirks. 'Yeah. It was a touching reunion.'

For a few seconds, nobody speaks. Taya clears her throat. 'Thanks for coming for us.' She says it quietly. 'Thanks for coming for me.'

'We tried patience,' I say, 'and then your finger turned up.'

She touches her bandaged hand again, almost involuntarily. 'The Five would've sent a team eventually.'

'Yeah,' Rafa says. 'And you still had nine fingers to get through.'

They share a look. Knowing. A decade of antagonism and recrimination between them dissolved: gone. They're tied together now, connected by something stronger.

'You guys hanging around?' Malachi asks.

Rafa nods. 'For the moment.'

'Nathaniel wants Virginia back. The room might be gone, but he still needs to know how they built it. And he'll want to talk to you. And Gabe and Jude.'

'Something to look forward to.' Rafa gestures to the back of the room. 'Is the bar open yet?'

Jude and Ez pull tables together and a few minutes later we're gathered around them, beers in hand. Rafa sits next to me, lets his knee rest against mine. It anchors me.

'What happened in there?' Jones asks the question carefully, respectfully. Rafa meets Taya's eyes. It takes him a few seconds to answer.

'As soon as we arrived in that room, Bel stabbed me again. And then Taya somehow managed to shift. Took them by surprise. I don't think they expected us to be able to get around in there.'

'Yeah,' she says, deadpan, 'it bought us all of a few seconds.'

'Long enough for you to rip the steel out of my gut mid-shift and start healing me.' He shakes his head. 'I've never seen anything like it.'

Taya shrugs off the compliment. 'We managed to shift half a dozen times—mended the worst of the initial damage—before they got syringes into us.'

'And then what?' Malachi asks.

'Zarael waited until we were conscious enough to feel pain, and then the real fun began.' She glances at Rafa. 'Neither of us could shift after that.'

Nobody speaks for a long moment.

'It's a shame you missed the best part.' Rafa squeezes my thigh under the table and recounts how Bel lost his head. Or at least the parts he remembers.

'How did you get out?' The question comes from a wiry

girl with short strawberry blonde hair whose name I can't remember. 'We came into the house to help, but Leon got that iron door shut again. We thought you were screwed.'

I go blank. I hadn't realized other Outcasts were inside the house. It means they know we got out of that room while it was sealed.

'Mya broke the wards with blood,' Ez says.

A collective pause. 'How?'

'Long story.' Ez drags her plait over her shoulder and fiddles with the leather tie. Meets my eyes, then Micah's. She's going to tell the Outcasts the truth. Even with Taya and Malachi in the room.

'Well, well, look who it is.' Jones is grinning at someone behind me. Daisy. 'You crossing over to the dark side finally?'

Ez lets her breath out, pushes her hair back over her shoulder.

'In your dreams,' Daisy says. She searches for Taya, relaxes a fraction when she finds her. 'Welcome home.' She nods at Rafa. 'You too.'

'We could've used you and those twin-sided sais in Iowa,' Jude says.

Something crosses Daisy's face—regret? 'I'm not like you: I like having a home. Not all of us can get away with defying Daniel.' She glances at Malachi.

'Come on Desdemona.' Jones pulls out a chair for her. 'Have a drink with us.'

Conversation fragments around us. Next to me, Rafa is

talking to Seth. Occasionally he taps the side of his boot on mine. I bump my knee against his.

'You're as bad as the Five, not telling them the truth,' Micah says quietly.

Jude peels a strip off the label of his Italian beer and glances down the table at Daisy. 'You think now's the time?

'Don't judge her. She's just trying to play this straight.'

'Which would mean telling Daniel anything she hears in here.'

'And Taya and Malachi won't?'

'You tell me.'

Right now they're deep in conversation with Ez, Zak, and an Outcast with a shaved head and multiple piercings. Jude rolls the wet beer label into a tight ball. 'What are the chances of us getting more time with Brother Stephen?'

'Really? Not enough crap going on for you right now?' Micah lifts his bottle, drains it, and then sighs. 'He'll be back in his cell by now.'

I nearly choke on my mouthful. 'They locked him up? I thought he didn't tell them anything?'

'He didn't. He's in the tiny wardrobe he calls his room. In a monastery they're called cells.'

Oh. I think I knew that.

'And if you're serious, we should go now before the rest of the Sanctuary starts filing in here for *aperitivo*.'

Rafa leans back as if he's stretching and rests his arm along the top of my chair. 'I'm in,' he says. 'I definitely want a chat with that sly old man before anyone else gets to him.'

FAMILY SECRETS

'We'll be back in a minute,' Rafa says to the gathering. 'Keep the beer coming.'

Outside, it's me, Jude, Rafa, and Micah. The wind whispers through the lavender, cold and persistent. Ez joins us about ten seconds later. 'Zak's keeping an eye on things in there.'

She and Micah lead us towards the front of the monastery, closer to the parking lot and the public chapel. The wind has picked up again and icy air bites my cheeks. Rafa and I walk shoulder-to-shoulder; his fingers find mine. We're passing along a cloister—yet another one—under lamps hung from rusty chains. The cobblestones are uneven here and the stone columns streaked black. This end of the Sanctuary is nowhere near as well kept as the rest of the place.

We're a little conspicuous moving along in our small

pack, but we don't come across anyone else—Rephaite or otherwise. We slip inside a building covered in a creeper vine and climb a steep, narrow staircase. The paint on the walls is peeling, cobwebs hang from the cornices. It's drafty, much colder than our building.

Jude picks at the flaking paint. 'Nice. The monks live in squalor while the Rephaim are in luxury a stone's throw away.'

'Steady on,' Micah says over his shoulder. 'The brothers have taken a vow of poverty. They don't want luxury.'

'Did anyone ask them?'

We reach the upper floor and Micah pauses in the gloomy hallway.

'You don't have to be here,' I say.

He lifts one shoulder, lets it drop. 'I'm up to my neck in this now so I may as well stay in the loop. And I'm not done with the good brother either.'

Brother Stephen's room is down the far end of the hallway. Micah knocks twice, waits. There's a cough and shuffling on the other side, and then the door opens. It catches on the carpet. The monk takes in the sight of the five of us and the color leaves his face.

'We're not here to hurt you,' Ez says.

He cradles his broken arm, draws a shallow breath and steps aside.

The room is so narrow we have to line up with our backs against the wall, wedged beside Brother Stephen's bed. It has a wardrobe, a small side table, shelves stacked with tatty books, and a tiny window. A single bulb hangs on exposed wiring. I smell camphor and liniment, and the oranges he has in a bowl by his bedside. I rub my arms through my sweater. How does he not freeze in here?

'You told Mya we knew the truth about her,' I say.

His shoulders are more stooped now, his movements slower. The dressing on his neck wound is puckered, matching his folded skin.

'She would have come for Virginia eventually. I made sure there was no violence involved.'

'What did you tell Daniel?'

'I told him the truth: that there was nothing I could do to stop her. He has no reason not to believe me.' He clasps his bony hands together—awkward with his sling—and lifts them towards Micah in a gesture of gratitude.

'How does lying fit with the oaths you've taken here?' Jude asks.

'I do not lie.'

'There are still lies of omission.'

'That is between me and God.'

Rafa knocks his boot against the monk's bed frame. 'You should've gone with Mya.'

Brother Stephen lowers himself onto the mattress, grimacing as he takes his weight on his good wrist. The springs squeak. 'Where would I go? Iowa? Los Angeles? I have known no other home but this since I was fifteen.'

'It's only a matter of time before it all comes out.'

The monk closes his eyes. 'I have served God to the best of my ability and will accept whatever consequences come.'

Micah glances around the room, the sparseness. 'How do you get information to your family?'

A deep sigh escapes Brother Stephen, like all the air is leaving him. Ez watches him in silence, her expression guarded.

'When I was first here, my mother or my sister would come to Italy once a year from America. I would arrange to meet them when it was my turn to collect supplies from the village.'

'How do you do it now?'

'Mobile phone.'

Of course.

'I would tell them about Nathaniel and what was happening here: training, missions, how the Rephaim were divided into different specialities.' He speaks slowly, as if every word costs him energy. 'In recent decades it has been about building the photo library. Understanding who is who and what each of your strengths are.'

'Why?'

His mouth twists a little. 'To better understand the enemy.'

'You think we're your enemy?' Micah sounds genuinely hurt.

'No, Micah,' Brother Stephen says, 'I have not thought so for some time.'

'But that didn't stop you betraying us.'

'I always believed I could honor the oaths made to this family, and to my own. In sixty years I have done nothing to endanger the Rephaim.'

'What about that room?'

The monk brushes his gnarled fingers over the blanket on his bed. 'I was not aware it existed. Virginia and Mya did not tell me, for my own safety.'

'Your family sent Mya here to tear us apart,' Micah says. 'Why a decade ago? Why not send her last century?'

'Because my cousin was already here in the brother-hood.'

'Who?'

He hesitates. 'Roberto.'

'Brother Roberto was a traitor too?' Micah's jaw tightens.

'Brother Roberto was a loyal member of this order. He was also a member of our family.'

'But your family was in Iowa. How did he end up in Italy?'

The monk points a trembling finger to a glass of water, half-full, on his bedside table. Ez hands it to him. The water sloshes up the sides as he raises it to his lips. He takes a sip and hands it back to her.

'Nathaniel came looking for the bastard child conceived

in our part of the world. He posed as an itinerant priest offering absolution. My great-grandmother had foreseen that Nathaniel would visit, so my great-grandfather, Heinrich, was prepared. He—'

'Was Heinrich the Lutheran minister?' I ask.

Brother Stephen falters. 'Yes.' He swallows. 'He told Nathaniel his daughter Martha had lain with a fallen angel, but that both she and the bastard offspring had died in childbirth. Heinrich offered up Roberto to serve, in whatever capacity Nathaniel saw fit, as an act of atonement for Martha's sin. Nathaniel brought him here. And when Roberto could no longer serve, I was sent to replace him.'

'So,' Micah says, 'first Roberto, then you, fed information back to your family and they plotted against us?'

'No, Micah, we gathered information. And we waited for signs.' He raises his watery eyes. 'And now I am old. My days here will come to an end soon. That is why Mya finally put herself in Nathaniel's path, in preparation for my passing. Her commission was to bide her time, become a trusted part of this society; work her way onto the Council of Five and slowly sow seeds of dissent.' He sighs. 'Not incite a rebellion in less than a year.'

'What happened to Mya's mother?' I ask. 'Martha?'

The lines around Brother Stephen's lips tighten.

'*Did* she die in childbirth?'

A long pause. 'She did not.' He closes his eyes, the paper-thin folds of skin momentarily shielding him from us.

'Brother,' Jude says. 'If your family receives messages from an archangel we need to understand how—and why.'

The monk meets his eyes. 'Dear Judah. Even without the knowledge of your past you still seek the truth. I have always admired that about you, even if your way of going about it was not always the most . . . efficient.'

I lower myself beside Brother Stephen. The mattress is hard, unforgiving. 'What happened to her?'

'I only know the stories as they were told to me.' He tries to straighten, but pain, or the weight of the moment, keeps him hunched. 'You need to understand, Martha was my great-grandfather's favorite daughter. Every day at dusk she walked the dogs between the crops and he would wait on the porch for her. On the Day of Great Transgression, the dogs returned in the darkness without her. Heinrich saw a strange light in the fields. The light was gone by the time he found her alone, lacing up her dress.'

'The angel just left her there to deal with him?'

'That is their nature, Judah. The Fallen do not take responsibility for their actions.'

'Did your great-grandfather believe it was an angel?'

'It would have been better for her if he had not. A tryst with a secret lover might have broken his heart, but it would not have burned his soul. Heinrich knew that an angel who lay with a human could only be among the Fallen, which meant both she and any resulting child would be despised in heaven.'

I run my fingertips across the rough wool of his bed cover. 'That's a big leap—that she would fall pregnant.'

'Heinrich was familiar with the Book of Enoch; he knew the last time Semyaza and the Fallen lay with women there were many offspring.'

'But why did he assume the child would be despised in heaven?' Jude presses. 'Everyone is so convinced we're abominations, but where is it written? Where's the evidence? Beyond the paranoia of a shamed minister and the guilt of the fallen angel who created this place?'

'Judah,' Brother Stephen says. 'The last time human-angel hybrids walked the earth, the archangels wiped them from existence.'

'Oh.' Jude breaks eye contact with him. He looks at me and then away.

'Hang on,' I say, 'I thought we could only die if we'—I make a slicing action across my throat—'and didn't the Nephilim die in a flood?'

'No.' It's Micah who answers. 'They were all executed by the Garrison before the waters rose.'

Executed. My insides quiver.

'Back to Martha?' Ez prompts and Brother Stephen nods, slowly.

'She *was* pregnant. Heinrich was willing to sacrifice his beloved eldest daughter to prevent her bastard coming into the world, but my great-grandmother threatened to starve herself if he did. So he bided his time. He knew both had to die: Martha for her sin, and the offspring for existing. He waited until the child was born and then he took his daughter's life.' His chin trembles. 'He and his brothers took the body to the field and performed a sanctifying ritual before cremating her body. They were afraid if they buried Martha any other way, her defilement would scorch the earth and kill the crops.'

I glance at Rafa and know we're seeing the same thing: the photos from the journal showing each stage of the burning and burial; of those men in their waistcoats and top hats in the cornfield, so grim. So self-righteous. I get a weird feeling in my chest.

'Afterwards he took the baby, Mya, to the altar in the old church.' Brother Stephen touches the fine fabric of his sling. 'Roberto told me that my great-grandfather cut her to see if she would bleed.'

'Oh my god.' Ez finds her voice. 'And you think *we're* the abomination?'

'That's when my great-grandmother fell to the ground and received the first revelation: the child was not the only one born to a fallen angel that month and our family, alone among all of those afflicted, had been anointed to keep the offspring of the Fallen separated. The baby in her husband's hands was the key to our bloodline fulfilling that destiny.'

'And what about Mya?' Ez says. 'How did she feel about that destiny when she was old enough to understand it?'

'Mya has had . . . a difficult time.'

'She told me about . . .' Ez hesitates. 'An incident when she was seventeen . . .'

Brother Stephen blanches. 'I am forever shamed that my kin were responsible for what happened that day. Heinrich overlooked it because the attack revealed that Mya had inherited skills from her Fallen sire.'

Mya told Ez the truth: that her cousins tried to rape her and the trauma of it triggered her first shift. Except she didn't leave home after it happened, like she told Ez. She lived for another century or so with the family who thought she was an abomination.

'How many were there?' Ez asks quietly.

Brother Stephen drops his chin to his chest. 'Four.'

I feel sick. Ez turns away. She's heard enough.

'Great-grandmother forbade any male in the family to have contact with her after that. The only exception was Roberto, and then me, but only once I had made my vows of celibacy and was accepted into the Order here.'

'Your great-grandmother must have had some clout,' I say.

'Roberto was entrenched at the Sanctuary by then. She threatened to get a message to him—have him tell Nathaniel about Mya. She was prepared for our family to forgo our destiny if she couldn't keep Mya safe from her own kin. But my great-grandmother could not undo the damage done.' He coughs, and his thin shoulders spasm.

'Mya was wild, and so angry. She fought with my great-grandmother, my grandmother, my mother, and then Virginia. She would disappear for weeks at a time, and then come home with stories of her promiscuity. Worst of all, she burned down the family church . . .'

I can't get a handle on how to feel about Mya. On the one hand, there's all the grief she's given me in the last few days. On the other, she's saved my life. Twice. I'm struggling to reconcile the Mya Brother Stephen's talking about with the Mya I saw in LA. I've experienced a few sides of her now but nothing to make me question her loyalty to the Outcasts—especially Jude. Has that all been a lie?

'Brother,' Micah says quietly. 'Do you think we all deserve to die?'

He struggles to straighten his spine, his eyes shining. 'I have lived among you for sixty-five years, Micah. I have seen the good and the bad. I have seen the confusion and the longing for answers. I believe the Fallen are the ones who bear the sin, not their offspring. No. I do not wish to see you dead or consigned to a fiery prison in the depths of hell.' He looks at me and then Jude. 'Regardless of what you have or haven't done.'

A gust outside rattles the latch on his window.

'Do you think Nathaniel's right—that delivering the Fallen to the Garrison will redeem us?' Jude is quieter now. 'Do you believe the only reason we've been allowed to live is to prove we're useful?'

The monk shakes his head, slowly. 'I don't know. But take comfort in the fact that God is merciful.'

Jude gives a short laugh. 'Maybe. But it's not sounding too much like the Garrison is.'

We head back to the commissary in silence. Wind whips around the cloister, carrying rain-sodden pine needles and dead flowers. The lamps swing; pools of light sway over cobblestones in a weirdly synchronized dance. Chains creak.

'She cares about us,' Ez says.

Nobody answers, our footsteps muffled by the wind.

'We've lived and fought beside her for more than a decade. We *know* her.'

'Clearly not,' Rafa says. He was conspicuously quiet in the monk's room. I have no idea what he's thinking.

'How many times over the years has she had the chance to hurt us? She planned our missions, Rafa, she could've led us into a trap a hundred times over. We were never coming back here, with or without her, so why stay with us if all she wants is to see us destroyed?'

We pass into the main piazza. We're almost back at the commissary.

Rafa shoves his hands in his pockets. 'Then why won't she talk to us and tell us what the hell is going on?'

'Because she doesn't think anyone wants to hear her side of the story,' Jude says. The light crosses his face and I can see his own guilt again.

'At least she knows what she's done,' I say, 'which is one up on us. For all we know—'

A blast knocks me off my feet.

I land on my backside so hard my teeth bang together. My ears thud. I sit up, arms aching and hands grazed. Confused. The night spins around me. Three more blasts— I feel them through my palms. The cloisters shimmer, orange and yellow. Something metallic coats my tongue. There's grit in my mouth. I try to focus on the building ahead, but the image won't sharpen. And then I understand.

The commissary is on fire.

OUT OF THE DARK AGES

'What the fuck?' Rafa springs to his feet, drags me to mine. And then we're running. Jude is with us, and Micah. Ez is gone, shifted; already in the commissary. Where we left Zak. And Jones. And Taya. And everyone.

Our boots pound on gravel where gravel shouldn't be. I breathe in dust and ash, stumble over a chunk of stone in the middle of the cloister. The air is thick, toxic. There's shouting now. The wind brings a wave of heat, the smell of burning plastic. My mind is blank. We burst through the commissary doors and skid to a stop. The scene is too much to take in—I can only process it in fragments.

The lights, out; windows, gone.

Blood. Glass. Groaning.

Tables and chairs overturned, scattered.

The kitchen, on fire. Men in white, shouting, blasting

away with fire extinguishers. The cloying smell of gas.

The silhouette of armed Rephaim, braced in front of jagged glass. Facing the night. Buffeted by cold wind.

And outside, white hair floats in the air like seaweed. Gatekeepers, everywhere. The black forest behind them.

Heat and smoke.

Fear.

Zarael. Inky hair against the shadowy forest. Face lit orange, grinning.

Another Gatekeeper—Leon—with a rocket launcher on his shoulder. Sleeker, shinier than ours. Russian lettering. Blue smoke twists in the wind behind and above him.

'Thank you for the inspiration,' Zarael calls out. His charred voice carries over the wind, the shouting, the hungry fire. 'Sometimes we overlook the obvious.' He nods to Leon.

'Incoming!' someone shouts and the Rephaim dive in opposite directions, parting like the Red Sea. Rafa pushes me down, covers my body with his. A rush of scorching heat passes over us and then, *whump.* The blast fills my ears, shakes my bones. Glass shatters. Another blast, louder. Hotter. Debris rains down around us. Jude is sprawled next to me, arms over his head protectively. An object, sharp and cold, digs into my hip. A fork.

'What's exploding?' Jude yells.

'Gas lines in the kitchen.' Rafa hauls me up. 'You okay?' But his eyes are already back on the demons beyond the gaping hole in the Sanctuary wall. Rephaim scramble to their feet around us. I can't find Ez or Zak. Or anyone. They're all shadowy figures bleeding into the darkness outside.

My stomach drops.

'Stay inside!' Daniel is at the back of the room, flanked by more Rephaim than I can count. Blades glint in violent orange light. Micah's with him—I didn't realize he'd left us. He jogs over, tosses swords to Rafa and Jude and then me. The hilt is rough, unfamiliar, but comforting.

'What are we waiting for?' Taya calls to Daniel. A sword hangs in her left hand, awkward. Malachi is at her side. I scour the shadows around them, no sign of Ez or Zak. A stab of fear.

'Do you think they've broken the wards?' I ask Rafa. My throat is cracked.

'I don't know—'

A Gatekeeper charges at the opening, sword drawn.

'Hold!' Daniel shouts. Beside me, I feel Rafa strain against the order. Combustible.

The demon grins and leaps at the opening in the commissary and—*thunk*. He bounces off something we can't see. And then he's flat on his back in the pine needles.

'Now,' Daniel shouts. 'Defend the Sanctuary and get that launcher. Retreat as necessary.'

Zarael throws his head back. 'Reload!'

There's too much happening. I can't form a coherent thought.

'Stick with me,' Rafa says and takes off. Jude and I glance at each other and then we're running after him. I dodge a table, jump an overturned chair. Vaguely wonder if Rafa is fit to fight Gatekeepers, if Jude is ready to face them again so soon after Iowa. If I am. None of it matters: it's happening anyway. My heart is in my throat. I strangle the katana. Smoke stings my eyes, burns my nostrils. I can do this. I have to do this. Everyone I care about is within these walls. Maggie. Oh shit.

Don't think.

Rafa leaps through the gaping window first. He blocks a strike before his feet hit the ground. I have a split second to take in the seething mass of Rephaim and demons and then I'm outside, on the wrong side of Nathaniel's wards.

'On your left,' Jude shouts.

I turn in time to see the Gatekeeper charge, eyes blazing, steel arcing down towards my face. I block it and my knees buckle. And then—finally—a blast of adrenaline. I burn with it, and the Rephaite strength it brings. I push back against the blade as Jude swings at the demon. The Gatekeeper spins and slashes, lightning fast. I strike again. Block. Jude strikes. Block. Sounds of fighting all around us, a blur of movement in my peripheral vision. We fall into a rhythm of attack and defense, drive the demon away from the building. Jude is intense, grim. Nimble.

A snarl behind me. A hellion.

Jude catches a glimpse of it over my shoulder as he ducks another attacking swing. I spin, see the hell-beast, all seven feet of it. I register yellow eyes and leathery skin over thick muscles before my eyes drop to the stump hanging from its left shoulder. It's come for me. I took the rest of that limb when it was trying to tear Daisy apart at the cabin on Tuesday night. It still has a mouthful of long teeth and one good hand with razor sharp talons. The bite above my collarbone flares white-hot. I glance over my shoulder. Jude is working double-time to keep the demon focused on him and not me. I shouldn't leave him alone. I should—

The hellion charges.

I remember the cage. My heart smashes against my ribs. I know what to do. I've done it before: hamstring it. It lumbers at me. Wait. *Wait.* Now.

The hell-beast leaves the ground the same time I launch myself sideways. Too late, I realize it's guessed my move or I telegraphed it. I make a split-second decision and change my grip on my katana. I drive my blade into its stomach at the same instant pain sears across my chest. I ignore it and use the beast's momentum to direct its bulk away from me. It lands heavily, taking my sword with it. I land on a bed of pine needles. I'm not pinned by the hellion, thank god, but shards of pain radiate up my neck, down my arms. I try to get up too quick. The forest reels, I stagger sideways, touch my chest. My hoodie is torn, bloodied. It hurts, but not like in the cage. The ground settles. The fire and fighting and chaos come back into focus. The hellion is trying to sit. I scramble to pull the blade free. I feel it slide back through flesh and tendons, almost gag. When I turn, sword raised to finish it off, a Gatekeeper is between the hellion and me. Our eyes meet—his flickering orange, full of violence—and I swing down. By the time the blade strikes where the demon should have been, he and the hellion are gone. I stumble forward into empty air, barely keep my feet.

It's not over.

Jude.

He's still holding his own against the Gatekeeper, further into the forest now. I risk a quick look around. Rafa and Micah are tag-teaming against Zarael. Ez— thank god she's okay—and Taya are side by side, fighting off a hellion and a Gatekeeper. I see red hair: Uri or Daisy, I can't tell. There are too many moving bodies between them and me. The forest writhes and seethes. We have more numbers but the Gatekeepers are so freaking *fast*.

And then the air is hot, crackling, blasting the side of my face. Another rocket. The explosion knocks me off my feet. Drives the wind out of me. I taste dirt. Grass. Pine needles. My ribs throb. My chest burns. I roll over, catch a glimmer of something in the tree above.

Leon. Reloading.

'Up there!' I raise the tip of my katana in Leon's direction and then run to help Jude. I'm two steps away when another Gatekeeper appears. I block a blow aimed for the back of Jude's head, kick out the demon's knee. I spin, cover Jude. The demon lunges again. I swing hard at his hip, force him to block me.

Where the hell is Nathaniel?

Jude and I are fighting back-to-back now, fending off attacks from both sides. Protecting each other. My arms ache. My lungs are about to burst. The scratches across my chest sting and tear with each swing and thrust. The tang of blood and sweat permeates the smoke. And yet, fighting beside Jude—the rhythm of it—feels familiar in a way nothing has since I found out I was Rephaite.

Behind me in the Sanctuary, something heavy collapses.

Jude takes a hit and slams into me. 'Shit, sorry.' We keep fighting. But I don't know how much longer we can keep this up.

And then the light changes. The forest is steadily bathed in blue-white light, chasing away the shadows and growing in intensity until my eyes burn and I have to shield them, even at the risk of it costing me my head. The Gatekeeper in front of me howls. I try to peer through my fingers, see enough to know the demon has gone, but it's too bright. Jude and I lean into each other. We're both panting, struggling for air. The light is unbearable, forcing its way between my fingers and under my eyelids. A gust of wind flattens my hair, whips pine needles against my shins. I hear shouting. And then everything eases a little. I squint, try to see.

The forest is bathed in a preternatural glow.

'Holy shit,' Jude whispers. I look up and forget to breathe. It's Nathaniel.

He's flying.

NEW TERRITORY

Of course he can fly: he has wings. I gape anyway.

Nathaniel swoops over us again, wings beating slowly. Stirring up the forest floor. He's shining like he was on the mountain when he drove the demons back at the cabins. It's had the same effect here: Zarael is gone. So are his horde and their hellions.

The commissary is a furnace, roaring and hungry. Rephaim are everywhere: limping to each other, climbing up from the dirt, looking around—ready to shift and heal but waiting for permission. There are sirens now, faint, distant.

Rafa hobbles over to me, a palm pressed to his abdomen. Leaves stick out of his hair, cling to his clothes.

'You all right?' I ask, but he's distracted by my tattered hoodie.

'What happened?'

'I got clawed, not as bad as last time. Are you all right?'
I repeat.

'I might have re-torn something, but I'm fine.' Rafa
gives Jude a quick once-over and nods, satisfied that my
brother is in one piece. He reaches behind him and pulls
the antique knife from his jeans. It's still in its sheath,
covered in blood. 'Got into a tight spot and had to use
this.' A quick grin. 'Protected the blade, though.'

Nathaniel is coming around again. He flies lower and
his wings beat backwards as he approaches the ground.
He's walking by the time he touches down, a seamless,
fluid transition. The wings fold behind him and disappear.

'Status report,' he says to nobody in particular.

Daniel jogs over, sleeves rolled up, shirt smeared with
dirt. Sword slick and dark. 'All accounted for.'

Everyone is okay—unless he's not counting Outcasts.

'Let them heal,' Nathaniel says and Daniel gives the
order.

'Have you seen Zak?' I ask Rafa. I touch the wound on
my chest. It's stinging like crazy.

Rafa scans the forest. 'Ah, crap.'

Two figures are huddled over a third at the base of a
pine tree. My heart lurches. Please no, please no . . .

Ez and Jones are trying to get their arms under Zak.
His broad shoulders sag. His thick hair is matted with
blood. Eyes closed.

'Bloody hell,' Jude says when we get close.

'He's fine, he's fine.' I say it as much to myself as to him. Where are the healers? The last time the Sanctuary Rephaim fought demons, the soldiers not on rotation healed the injured. But everyone who could swing a sword was out here defending the Sanctuary, so tonight the injured have to heal each other.

'He's unconscious,' Ez says and lifts her face. Blood trickles from a split above her eyebrow. Her eyes are wide, worried, but she's trying to keep it together. 'I need to get him to Brother Ferro.'

Rafa kneels but she puts out a hand to stop him helping. 'You don't have the strength to spare.'

'I do.' Daisy is behind me, twin-bladed daggers still in each hand. The sirens are closer.

Ez nods. 'Thank you.'

'This is bad,' Jones says and then the four of them disappear. I don't know if he means Zak's injuries or the fact Zarael's figured out modern weapons can damage the Sanctuary. How much of the place does he have to destroy before the wards break?

Calista, Uri, and Daniel are deep in discussion with Nathaniel, their faces lit by the blaze. Calista looks up, sees us. 'This is what happens when we break ranks and act on impulse,' she says.

'You think this is *our* fault?' Anger burns through my worry over Zak.

'If you hadn't destroyed that house, Zarael would never have thought to use a rocket launcher on the Sanctuary.'

'Then he must be the dumbest demon this side of hell.'

'You pushed him to the point where he thought it was a viable option.'

She says something to the others, and then all four of them walk towards us. I meet them halfway, hear footsteps behind me. 'We've got your back,' Jude says. I know without looking that Rafa's with him.

I point at Nathaniel. 'You're just upset that you didn't get to keep the iron room. But if you'd done in Iowa what you did here tonight, we could have rescued Rafa and Taya with a lot less stress and you could've seen that room for yourself.'

'You did not have to destroy the farmhouse today,' Nathaniel says.

'We should have left the threat to hang over all our heads? Didn't you hear what was going on in that place?'

'We could have returned to destroy it if and when the Garrison commanded me to do so.'

'The Garrison? Seriously, Nathaniel, when was the last time you even heard from them?'

'I do not have time to argue with you, Gabriella. I must prepare the brothers before they speak with the fire brigade.' He shifts before I can push the point.

'I really expected more from you, even without your memories.'

'That's enough, Calista,' Daniel says before I can bite back. 'Emotions are running a little high right now. Let's not make this any worse.'

Another explosion in the commissary. We all flinch. It's a war zone, all smoke and flames and rubble.

Rafa catches Daniel's eye. 'When's the debrief?'

Daniel checks his watch. 'Let's make it twenty minutes. You and your people should be there.' He nods at me and then shifts without warning. Calista scowls and does the same. Yep, the courtesies are out the window now.

Jude scans the shadows beyond the glow of the fire. 'What about Zarael?'

I think about how many rockets there are in the world—and how easily Leon could get them.

Rafa shakes his head. 'He won't be back tonight. Not after he and the horde scored a full dose of Nathaniel.'

'What *was* that?' Jude asks.

'Angel mojo. It's usually deadly to pit scum, but after his own stint downstairs Nathaniel's only got enough juice to burn their eyes. They'll recover, but it'll take a day or so.'

'Why would they risk Nathaniel doing that to them?'

'They know he's slow to get involved.'

Another blast from the house and a ball of fire spews out of the gaping window, driving us further back. The Sanctuary was supposed to be the one place the Rephaim would always be safe. It was—

'Maggie.' Shit. Shit. Shit. I have to get to her.

'Gaby, wait—'

I feel the pull before I realize I'm even trying to shift, and then I'm in the maelstrom. Right in the thick of it. Alone. My skin feels like it's being stretched from my body, my hair pulled. Sleet hits me from impossible angles. Focus, focus. I think of Maggie. The room. The room. Beige walls, beige carpet. Warm air—

My knees slam into something and I pitch forward into a soft landing. The wind is gone; so is the ice. I'm dry and the air is toasty. I finally stop moving. I open my eyes and the walls swerve by once, twice and then stop. It's Jude's room, but it's empty. I know it's Jude's room because his books are still scattered on the blanket next to me.

'What the fuck, Gaby!'

Rafa and Jude are standing by the window.

'You could've ended up anywhere.' Rafa is rattled. Jude's not much happier.

I roll over and sit up. 'But I didn't—I'm here. And they're not.'

Jude turns to the window, checks outside. The commissary is down the other end. The air in here smells faintly of smoke. 'They would've heard the explosions,' Jude says. 'Jason would have had them gone three seconds later.'

I flop back on the bed. Adrenaline burns through me. My sword is still caked with whatever black gunk runs through hellions. It's all over the blanket now. Sirens, muted through thick glass, have reached the front parking lot. I close my eyes, feel the battle settling into my body, becoming part of me. But I don't want it to be part of me. I'm tired of fighting for my life, of fearing for everyone I care about.

A weight settles next to me on the mattress. 'You scared the shit out of me.' Rafa's voice is tight. I open my eyes, see the tension in his face. He offers a hand and I let him pull me to a sitting position. 'How about you try *calling* Margaret.'

I feel for my phone. Incredibly, it's in my back pocket, intact. My fingers shake but I manage to call up Maggie's number.

'Gaby,' she says before it's even rung at my end. 'Are you okay? What happened?'

I explain.

'I thought . . . I didn't know . . .'

'I know, I'm sorry. Where are you?'

'Rome. It's—Oh. Jason wants to speak to you.'

He comes on the line and I tell him what's been happening here.

'Is it safe?' he asks.

'As much as it ever was.'

'Dani is insisting on coming back.' He doesn't hide his frustration. 'There's no talking sense to her when she's like this, but I'm not bringing her to you if the wards are down.'

'They held, Jason. We saw a Gatekeeper hit an invisible barrier. They still can't get in, at least for now.'

A terse sigh. 'Fine.' The phone disconnects and then

the four of them materialize in the middle of the room: Jason, Maggie, Dani, and Maria.

'Gabe,' Dani says. 'I think I—' Her eyes roll back in her head and her body goes limp. Jude lunges forward and catches her before she hits the carpet.

'Oh god.' Maria drops to her knees beside them. She presses her fingers on Dani's neck. 'Her pulse is crazy. Everything is so much more extreme for her in this damned place.'

'What's happening?' Jude asks, alarmed.

'It's a vision.'

I brace myself for Dani to start convulsing or vomiting or something, but she stays slumped in Jude's arms as if she's asleep. He sits down on the bed, carefully holds her across his lap. I can't bring myself to look at Jason.

'How long does this usually last?' I feel a thread of panic. What if she doesn't wake up? Maybe this has been too much for her. Maybe I've done irreparable damage asking her to project her mind into a room full of demons. We wait in silence. It could be a minute, it could be five. The thread wraps around me, pulls tight. And then Dani's eyelids flutter open.

She frowns, swallows. Her eyes are bleary, as if she's been in a deep sleep for hours. She focuses on Jude and then sits up so fast she almost head-butts him. 'Gabe.'

'I'm here, Dani. What did you see?'

'Zarael and the Gatekeepers.'

'Are they coming back here?'

'No. They're going to Pan Beach.'

I can't breathe. 'How many?'

She squeezes her eyes closed and her lower lip trembles.

'All of them.'

A NEW LINE IN THE SAND

I can't stand still.

I fidget with the leather on my sword hilt. Toss the katana from hand to hand. Tap the flat of the blade against my calf.

'Calm down,' Rafa says. I'm between him and Jude. The Outcasts are here in the chapterhouse too, except for Zak and Ez: Zak's still in the infirmary, Ez at his side.

'Yeah,' I say, 'because you're an expert at patience.'

'Which is why I look to you to set the example.'

'Oh, fuck off.'

His mouth quirks.

'You two all right there?' Jude asks.

'Yeah,' Rafa says. 'Baiting your sister has always been the best way to distract her when she's wound this tight.'

We're waiting to be debriefed. It's been twenty-five

minutes. The mood in here is pensive, the chatter low and intense. Daniel, Uri, and Calista are on the dais, their backs to us. Taya and Malachi are in the middle of a crowd of Sanctuary Rephaim. Everyone's cleaned up and bandaged. My chest is tender, but not too bad thanks to a shift with Rafa. Just what I needed: more scars.

At the other end of the Sanctuary, fire fighters are battling the blaze in the commissary; as far as they know, the only other people on the grounds are the half dozen monks evacuated into a makeshift shelter in the parking lot. But Simon, the Butlers, and their crew are in the infirmary with Brothers Ferro and Benigno, and Brother Stephen is still in his cell.

Rafa leans in close. 'You still okay about . . . before?' He doesn't touch me, which makes the question even more distracting.

'Is this another tactic to *unwind* me?' My eyes drop to his mouth and he smiles.

'Is it working?'

'Maybe.'

'In that case, I have a few ideas on how to spend our time when we get to Pan Beach.'

For a few heat-filled seconds I'm far from the chapterhouse, thinking about Rafa's lips and hands. And then the side door opens and the urgency of the moment jolts back through me. A gust of wind catches the door and slams it open, bringing with it the stench of the fire.

Nathaniel closes it behind him.

I tap my blade against my leg again and wait as the fallen angel climbs to the dais. His boots echo on the stone steps and the room falls quiet. He takes in the crowd, gives nothing away.

'Good work tonight,' he says. 'We have now seen the desperation of our enemy. Our mandate—'

'Why couldn't they get inside?' The question comes from someone in the front.

Unbelievable. The Sanctuary Rephaim still don't know about the wards.

'Let Nathaniel speak,' Daniel says, but I can see he's realized his mistake. I stand on my toes and try to see who spoke. The Rephaim closest to the dais—all of them loyal to the Sanctuary—wait for Nathaniel to answer.

'The Sanctuary is warded against demons.' The fallen angel says it matter-of-factly.

'Since when?'

'Since the day the monks agreed to shelter me.'

A strange silence follows.

'But . . . we've brought hellions here.' Another voice, from the back this time.

Nathaniel nods. 'And you have always been required to seek my authority to bring a creature from hell inside these walls. Now you know why: my will, and my will alone, can alter the wards, if only fleetingly.'

Malachi and Taya exchange a glance, pieces sliding into

place for them. That's great. But it's not what we're here for.

'Have you heard from the Garrison?' I ask.

Nathaniel's eyes meet mine. 'No, and I would say their silence speaks volumes.'

'You think they disapprove of us rescuing Rafa and Taya?'

'I doubt they would approve of risking the lives of every other Rephaite by bringing Zarael to our doorstep with a rocket launcher.'

I check the faces around me, try to read the mood. The Rephaim shuffle and fidget, agitated and unsure. On the dais, Calista and Uri stand perfectly still. Daniel watches me carefully: he thinks he knows where this is going. He has no idea.

'So we should have left them there?' I ask.

'You should have exercised patience and discipline.'

Daniel catches my eye and shakes his head in a warning. But I'm out of patience. And discipline.

'Dani had another vision.'

The fidgeting and shuffling stops.

'The Gatekeepers are going to Pandanus Beach to kill as many men, women, and children as they can find.'

Nathaniel doesn't blink. 'They would not risk it.'

'They would and they will—to punish me.'

'Not everything is about you,' Calista snaps.

'Zarael wants payback for us destroying the house— you said it yourself, Calista. He's wreaked havoc here, but not enough to give him access to us. The only other place he knows he can bait us into a fight is Pan Beach.'

'No, that's the only place he can bait *you* into a fight. You and Rafa are the only Rephaim with a connection to it.'

'And me,' Taya says. 'I have an attachment.'

'When is this supposed to happen?' It's Malachi who asks.

'Dani says it starts on the beach during an electrical storm. We've checked: there's one forecast for Wednesday afternoon.' Which on Pan Beach time is two days away.

'Storms are not uncommon in that part of the world at this time of the year,' Nathaniel says. 'I could help pinpoint the event more accurately if you would allow me to search her mind.'

'You can't. She's gone.'

I'm not lying. Jason has taken her back to Rome with Maggie and Maria. They won't be there long. Regardless of the threat—or because of it—Maggie is desperate to get back to her mum in Pan Beach. God knows what she plans to tell her. And Maria is desperate to take Dani anywhere we aren't. I have no idea how that discussion is going to play out with Dani.

Nathaniel stares at me. It feels like the air has dropped a few degrees. 'I must wonder, Gabriella, if you are intentionally blocking my access to anyone who claims to receive visions and revelation. You hid this child seer from me. You did not tell me about the women in Iowa until it was too late, and then you destroyed the iron room before I could study it. And now you tell me about an attack on humans—an unprecedented and brazen attack—and will not afford me the opportunity to examine the one who has seen it. I acceded to your wishes to let the child stay here on the understanding I would speak with her in time, and now you have allowed her to be removed—'

'We need to go to Pan Beach.'

'No, Gabriella, we do not.'

Is he kidding? Not taking on the demons in Iowa is one thing, but refusing to protect humans when there is a clear threat?

'If they attack Pandanus Beach, the Gatekeepers and their hell spawn will bring down the wrath of heaven.' Nathaniel looks around the room. 'None of you want to be caught in the crossfire when that happens.'

'If the Angelic Garrison gives a crap about us, or humans, they'll drag their shining arses down into this world and back us up.'

'Gabe, enough,' Daniel says.

I ignore him, approach the dais. Jude and Rafa follow and the Rephaim part to let us through. We stop at the foot of the first step. 'Are you worried that taking on Zarael in a full battle will trigger some promised war between angels and demons?'

'It is not "some promised war", Gabriella. It is the final battle between heaven and hell you speak of so lightly. And it is not your war to fight until you have earned your place on the battlefield. You have the authority to defend yourselves against demons: you have no mandate to attack—no matter what the cause. That is for the Garrison alone.'

'You know what I think?' Jude says. 'I think you're worried the world might end before you've had a chance to find the Fallen and redeem yourself.'

'That is not my concern alone. Finding the Fallen is your only road to redemption too.'

'Says who—you? What if you're wrong, Nathaniel? What if that was never what the Garrison intended for us?'

'Then we will all be dragged to hell together.'

The mood in the chapterhouse shifts to something darker, more apprehensive. The silence stretches out for five seconds, six—

'You're going anyway, aren't you?' Taya says.

Jude nods. 'Me, Gaby, and Rafa.'

'And me,' Jones says, stepping forward.

'Count me in.' It's Seth. He gestures to the Outcasts around him. 'We're all in.' They're as intent as I've seen them. It could be about making a point to Nathaniel—it wouldn't be the first time—or because they know it's the right thing to do. Either way, I'm grateful they've got our backs.

'And us.' Ez is by the main doors. Zak has one arm around her, the other braced against the wall. His head is bandaged and his shoulder strapped.

'Just give me a couple more shifts before I have to swing a sword,' he says.

Taya clucks her tongue. 'You idiots. You're going to get yourselves killed.'

I turn back to her. 'You going to stop us?'

'No, *Gaby*, I'm coming with you.'

I blink.

'You heard me.'

I swallow. I do *not* have a lump in my throat over Taya.

'Not without me,' Malachi says.

'Or me.' Micah.

Warmth spreads through me, driving away the chill of Nathaniel's stare. I can't help it, I look around for Daisy. She's to my left, eyes fixed on her boots. Straight red hair falls in a curtain around her face so I can't see her expression, but her hands are tight fists. She's struggling.

Nathaniel doesn't say anything. He's waiting, as if he doesn't quite believe we'll do this—or at least that Taya, Malachi, and Micah will disobey him.

'Let's go,' Rafa says.

My eyes drift to Daniel. There's something in his eyes, a shift. He's not entirely on board with Nathaniel's decision-making here. I hesitate a few seconds longer, give him time to act on whatever he's feeling. Or for Daisy to join us. I hear the others moving towards the main doors, wait another heartbeat. But Daniel and Daisy stay silent.

I turn away, unsurprised. And a little disappointed.

UNEXPLODED INCENDIARY DEVICES

We gather outside in the cold. The defiant: me, Rafa, and Jude. The Outcasts. And Taya, Micah, and Malachi. There are twenty-six of us now.

'You know, life was a lot simpler when you guys were just arseholes,' Malachi says.

Rafa gives a short laugh. 'Likewise.'

'When do we leave?'

'Ten minutes. Meet you in the library. We'll go get the Pan Beach boys from the infirmary.'

'What's our arrival point?'

Rafa looks to me and I check my watch.

'It's about eight a.m. at home, so we'll need to be careful how we introduce this crowd to the town. Let's divide everyone between your place and mine and go from there.'

'You want me to call Mya?' Jones asks.

Jude shakes his head, glances at Rafa. 'Nah, mate, I'll do it when we get there.'

The Butlers and their crew fall over themselves to get organized when we tell them what's going on.

'We'll get the gear from camp,' Mick says, struggling to put on a sweater. 'We can set up positions around the beach and blow the fuck out of them.'

There's no way those boys are getting their arsenal anywhere near the esplanade, but we can argue tactics when we're home.

'I can't believe the cocksuckers got Russian RPG-7s.'

I don't know how Mick knows this and I don't ask.

'They put the fire out yet?' Rusty asks. 'Smells like it.'

'Not sure,' I say. 'But the kitchen's stopped exploding.'

Simon is dressed in jeans and a too-big woolen sweater. He's on the floor tying his bootlaces. The stench is gone so I'm assuming the poultice has too. 'We have to warn the town,' he says.

'I know. We'll figure it out.'

'Do you want me to take you home before I go to Gabe's place?' Taya is standing over him, watching him finish with his shoes. Is Simon one of the reasons she's willing to defend Pan Beach? I did find them almost-flirting on the couch that time.

'That'd be good. Your room's still there if you want it,

too.' Simon's eyes flit to her bandaged hand. 'Are you sure you're up for another round?'

'This?' Taya holds it up. 'It's a finger, Simon, not a leg. Don't worry your pretty head about it.' She smiles, very un-Taya-like. And despite the fact his town is about to be the center of a showdown between Rephaim and demons, Simon blushes. Rafa sees it and smirks, but resists the urge to give him a hard time.

It's a parade of the walking wounded as we lead the boys from Pan Beach to the library. Mick with his half-beard and his arm still strapped to his chest, sucking down a cigarette he bummed from Brother Benigno; Rusty, nursing his chest wound with one hand, carrying Mick's rocket launcher with the other; Woosha, missing a thumb, his dislocated shoulder strapped; Joffa, still in bad shape with his burns, broken nose and laceration to his thigh, supported either side by the blond mullet and the big guy with tribal tatts. The poultice may have helped with Simon's bruised ribs, but he still walks gingerly.

This is the guys' first trip outside the infirmary but there's not much to see. The wind is still too thick with smoke and ash.

'Someone has to break the news about the rest of the boys,' Rusty says.

'Save the town first,' Mick says and draws the cigarette down to the filter. The lit end flares, momentarily lights up his face. He blows the smoke out the side of his mouth. 'Shitty news second.'

Everyone's waiting for us in the library. The place still smells of mustiness and dried paper, now with a top-note of smoke.

'Fuck me, there's a lot of you bastards,' Mick mutters.

'This isn't a lot,' Rafa says, 'but it's all we've got.'

Ez and Zak meet us in the middle of the room. Zak doesn't need help to stand anymore but they still have their arms around each other. It makes me happy in a way I wouldn't have thought possible a week ago. I glance at Jude and then Rafa. Feel strong, like I belong wherever they are.

'We ready?' Rafa flattens two pieces of paper on the nearest desk and we gather around. Each page has coordinates and a mud map of Pan Beach: one to the shack where he's been staying and one to the bungalow Maggie and I share. Rafa describes the lay of the land and layout of each and then we work out who's going where. Jude, Simon, and the Butler crew are coming to the bungalow with me, Micah, Ez, and Zak. Everyone else is going to Rafa's place.

'It's tiny, so no bitching about cramped space,' Rafa says. 'It's a place to stay out of sight until we work out a plan.' He walks over to Jude and me. 'Jude, you good?'

'Yeah, mate.' Jude tests the weight of his sword, looks from Rafa to me. He feels it too: there's something *right* about the three of us standing here together, ready to face whatever's coming our way. There's a ripple of energy—nervous, impatient. Everyone's ready to be gone.

My stomach drops and cold air stirs at my feet.

'One last thing before you leave.'

Nathaniel is standing a few paces away. Daniel, Calista, and Uri are with him, along with a dozen armed Rephaim. Daisy is among them, avoiding eye contact with our side of the room. Daniel is working hard to look impassive but he's rattled. The tiny flare of his nostrils gives him away. Is he unsettled because he knows what Nathaniel's going to say, or because he doesn't?

'Knock yourself out,' Rafa says.

'Holy shit, is that the angel?' Rusty whispers it too loud.

Nathaniel's attention settles on me. 'Do your Outcasts know the truth about Mya?'

I take a moment, try not to react. Jude steps forward. 'What truth would that be?'

'That she is a conspirator with the humans who built the iron trap.' The fallen angel's gaze rakes over the Outcasts. 'Mya is not here because Gabriella and Judah know the truth about her and she is ashamed to show her face. A truth they have chosen to keep from you.'

'What's he talking about?' Jones asks Rafa.

'The women who created the room in Iowa share the same human bloodline as Mya,' Nathaniel says. 'You think I did not know that, Gabriella?'

He's baiting me. 'That's a stab in the dark.'

'You forget that the Garrison led me to each of you.'

'So?'

'They led me to Iowa. To a babe I was told died in childbirth. I did not see a body and I never believed the story. That is why I brought Brother Roberto here, to retain a connection to the family.' He pauses to let that bitter seed take root. 'When Mya appeared twelve years ago, it was obvious she was that child. But I did not understand her role in creating the schism.'

'You assumed Mya was that child because she was the only one you knew about but didn't find. How do you explain Jason?'

'It is true that when I realized this lost Rephaite was familiar with the Iowa family, I wondered if I had been wrong and he was indeed the missing child. But then it was Mya who took Virginia from here tonight, not him.'

'And you think that was out of character for her?'

'Gabriella, in the last fifteen minutes I have had the opportunity to speak further with Brother Stephen.' He gives me a knowing smile and my insides turn to ice.

'Did you hurt him?'

'I did not need to. He was grateful to unburden himself.' Nathaniel waits, lets the moment build. 'He confessed that Mya is his kin.'

I focus on the books behind him, the faded black and

navy spines, the flaking gold lettering. I sort through a storm of thoughts and find the most important: Brother Stephen didn't tell Nathaniel that the Rephaim need to be unified before the Fallen can be released from wherever they're trapped.

Or he told Nathaniel, and the fallen angel isn't sharing.

'Is that true?' Jones asks.

'We don't know for sure,' Ez says. 'We haven't heard her side of the story.'

The Outcasts whisper to each other, mutterings of confusion and disbelief.

Ez turns to address them. 'She's risked her life for us more times than I can recall. She's my friend and I'm giving her a chance to explain before I turn my back on her.'

'Taya, Malachi, Micah.' Nathaniel's voice is softer now, conciliatory. 'Are you willing to trust your lives to Rephaim who have spent the past decade following a girl whose family wishes to destroy us? A girl who has lied to them about who she is and what she has done?'

Blood pounds at my temples and I feel the heat in my face. 'Are you kidding? *You* want to talk about secrets and lies?'

'Gaby.' Jude puts his hand on my arm. Our eyes meet and he reads my intention, nods. 'Make it count.'

I push a chair aside so there is nothing between Nathaniel and me. 'When are you going to tell the Rephaim you murdered their mothers?'

The accusation sucks all the air from the room.

'Gabe, are you insane?' Calista says it barely above a whisper. 'That's . . .' she struggles to find a word strong enough. 'That's . . . *blasphemy*.'

'Is it?' I ask Nathaniel. I keep my eyes on him. He remains unmoved and unmoving. Even his irises are weirdly static.

'Is that what Mya is claiming?' Daniel asks.

'No,' I say. 'Jason.'

The doors bump against the wind, stronger now. It's the only sound in the library for a few long seconds. I can't tell if Nathaniel is looking at me or not, but I push on.

'Do you remember finding Jude and me in Italy, Nathaniel? Well, we weren't the only ones there. *Two* of your Fallen brothers found willing girls there: our mother, and Jason's. They were cousins.'

Nathaniel doesn't respond although his eyes flare and resume flickering.

'Jason's mother was away from the house with him when you stole Jude and me and killed our mother—like you killed all the women who hooked up with the Fallen.'

Nathaniel blinks. Once, twice. Daniel looks to him, waiting for the denial. It doesn't come.

'Fast-forward a few years and Jason's mother has another baby. That child is the first in a line of girls to have visions about angels and demons . . . and now Rephaim.'

'The child who was here—' Daniel stops. 'She's related to you? How long have you known about her?'

'Does it matter? Nathaniel has lied to all of you from the day you were old enough to understand him.'

Jude stands beside me, calm. Steady. 'If you're really in contact with the Garrison,' he says to Nathaniel, 'call them down so they can explain what they want from us. Let them explain why they led you to our mothers only to kill them, and why we have to jump through their hoops to justify the air in our lungs.'

'The Angelic Garrison cannot be summoned.' Daniel says it more out of habit than conviction. He's adrift. I think he's thrown as much by Nathaniel's silence as our accusations.

'Call them down, Nathaniel.' Jude gestures to the Rephaim around him. 'We'll wait. If they don't show, we'll know once and for all we're on our own, and you can let the rest of your Rephaim decide whether they want to help us save Pan Beach or not, without worrying about what kind of statement it makes.'

'Gabe.' There's unease in Daniel's voice now. 'This is history repeating itself, only this time you're on the wrong side.'

'Am I? Did you not hear what I just said about our mothers?'

Calista crosses to Taya, her lips pressed into a thin line. 'They're tearing us apart all over again, and this time they're taking more of you. Are you really going to be complicit with that? Mya is a traitor!'

Taya shakes her head. 'This isn't about Mya. And I'm not going to Pan Beach to join the Outcasts—I'm going with Rephaim who want to protect humans from Gate-keepers.' She holds up her bandaged hand. 'They tortured me, Callie. I know what it's like to be helpless against them. Maybe the Garrison will stop Zarael if we do nothing, but I don't want to take that chance. And when it's done, I plan on coming back. If I'm still welcome here. We can sort out everything else then.'

I check around the room: we're right on the edge. The Rephaim are caught between what they've always believed and what they're willing to accept, desperate for a foothold as the ground gives way beneath them. Even the Butlers and their crew are engrossed. Thank god Mick and Rusty have the brains to keep out of the firing line.

'We're not the only players in this game, Daniel,' Jude says. 'Somebody's giving visions and revelations to Jason's family and, apparently, to Mya's. Somebody turned Gaby and me inside out a year ago, gave us fake lives, and made us think we'd lost each other—made us think we were human. There's too much we don't know. Maybe it's the archangels doing all these things, maybe it's not. Either way, they know what's going on and it's time we were in the loop. Don't you want to know?'

Daniel looks to Nathaniel again—everyone does.

They want him to explain it all. They want meaning and certainty, even if it means he's lied to them.

Nathaniel breathes in and out slowly. 'I will not "call down the Garrison" as you so crudely put it.' His voice is wintry, hollow. 'There are matters between my brothers and me that are not of your concern. I have kept you and protected you from the moment you came into my custody. Do you think it was an accident I found each of you? It was destined, and every decision I have made was for your good, to give you the chance of redemption.'

'Redemption for sins we didn't commit,' Jude says.

'Together, we will find your fathers,' Nathaniel continues. 'We will hand them over to the Garrison. Only then will you have the freedom and knowledge you so desperately crave, Judah. And you cannot achieve that if you are dead.'

'I don't plan on dying in Pan Beach.'

'That does not mean it will not happen.'

'Did it ever occur to you that our fathers' sin was not in seducing human women, but in failing in their role as watchers and protectors? Gatekeepers are planning to attack a town full of people. If you let that happen, aren't you falling all over again?'

'Do NOT lecture me.' Nathaniel's voice is coarse enough to flay skin. 'I watched over this planet when the sun was young and men remembered there were worlds they could not see. You are a *child*.'

It's as if the room snaps frozen. Nobody moves. Nobody breathes.

'Being young doesn't make me wrong,' Jude says.

'Perhaps you should reserve such sweeping statements until you know the magnitude of the havoc you and your sister wrought a year ago.'

There's no answer to that.

I say carefully, firmly, 'We're going to Pan Beach.' I scan the faces of the Rephaim on either side of Nathaniel. All conflicted. 'Anyone else is welcome to join us. It's not about choosing us over the Sanctuary—or at least it doesn't have to be. And we could really use the backup.'

We wait. Still nobody moves. Of course they don't. It's too much to expect—

Daisy steps out from the line of Rephaim.

Our eyes meet and I let her see how much this means. She crosses the floor with stilted steps. Jones nods his approval and makes space for her beside him. Nathaniel watches without a word.

'We need to talk about Mya,' Jones says to Jude.

'We will. Not here.'

I'm ready for Nathaniel to issue an ultimatum. He doesn't. He waits, and the rest of his Rephaim wait with him. Is this what it was like when the Outcasts walked out a decade ago? Daniel is fixated on a spot somewhere above my head, lost in his own struggle. It's not about joining us—I doubt that option has even entered his head. But maybe he's reframing how he sees Nathaniel, and that alone would be a seismic shift. Uri's attention strays to Malachi and Micah. Calista catches Taya's eye one last time, urgent. Taya shrugs.

Rafa cracks a knuckle, puts his back to Nathaniel. 'All right, enough with the drama, let's get out of here. Everyone know where we're going? Good.' And then to me, quieter: 'You sure you two want to do this without a parachute?'

I nod. If there's one place I'll be able to shift to it's that bungalow—the only place I've ever thought of as home. And Jude's been to Pan Beach so all he has to do is trust me to guide us to my kitchen. I know it's a risk but I want to do it. I need to.

Rafa puts a hand in the small of my back, leans in close. 'I'll see you at your place after I get the crew settled. Got your phone?'

My nerves crackle a little now. 'Yeah.'

'You two go first.'

Great. I get to shift with an audience of Nathaniel, Daniel, agitated Sanctuary soldiers, and impatient Outcasts.

'Come on,' Jude says. 'Let's do this.' As always, he's up for anything. He faces me and for a second I'm back in that cable car with him, about to fall into a gaping chasm with only a bungee rope to stop us smashing into the river below. We grip hands and he gives me a wry smile. 'Three . . . two . . . one.'

I picture stepping through the imaginary curtain into my kitchen. Sunlight streaming onto the red laminate. My library swipe card on the bench. Dirty coffee cups in the sink. The floor of the Sanctuary drops away, quick and violent. The cold rushes in: the wind tears at me. I can feel Jude's hands still in mine. I'm doing it. I'm doing it. I'm—

Everything stops. And I'm in darkness.

AND NOW I SEE

The hurricane has frozen. Not disappeared as if we've arrived at the other end: frozen. I can't open my eyes. Can't feel Jude. Can't speak. Are we stuck? My breath hitches, sticks. I'm suspended in a giant block of ice. In blackness. Total blackness. My head pounds at my temples, the base of my skull, the bridge of my nose.

What did I do wrong? Are we trapped on the other side of the curtain? That thing Rafa said never happens? Are we trapped with the Fallen? I can't breathe, can't think.

Then I feel it. A touch on the nape of my neck, on the scar where my Rephaite mark should be. I can't tell if the thing touching me is warm or cool. Living or dead. I'm numb, either from the lung-crushing coldness, the lack of oxygen or that touch. But the scar flares unbearably hot for a split second.

And then it's over.

I'm back in the maelstrom, Jude's hands in mine. And then . . . we're in my kitchen. An impossibly gentle arrival.

I blink against the sunshine, rest for a second against the bench. My fingertips, still numb, trace the scratches and wine stains on the red surface.

It's all familiar.

Except it's different. All of it. The jacaranda tree outside the window, the sound of the surf down the hill a block away, the smell of coffee grounds. I let go of Jude without looking at him and go to my room, hear the chatter start up in the kitchen behind me as the Butlers catch their breath.

My room is exactly how I left it. The beat-up desk from the market covered in clothes and books. Faded curtains. Dirty coffee cups on the floor. But none of it feels the same.

'Gaby?' Jude is at the door. We lock eyes and I see I'm not the only one feeling it. We exchange a long, silent look. He grips the doorjamb, waiting. He knows the world is about to change.

Because I remember.

Everything.

ACKNOWLEDGMENTS

I've hopefully expressed my gratitude to each of you individually, but for the record, my heartfelt thanks go to:

My editor, Mandy Brett, and the rest of the awesome team at Text Publishing including Anne Beilby, Rachel Shepheard, Alaina Gougoulis, and Steph Speight.

The team at Orion/Indigo Books, particularly my editor Jenny Glencross and senior publicity manager Nina Douglas.

Thanks, too, to the supportive team at Tundra Books/ Penguin Random House: Publisher Alison Morgan, Editorial Director Tara Walker, and Publicity Manager Pamela Osti, as well as Val Capuani. And of course for the tireless enthusiasm and professionalism of Publishing Coordinator Sylvia Chan.

My agent, Lyn Tranter (Australian Literary Management), and Jane Finigan at Lutyens & Rubinstein Literary Agency in the UK.

For invaluable input into early drafts of *Shimmer:* Alison Arnold, Rebecca Cram (Place), Michelle Reid, and Vikki Wakefield. Special thanks to Michelle for going the extra mile.

My nephew, Aaron Minerds, who kindly explained to me what happens when you fire a rocket into a building. (It's okay, he has a military background.)

My family and friends, whose enthusiasm for my writing never fails to make me smile.

Murray: thank you for your love, good humor and endless patience—and the steady supply of espresso and pinot noir.

And, again, to all the readers, bloggers, reviewers, booksellers, and librarians who continue to support the Rephaim series. Thank you.

LOOK FOR BOOK 4 IN THE REPHAIM SERIES,
BURN

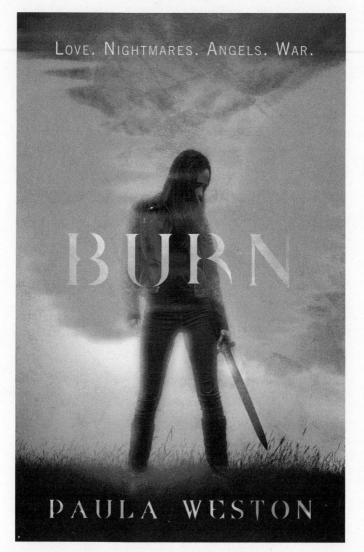

LOVE. NIGHTMARES. ANGELS. WAR.

BURN

PAULA WESTON

Cover design: Us Now • Cover image: Stephen Mulcahey © Arcangel Images

ISBN: 978-1-77049-851-8 • eBook: 978-1-177049-853-2

AWAKENINGS

Jude and I are looking at each other. Watching. Sunlight streams through the window, warms my back. I can hear the surf pounding the beach a block away. A magpie somewhere outside. My room smells of stale coffee and the half-melted vanilla-bean candle in a mason jar by my bed. My chest is a storm of emotion, thunderous and insistent.

'What do you remember?' Jude keeps his voice low, doesn't move closer.

I bite my lip. Memory after memory rises up like a wave, crashes down, replaced by another. They just keep coming.

'Gaby, we need to talk.'

'I know. Just . . .'

I close my eyes. I'm unhinged, spinning. There's a tornado under my ribs, surging and tearing at me. Voices in the kitchen, louder now. Mick Butler. Zak. Micah. Daisy.

Footsteps in the hallway. I force my eyes open, let the world back in.

'Gabe.' Ez steps into the doorway. 'What do you want us to do with the Butlers and their crew?' Daisy appears between Ez and Jude, still rattled about having chosen to defy the Sanctuary and come with us.

I cast around for some thought to anchor me to the moment. *Demons are coming to tear Pan Beach apart.*

That'll do.

I remember where I am. *Who* I am. 'They're human. They need to go home and sleep. We'll catch up later at the Imperial.' My voice is steadier than I expect. 'Tell Mick to stay off the mountain.'

Ez frowns. 'Are you okay?' She looks at Jude and then back at me. 'What's happened?'

I shake my head. Swallow. My heart is racing. Ez and Daisy are going to hear my pulse if I don't get out of here. 'Just relieved to be home.'

Home.

'When are you going to Rafa's?' Ez asks.

My stomach does a neat somersault. 'Soon,' I say. 'I need a run.' Because if I don't burn energy soon, the chaos in my gut is going to rip me open.

'A run?' Daisy says. 'Like, *now*?'

'Yep.' My mouth is dry.

'What about everyone else? Shouldn't we be—'

'You can all chill for half an hour. We'll work out a

plan when I'm back.' I'm talking too fast. I look around for my running gear, spy three-quarter tights in the pile of clean washing on my desk. 'I need to change.' I force myself to make eye contact with Daisy. 'I won't be long.'

'I'll come with you.'

'*No.*' It comes out too loud. Daisy stares at me, her straight red hair tucked behind her ears. Freckled cheeks flushed. 'I need . . . space.'

Ez's forehead is still creased. 'But you'll call into Rafa's?'

I nod, noncommittal, and kick off my boots.

The voices in the kitchen are louder. Micah's arguing with Rusty. Ez gives a meaningful glance in their direction. 'I need to sort out these clowns. Daisy—a hand?' Ez disappears back down the hallway. Daisy catches my eye for a second, shakes her head in frustration, and follows.

Jude stays. 'Can we talk?'

Anger stirs—or the memory of it. I can't tell what's real and what's an echo right now. 'Let me get my head straight.'

'Gaby—'

I grab a T-shirt and my running shoes and shift next door to Maggie's room without looking at him. I stand for a moment, my breathing quick and ragged, thoughts tumbling.

Maggie's bed is neatly made but her work table is a jumble of cloth bolts and patterns. Her sketchbook is closed, half-covered by a crimson shawl she started knitting last week. Chanel No. 5 still lingers. It brings another flood of memories—more recent—of cooking with Maggie in our kitchen, walking down the hill to work together, sharing the bathroom mirror. Drinking beer in our regular seats at Rick's, overlooking the esplanade.

My throat tightens. I need to run. *Now.*

I shift with the shoes in my hand. It's easy now, like walking. I pinpoint my arrival to a spot behind a hulking fig tree on the rainforest track. The path is empty under the leafy canopy. I stomp my foot on the trunk to jam my heel into the runner. I don't realize how much I'm shaking until the third time I fumble the laces.

Quick hamstring and calf stretches. I fix my eyes on the track, anticipating the cool air against my skin, the burn in my muscles. I need the release. I need the escape.

But I already know I can't outrun the thing I'm trying to avoid.

The truth.